Unicorn Joes

By Sonny Day

Copyright © 2022 by Sonny Day

All rights reserved. No part of this publication may be reproduced, distributed, or transmitted in any form or by any means, including photocopying, recording, or other electronic or mechanical methods, without the prior written permission of the publisher, except in the case of brief quotations embodied in critical reviews and certain other noncommercial uses permitted by copyright law.

Book Design by HMDpublishing

FOREWORD

"Unicorn Joes" was conceived and commenced in 2106, pre-Covid pandemic. I re-started and completed it in 2022 but decided to leave the story set in London in 2016.

I like diversity in characterisation; my portrayal of two young Englishmen, one of Indian heritage, and two foreigners, a young African and a young Chinese lady, is not meant to draw racial stereotypes. I mean no offence; their characters and traits could easily have been switched. I hope you enjoy Spencer, Surjit, Innocence and Mae Li for who they are; ambitious and talented young people willing to take a risk and create wealth whilst befriending each other because of this.

I hope you find their story irreverent, amusing and worth your time to read it.

Thank you and be lucky,

Sonny

Dedication

*To Robin Oliver and Richard Binley,
thanks for giving me a go.*

CONTENTS

FOREWORD 3

MONDAY 6

TUESDAY 77

WEDNESDAY 114

THURSDAY 148

FRIDAY 196

SATURDAY 229

SUNDAY 250

MONDAY

The girl with the long, wavy red hair looked up at him with mischievous green eyes, their lashes emboldened with thick mascara. She offered a saucy smile, followed by a minxy wink before peeping down her top and then, without moving her head, looking back up at him. She bit her bottom lip, overacting the suspense and tossed her head up and around to the side to send her flailing hair back over her shoulder. The rest of her face was revealed, pale and faintly freckled. Her Lalita-like leer morphed into a sultry stare, and her fingers played temptingly at the tiny clasp straining to contain her boastful breasts. She held this pose briefly before her fingers fumbled at the fastener, threatening to free her orbs, frustratingly out of touch from his grasp. Like the penny falls, each simple move left the prize dangling agonizingly within reach. Just one more tilt, a few pennies more, one more coin in the slot, and on this occasion, one more button, and they would be bound to spill out completely. Her fingers played at her silvery-blue chemise, teasingly at the final release as she smiled more, looking up at him.

"Get on with it, for fuck's sake, you're not winning a BAFTA for this performance," sighed Spencer, one of her several spectators, each observing remotely and isolated from each other. Most sat in silence with keen ears listening for a partner's impending steps before the door handle might turn abruptly. This would trigger a scurry of activity that would simultaneously close the webpage, zip up trouser flies, and delete the browser history with the speed of a magician's fingers. Spencer sat in an office chair and lifted his hips to arch his back so that his long, slender right-hand fingers fumbled deep into his trouser pocket.

The red-headed girl's routine ran its course, and at last, the breasts were untamed, hanging pertly forward and swinging with the firmness that her youthful looks suggested they might. She let them ride some more, her face closing in on him, and then sat up laughing as she shuffled her shoulders clear of the untethered top that slid down her back and onto the bed where she knelt.

Spencer's eyes diverted to a photo of a mature and full-figured woman adorned in an ill-fitting negligee and aligned next to the now topless red head's frame. His hands withdrew from his pocket and held a scrunched tissue. He sat upright, his long legs astride but immersed under the desk.

"Mature 43 years old woman wants shag within 3 minutes of you, call now? If you're forty-three, I'm Harry Kane, but that doesn't matter, make a note of the website address," he mumbled and added the details into his spreadsheet before selecting the next model. Spencer toggled to other live performers, more sexually encounter-themed ads popped up, and he tapped more data into his file.

He opened the tissue to observe the pale gooey content before squeezing it shut and pushing it towards the boundary of the desk's surface. Then, finally, he withdrew another tissue from the cellophane packet perched on the beech veneered desk where he and his Macbook sat and blew his nose loudly.

"Man, this hay fever. The smog doesn't help either, filthy London," he coughed before pinging the used tissue with the same aplomb towards the perimeter next to the previous one.

Sat opposite him at the shared table stared a bemused young Asian man. They were at the open-plan floor of the Hive, a business hub for emerging technology entrepreneurs and their companies who rented desks for £15 per day, free coffee and tea included. On balance, it was cheaper than hanging out in Starbucks, and you got to charge your laptop and phone guilt-free. Spencer glanced back at his screen. A blond-haired girl with heavy makeup and an even heavier girth relaxed, lying on her back, exposing another unclothed part of her anatomy before he clicked away, searching for other pop-up advertisements.

A young girl wearing a dark blue French beret and a lightweight coat matching in colour pushed past the back of Spencer's chair as she made her way to an adjacent desk and glanced at his screen with the innate nosiness possessed by us all; she could not help but do so. Then, as she was ready to shuffle on, her eyes glanced at the screen content that stopped her in her tracks. She pulled a disapproving frown and stabbed a pointed forefinger towards the tilted display on Spencer's laptop.

"That's disgusting, do you mind? Stay in your bedroom if you want to watch that filth; this is supposed to be a place of business!"

Spencer spun around in his chair, and he looked up, puzzled.

"Eh, what? Oh, it's research, and this is business," said Spencer deadpan.

"Is that what you call it?" she was then drawn to the used tissues stuck together on the desk, and Spencer was too late to anticipate the conclusion she had drawn.

"I've got hay fever," he offered flatly in a nasal tone.

"This an office, wank from home, if you can't respect that," she replied contemptuously and walked on to the next aisle of desk space and sat down to arrange her things from her matching blue bag. As she did, she looked up and across at him, evidently tall by the look of his slim frame and with dark black shoulder-length hair hung around a fair face. He was fit and good-looking. What a shame he was a pervert.

Spencer quickly retrieved another tissue and made an overplayed attempt to blow his nose to corroborate the unlikely truth. Why were his airwaves suddenly as free-flowing as a new Dyson upright when he needed a thick glob of mucus? Spencer felt hungry and thought about something to sustain him, having arrived at the Hive for the first time when it opened at six o'clock that morning. It was now eight o'clock, and his enthusiasm waned as his hunger grew. On Friday, he'd have less than an hour to persuade investors that his idea was worth their capital to finance his plan. A business as old as the world, but one that the digital age has changed. He'd thought it a novel idea, an intelligent app, and a small slice of the two hundred billion dollars generated by internet porn each year was all Spencer Churchill needed to retire at 24. An early high net worth retirement offered fast cars, fickle women, and a hedonistic lifestyle that would shame the devil. He'd waste the rest to quote a famous and now dead Irish footballer.

"Fuck this, I need a coffee and a bacon sandwich," he announced, and with the stamina of an old man who had been up all night, not the two hours since this young man had arrived into the office from Barnet, he pulled himself out of his chair and arose with another yawn.

"Can you keep an eye on this?" he nodded at his Macbook to the Asian guy sitting opposite him. The guy looked back blankly and nodded before staring back at his screen with a sigh.

A mile away, a motorcycle weaved its way in and out of the inaptly termed "rush hour" traffic that dawdled its way down the Grays Inn Road, flanked by the buses and black taxis sauntered along their separate lanes. Cyclists rode their bikes and their luck within inches of their lives and of being maimed by the angry traffic, some to save a few quid, most to save time. Money in the city of London could be limitless; time was not. The motorcycle took the bisecting lines between the north and south road directions that spurred from Euston Road to its North to Holborn at its South. It darted back into the cover of the slow-moving traffic when it met another oncoming deploying the same tactic. The rider bobbed forwards and sideways to manoeuvre the purring machine quickly down the four hundred meters past Calthorpe Street before swooping into a slight gap in the traffic to swing left into Clerkenwell Road. The ubiquitous white van with a fat-shaven-headed driver braked suddenly, releasing its frustration with a long, loud honk from its horn, which surprised some of the dozens of pedestrians waiting their turn to cross the junction. These rare few scuttled along the streets without earphones attached like life support to smartphones and drip-fed their patients with a relentless and insatiable digital din. The open-eared walkers were startled back to their starting blocks. The motorcyclist was not bothered and acknowledged the van driver with a solitary finger raised from the lefthanded black leather gauntlet while the other twisted on the throttle to speed it away. It tore a further half mile along, accompanied by another single-finger salute to an aggrieved Mercedes driver at the Farringdon Road crossroads before dashing across an amber traffic light at the Goswell Road junction and into Old Street. The final straight was a half-mile and less than 30 seconds to complete the journey that ended before the roundabout that bisected its West and Eastside and the City Road that ran North to South through it. The black leather-clad rider peeled left across the bus lane, carefully over a leafy pavement and into a side road that ran parallel with the Hive and to Baldwin Street at its far end. The big bike released its last roar from its powerful lungs and parked in a marked bay before its lights and engine extinguished. The rider sat upright and removed her black onyx helmet with the dark frosted visor. Once untethered, her hair was shaken and released like a cliché in a shampoo commercial. It was jet black and wavy with a silk-like gloss. Her facial skin had a flawless olive complexion, and her eyes narrowed but a beautiful brown that could cut through machismo at thirty paces. She was a tall Chinese girl, six feet in dark black leather knee-high boots that matched the taut, tight trousers overlapped by a black nubuck jacket that bestrode a supermodel figure. She swung her right leg up and over the back of the cooling machine like a back kick by Uma Thurman in Kill Bill, either volume.

As she strode toward the swing door entrance of the Hive, the revolution of its turning panels quickened enough for her to check her stride, her hands planted impatiently on her hips, cradling her helmet as the cause of its accelerated spin strutted through. The young man, similar in age to Mae Li, bounced boyishly out into the emerging April morning sun, his shoulders rocking in unison with each stride singing "Every day I write the book" by Elvis Costello. "He'll have a bad back with that posture," she thought, "but nice voice and arse" as he strode in straight fitting ripped black jeans towards the tube station to retrieve a coffee and bacon sandwich. Mae Li, founder, Chief Executive, and sole employee of 888 Media Technologies, not yet incorporated, stepped into and through the turning doors. She flashed her pass at the turnstile, then skipped up the stairs, two steps at a time. She arrived without any increase in her breath at the open-plan floor five stories up, adorned with long tables, and each sat under bare ceilings. Aluminium air conditioning piping and black dish-like lamps hung over the room, casting ambient light and heat to incubate the dreams hatched in the battery farm-like bays below.

She made her way to a vacant chair next to the Macbook with its lid open and the screen saver with "back in a jiffy" entitled across a cartoon picture of a limp phallus, hung well below the blotchy testes, encased in a flesh-covered condom. Mae Li sat down and tutted. The laptop belonged to a bloke; why were men so immature? They never grew up, and everyone she met was like Peter Pan, who wanted her to be a mother they could shag, a combination of Wendy and Nanny if Nanny were not a St Bernard dog. She placed her crash helmet on the table and retrieved her laptop from the leather bag strapped across her shoulders before looking at the East Asian-looking guy who sat diagonally opposite. He had a fair face encased by fine black hair that sat like a bowl over his head, "why did Chinese men never do anything with their hair" she thought. He was Chinese, wasn't he?

"Nǐ shì zhōngguó rén ma?" she remarked inquisitively.

"I'm sorry?" replied the young man.

"I asked if you were Chinese, but I think your reply answered my question," replied Mae Li smiling politely.

"No, I'm from Luton," he said before returning to his screen. "I can't wait until I can afford my own office," he thought before peeking back at the beautiful young lady sitting across from him.

Mae Li flipped the lid to her Mac Pro and opened the most important presentation of her short work life so far. More hard work was needed before it was compelling and ready to share at her appointment with the investors who loomed in judgment at the end of the week. There were just four more workdays to finalize it. She was determined to show her father that she could independently succeed with drive and initiative. Although she accepted the financial support that provided her motorcycle and the flat on Midhope Street, convenient for University College, where she had graduated a year earlier, she did not want to return to China to work for her father's manufacturing electronics business. Neither did she want to stay in London only to be its European representative, as was his wish. He had reluctantly agreed to allow her one year to establish her own business before he terminated the financial pipeline and the flat sold unless she agreed to his plan. The prospect was unthinkable, so these final few days were going to finalize a proposition that would garner the support to launch her web service and grow into a lucrative business within three years meaning respect from her father and, above all, independence from him.

Innocence Ndlovu bounded out of her shared flat in Dalston Lane to stride the two miles between her work. Before closing the door behind her, she reminded herself of a simple arithmetical sum, $2 + 2 = 4$ and $4 \times 80 = 320$. Two miles to work and two miles back equalled four and 80 calories burned for each mile for a woman of her average size; walking at a brisk pace meant 320 calories expended. Her daily commute allowed the consumption of two small Cadbury's caramel bars, one bar, to be consumed within seconds of arriving at her spot in the Hive with a cup of weak milky tea, the bag dipped and discarded almost before the water turned brown. The other was stored into her Cadbury's deposit account to be withdrawn from her special chocolate tin, placed at the back of the cupboard, and binged when needed. It wasn't as if she was plump or required to be overly vigilant regarding her calorific intake, but like most women, a female mirror cursed her. This one hung inside her bedroom. The female mirror could reflect Aphrodite herself, but the recipient would search for an imperfection, something that would gnaw away at her confidence and inflamed like fat on fire by the casual and chance remark from a man, or worse still from another woman. Men, well, they were the opposite. The male mirror always found something positive to reflect.

Even the most out-of-shape and unashamedly gruesome man would regard something flawless from the same sheet of glass. Male mirrors were dangerous, encouraging overweight, slack-stomached men to tuck close-fitting t-shirts into jeans that were too tight to rise above hips. Our heroes slung them under their bellies. Loose jowly cheeks shaved when pulled taut in a pattern to form a virtual jawline. Shirts were flayed open to the chest where bristling brushes of hair intended to show off masculinity became sweaty and matted, catching food particles or small insects as the days in London became muggier. Lonely strands of cranial hair combed over balding crowns, trousers tucked under guts, jackets stretched over slumped, rounded shoulders, the male mirror knew no bounds when it came to breathing confidence into the most challenged from the gene pool of XY chromosomes. It was why men bought the size of clothes that they wanted, not what they needed, because the male mirror never failed to deceive its reflection.

Innocence made her way across Kingsland Road onto the West side of the street before she turned into Stamford Road. That led her to her favourite sounding street, De Beauvoir Road, whose boxy Georgian-fronted townhouses and trees stood randomly along the pavement as if they were uprooted and moved about in the night when nobody was watching. It sounded sophisticated and grand and shared its name with De Beauvoir Town, the southwest corner of Hackney, which stretched to Kingsland Road to its east, Southgate Road to its west, up to Balls Pond Road in the north, and the Regents Canal, which she crossed to its south. Innocence researched its history and discovered that Richard de Beauvoir had inherited the land developed during the 19th Century. Where once grew a leafy suburb of London now contained a mix of residences owing their character to Tudor, Jacobean, Georgian, Italianate style Stucco villas and scarred by high rise residential blocks erected in haste during the 1960s, like many ugly buildings from that decade. Most people did not notice its eclectic yet distinct style. Still, Innocence did. She was fascinated by its history and often detoured via it to Dalston Lane if there was more time to explore the few dozen streets that could tell thousands of people's stories from a city that could recount many millions more.

Innocence sang in accompaniment, buoyed by gospel music from her native South Africa, and played joyously into her ear pods from her phone. The words rang out the same, but the equivalent note or key was not often matched. The euphony mattered less against the backdrop of the thousands of disgruntled diesel engines that rattled their way up and down the A10 that ran parallel a few blocks away. Although it was unkind to consider which was more tuned, it was true. Innocence loved the feeling of the start of a new week, and this one was one of the most significant of her 23 years of life so far. A meeting with an investment panel from an incubator start-up funding company approached a few days away. At that point, she would introduce the beta version of her game and, more importantly, the financial numbers that would multiply a handsome profit, assuming it grew with expectations. Her step quickened as she considered the urgency of claiming a vacant seat at her before they became oversubscribed.

The Hive consisted of 5 floors of a corner building in Old Street, a vibrant hub of entrepreneurs and start-ups. The office had an industrial feel with stripped-back walls, graffiti, and exposed piping. The fifth floor hosted the hot desk area, the cheapest area to rent, with the first-come-first-served desk space. Although the capacity to cope with busy demands, Monday morning was the most dynamic. Innocence knew that she had to claim a desk before 8 o'clock or face waiting for somewhere to perch like a game of musical chairs. Emerging from the stairwell, she surveyed the large floor plan, as expansive as a five-a-side football court. She noticed a spare chair opposite a Chinese girl adjacent to another East Asian-looking guy who sat opposite an empty seat where a laptop claimed its place. Innocence bagged the vacant seat by placing her coat around the chair and rifled into her bag to produce her computer, which she lay on the table, and a small chocolate bar before heading off to the coffee machines. She returned shortly after with a cup of milky tea and peeled the wrapper off the chocolate bar. The slow, precise tears of the silvery foil caught the attention of the pretty Chinese girl sat diagonally opposite, and as their eyes met momentarily, Innocence beamed across and piped,

"It's never too early for chocolate," she said, dipping the bar into the hot milky tea.

"And it's never too late. So I've taken it to indulge in bed, " smiled Mae Li.

"You need to gobble it quickly before it melts in your hands," giggled Innocence naively.

"Oh, I do. I like to hold it on my tongue for so long as it takes to dissolve and trickle down my throat," whispered Mae Li while Innocence held the chocolate erect in front of her open mouth and nodded approvingly. Innocence kept the chocolate in suspense and looked at it, pondering what Mae Li had suggested. The top of the bar was softened and steamed slightly. The guy from Luton could not help but listen, looked up and across at Innocence. She looked back across at him and looked back at the chocolate tantalizingly before she tore the top chunk off with a grin and smacked her lips. "Mwah." she looked up and blissfully smiled as she sucked hard on the warm melting chocolate. Innocence snapped off another chunk, stirred her tea with it, and prepared for another go.

It was still early in the morning, but this was already enough for the poor distracted chap from Luton, and he pushed back his chair with a squeal against the wood-panelled floor and flipped the lid to his laptop shut before sliding it into his bag while recoiling the power supply. He was upgrading to an individual room, the single occupancy pods on the third or fourth floor, and with it, the peace to focus on his project devoid of disruptions from strangers.

Surjit Ghosh momentarily lost balance, jerked by the sudden pull of the 20-year-old rolling stock on the Northern Line. As the trains pulled out from any of its 50 stations that straddled the line, standing passengers braced themselves for an unhinged tug that might catapult them into the arms or laps of other commuters. Depending on their outcome, this experience could be mildly enjoyable, unpleasant and perhaps painful. Surjit held the horizontal supporting rail that runs parallel to the ceiling directly above the front of the seats that run along the side of the carriage, each of them occupied this morning as would be expected soon after seven o clock. He was well under average height for a male at 5 feet 4 inches, and his slender arm was at full stretch to hold on to the rail. The heels of his shoes gave him an invaluable extra inch for which all short men were grateful. He alighted at Elephant and Castle. Although it served as the terminus for the Bakerloo line, he was several stops into a south Londoner's journey north, on the aptly named Northern line, having started at Morden, south of Wimbledon. It was not often that he had the opportunity to take a vacant seat, but with only five stops and 15 minutes to Old Street where he disembarked, he was unconcerned with contesting a seat should one be available. The train's jolt swung him sideways so that his right leg momentarily became engaged with that of the pretty young lady who sat with her eyes shut below him. He shot her a nervous glance, ready to roll his eyes upwards and mouth the word "sorry" across the rising hum of the train and the music which shrilled loudly from under her wavy ash-coloured hair. He held the word on the edge of his tongue for a few seconds more before looking away while readjusting his feet to support a more independent position. She had either not noticed the interaction or was not overly bothered by it. Surjit felt this moment of contact summed up his entire experience with women of his age group. He was either unattractive or anonymous and yearned to embrace a girl who could love him as much as he imagined he would love her. His mother's expectation only magnified the pressure he felt from within himself to achieve such an aspiration. She would bark endlessly, "Surjit, when will you find a girl, get married, and get a proper job? You are 25 years old, and life is passing you by, my boy." Having gained a 1st class honours degree in computer science from Manchester, Surjit was not without options regarding employment inference. Still, a spirit in him fuelled his ambition to develop something new and clever, empowering people through their mobile devices, which were carried everywhere as a part of life. He had been coding something extraordinary and was ready to present a plan to investors this week to gain funding to develop something that could enter commercial production.

Surjit stole another glance at the girl with the previously engaged leg with him and the tinny music emitted from under her hair. She chewed slowly on, presumably, some sort of gum, maybe nicotine, an early morning fix to satisfy the addiction that such a controlling parasite held on its host. He recalled how people reacted in horror to examples of parasites that ingested larvae into insects that would eat them alive from within. He thought it morbidly ironic how people would pull on their cigarettes and joints that dispelled hundreds of toxins into their lungs that might spore and invoke unlimited cell reproduction. These would form tumours that would inevitably suffocate and eat them alive like parasites devoured the insects. Alcohol and other drugs were no different, so he abstained from indulging in them. He never had and never would.

The train bumped to a halt. Surjit looked up, and they were by now at London Bridge. A few passengers stepped out from the doors and pushed past the multitude of others that hung outside, jostling to replace them and head under the river. Surjit observed how the train's initial motion choreographed a wave of passengers' heads, peering down into mini-screens.

Their Gods demanded attention and averaged a homage of over 100 times a day by their worshippers who received the Word not through a testament of books but from a gospel of apps. Matthew, Mark, Luke, and John no longer kept the faith; Facebook, Snapchat, WhatsApp, and Angry Birds had replaced them. These and a biblical denomination of 2 million ever-changing programs from which 140 billion downloaded across the planet this year. No religion or cult on Earth could compete with absolute devotion and widespread zeal. The second coming had come. It thundered across the earth and carried upon its four horses, only for Death, Famine, War, and Conquest to be substituted by Apple, Samsung, Nokia, and Huawei.

As the train lurched into Old Street, Surjit stopped pondering the apocalyptic reality brought upon by the device he was to make his fortune from and focussed on heading up to the Hive. He needed to secure a good spot to work from and check in on Digamber, the software developer Surjit had contracted with his meagre savings to help cut and test code from Pune in India. The fifth floor was busy this morning, and it always was on Mondays, the herald of a new week met with renewed optimism and determination. Surjit scoffed that by Thursday at half-past three, there would be more empty desks than occupied when dreams were left pending for the diversionary draw of the big night out in the city that came alive to the crowd of the bars and clubs that throbbed until the early hours. No longer, New York that never slept, he could choose any seat from which to work and another upon which to sit to and from the Elephant and Castle on Friday morning. There was no chance of an indiscrete encounter on Fridays. He stood at the doors of the fifth floor. He surveyed his options like cinemagoers choosing seats, looking up at the banks of seating, calculating who looked like they bathed regularly and who were not holding a bucket of popcorn or noisy sweet packets? Surjit was not concerned with confectionary but was looking out for the murmurers. The rules and protocol of the hot desk floor meant people had to leave to make and receive business calls on their phones, Skype, or Zoom, but this did not dissuade some people from mumbling to collaborators or prospects when texts and instant messages couldn't do. The tables had filled quickly, but one worker, a Chinese-looking guy who appeared agitated, was already packing his things to go. Surjit shuffled to claim the seat next to the black girl wearing the pink sweatshirt printed with multi-coloured sweet wrappers and bearing the words "Sugar Rush." Quite apt, he thought as he noticed she was dipping a chocolate bar into a hot drink and smiling gleefully. Surjit momentarily considered the spike of endorphins created, her beaming smile born from processed sugar and cacao beans. Perhaps this was why men bought women chocolate? How much chocolate would he need to buy a girl and for her to consume before she sufficiently stirred to find him attractive enough to succumb? Could a girl eat that much chocolate? He made a mental note to explore this topic; he was on to something further. He pulled out the chair and sat down, and the seat was still warm, which made Surjit feel a little uncomfortable. Had it been temperate from the bottom of the beautiful Asian girl working diagonally opposite him, it would have felt perversely gratifying to share on her behalf. However, the slight balminess emanating from the surface through his buttocks was a legacy left by that stressed-looking Chinese guy who did not sit comfortably with him. Surjit made another mental note, only take chairs vacated by females, preferably attractive ones. He looked across at the girl, and she had beautiful unblemished skin, such a fine jawline and bone structure that looked like a grandmaster had sculpted her. She did not return his glance, and Surjit felt the familiar take of anonymity. He cleared his throat slightly and followed this with a calm excuse, and while his eyes met his screen, it was a glass-like stare where your attention was at the far corner of your peripheral vision. Nothing, nada, not a carrot. What would it take for them to notice him? Just for once, to be acknowledged as a person as much as a man. There was work to be done, thought Surjit. The recognition you crave and deserve will come during the investors' meeting on Friday. Yes, that made sense, but no, it could wait another minute. Just one more attempt, a last-minute request for the bar to be raised, the arena to be peaceful as Surjit Gosh went for gold in the award of best anonymous male to be noticed by an unfamiliar beautiful female. He pushed the chair out from under him, bowed slightly, and sought to bring it back under him while scraping it across the wooden floor, which would emit a screech from which he could apologize. Clumsy? Inarticulate? Desperate? Yes, but so what? Just to get a reaction, any response. Even a "quieten the fuck" up would suffice. Surjit realized it was slightly heavier and more awkward to retrieve, pushing the chair back. He tensed his thighs and tightened his stomach to exert the necessary force to complete the exercise. And that's when Surjit received the attention he so desperately sought from both ladies, although it could never be for the simple apology that failed to be uttered from his astonished lips. The chair barely made a sound as it somehow glided across the surface, but the additional thrust required to propel it forward caused an unplanned "Parp" from Surjit's strained buttocks squeaked with perfect clarity and pitch. Surjit was in shock; he had just audibly farted in public. Now, when all he ever wanted for that moment in the world was to go back to being unrecognized, the epitome of the invisible man, he felt like all the world was looking at him. It wasn't, but three of its population were.

"That's working now, try your lights," snapped the tall young man who appeared behind him with a folded white paper bag under his arm and clutched a takeaway coffee cup by its cardboard sleeve.

Surjit looked up, and the same guy sat opposite him, placing the contents onto the table before his long, elegant fingers retrieved a thickly sliced bacon sandwich from the bag. He had dark raven-coloured shoulder-length hair, brown eyes that hinted mischief, and a disarming smile. Surjit half smiled in return before shooting his gaze back at his screen, and he was sure there was more than a fair chance that he would die of his embarrassment as he felt his head bursting with all the blood that had rushed to its aid. He heard a faint giggle from the black girl to his left, but he dared not peek up. Perhaps it was best to get up, leave and never come back. There was another pay-as-you-work location in the city, but he needed to work without disruptions during this critical final week. Spencer's jaws broke the silence, wrestling with the doughy bread that encased the fried bacon emulsified with brown sauce. He'd bitten off more than he could reasonably chew, and although the outcome was never in doubt, the first seconds of the bout saw the sandwich put up a fair fight, as could be seen through Spencer's open mouth. Mae Li let out a slight sigh, not caused by managing her presentation but by the boyish buffoon with the silly screensaver and the noisy breakfast habits.

"Sorry, I won't be a minute with this. I know you are not supposed to eat at the desk, but then I thought I'm new here, and what the fuck, we're not in North Korea, oh no offence," mumbled Spencer through a combination of chewing, swallowing, and speaking.

"I'm not Korean, I'm Chinese, and you should not speak with your mouthful," rebuked Mae Li quietly, who had noticed the singer with the arse as tight as a tambourine. She thought she could dig her nails into that and puncture its skin.

"That's what I told my girlfriend last night," batted back Spencer, hesitating before taking a smaller bite of the remaining snack. Then, finally, he looked up at Surjit and raised his eyebrows in glee, who shot a glance back, relieved that this conversation was at least dowsing the flames that were his discomfiture from breaking wind in the presence of one of the most beautiful girls he'd ever met. Assuming "met" was an appropriate word since their introduction was an unsolicited audible emittance from his arsehole.

"What a lucky girl, whoever she is?" retorted Mae li.

"Thank you, her name's Chantelle," replied Spencer.

"It would be," remarked Mae Li sarcastically, looking across at Innocence, who smiled nervously back.

"Here she is," slurred Spencer finishing the last morsel and licking the spot of brown sauce from the side of his mouth before turning his laptop to face Mae Li. The picture was of a Rottweiler wearing a huge grin, its tongue lolling out of its baggy chops as it perched awkwardly on a living room couch.

"Oh, I think you're punching above your weight," remarked Mae Li. Spencer smiled at Mae Li and then looked at the picture.

"Oops, that's Daisy, my mum's dog. But, being candid, I love her more than Chantelle. So here she is," The photo on the screen was of a pretty blonde-haired girl with lots of make-up pouting at the camera wearing a leopard spot printed top and a necklace from which hung the letter "C."

"Charming, I'm sure you make a great couple. I need to focus on my work now, thank you," remarked Mae Li, who returned her focus to her screen.

"Me too. I've got a meeting with investors this Friday. Round one funding for my online business. It's a no fucking brainer, but then you can never do enough preparation. My Dad says he always remembers the five P's in the Army. So, proper preparation prevents piss poor performance."

Mae Li could not help herself. "Six," she corrected him.

"What?"

"That's six Ps. Proper preparation prevents piss poor performance" she counted each word on her fingers and hushed and mouthed the word piss.

"Well, perhaps it's meant to be five, but I think he added piss for dramatic effect," replied Spencer nonchalantly, "Either that or he couldn't count," and hmphed before smiling across at Surjit, who thought this was brilliant. He'd received an acknowledgement, and his indiscretion was side-lined by this exchange. Surjit smiled hesitantly back.

There were a few moments of silence, and it appeared the interpose was through with, but Innocence had contemplated what Spencer had said.

"I thought the five P's of strategy were the plan, ploy, pattern, position, perspective as attributed by Mintzberg," remarked Innocence.

"No, not according to Winston Churchill, it wasn't," replied Spencer.

"I don't recall Winston Churchill noted for such a saying," frowned Mae Li raising her eyebrows towards Spencer.

"Winton Churchill is my father," replied Spencer.

"Your father is Winston Churchill? He can't be. He died in 1965," said Mae Li.

"No, not Sir Winston Leonard Churchill, wartime leader and one of Britain's greatest statesmen. I refer to Winston Derek Churchill, a plasterer from Watford. My Dad. Well, he was a plasterer. He's retired now. His shoulder's fucked" nodded Spencer.

"Your Dad is called Winston Churchill?" confirmed Innocence.

"Yes, my family name is Churchill. When Sir Winston Churchill died, as you correctly stated, in 1965, my grandfather named his first son my dad, born that same year, Winston. I'm Spencer, by the way," and he held his hand out to Mae Li. It was rude and awkward not to accept his offer to introduce himself.

"Mae Li." She replied, extending her hand and fingers confidently, her nails beautifully manicured, which Spencer noted.

"And I'm Innocence," beamed the lovely black girl from across the desk. Although there was a pause before they each looked across at Surjit, it seemed appropriate to do so.

"Hi, I'm Surjit."

"I think you've introduced yourself already," laughed Spencer. Surjit's heart skipped, and he felt his blush return to his face.

"I'm so sorry." He apologized.

"Don't worry, everybody farts, even Mae Li and Innocence, isn't that right, girls?" added Spencer, but there was no answer from either of them.

"Can we get on with our work, please?" replied Mae Li, and the please was elongated to accentuate the request. Spencer returned to his screen and picked up his coffee. He slurped some hot black coffee through the perforated flap on the lid and shuddered as the hot liquid scalded his throat. Spencer looked across to where the girl with the blue beret sat, and it appeared she concentrated on her work. Spencer waited, looked up, and then looked back when she noticed he was looking over at her. That look was enough for him. All he had to do was wait for the right moment, and if she were interested, and he was sure she was, she would make sure that moment came. His phone wolf-whistled, alerting a text. Mae Li breathed in a little deeper.

7.43 CHANTELLE   *how r u, babes? xxx C*
7.43 SPEN   *busy talk later x*

The phone wolf-whistled again,

7.44 CHANTELLE   *how is your new job?*
7.44 SPEN   *not really a job is it but busy talk later x*

Another whistle and Mae Li closed her eyes slowly.

7.44 CHANTELLE   *missing you already xxx*

One more alert, and Mae Li slowly clenched her fingers.

7.45 CHANTELLE   *missing me?*

There was another wolf whistle, and Mae Li breathed more profoundly and drummed her fingers.

7.46 CHANTELLE   *Spen?*
7.46 SPEN   *FFS, busy, talk later*

Mae Li turned to Spencer.

7.47 CHANTELLE   *wot no kiss?* ☹ *xxxxxxx*

7.48 SPEN   *ffs xxx*

"Spencer, can you switch off your alerts, at least while at this table?" hissed Mae Li.

7.49 CHANTELLE   *Luv u hun xxxxx*

"Pardon, yes, fair enough, there, it's sorted," he replied deadpan slowly and adjusted his phone settings. Mae Li looked up at Innocence, expecting some eye contact support, but she had become immersed in a world of puppies, kittens, and lollipops.

Surjit felt comfortable with the group of people assembled at this table. They acknowledged him, and he'd had to fart to utter six words and become a part of a conversation. He looked up at Spencer and Mae Li, they were the catalyst for it, and he was sure something else repeated offered another opportunity to interact. Spencer's irritating text alert had nearly kicked things off again, but then he had acquiesced when asked to quieten it down. Spencer leaned back in the chair, his head resting on the back to appear almost horizontal while peering over the desk at his screen. Mae Li sat upright, tapping intermittently on her keyboard. She seemed to be editing something. Surjit glanced to his side; Innocence's screen was awash with small cartoon furry animals. They looked like cats and dogs interspersed with candies. How could she be playing a game at work? Granted, it was still early in the morning, but time was money; perhaps this is how she warmed up for the day like some people do Crosswords, Sudoku, and drink coffee.

Innocence was contented. The chocolate had kicked in, its glycaemic effect coursing through her veins. The prototype of her game was functioning well with enough inaugural features operating as expected, puppies and kittens competing for candies. The world was full of cat and dog lovers; for most of them, you either loved one or the other, meaning a vast market potential. The game developers in South Africa had completed a good prototype, and she hoped the success of "Sugar Rush" would leverage more opportunities for them. It had to; the money saved hard from long shifts waiting tables had run out. However, there was enough content to appreciate the concept, and it just required more work building the business case for the investors to consider. She had a few days to finalize the plan before the meeting on Friday.

Mae Li glanced at the busy people in business attire, holding mobile phones, some smiling, some pointing, then focussed her attention upon the heading of the title slide, "Veracity – an investment opportunity by Mae Li, CEO 888 Technologies". Maybe calling herself CEO was a little hyperbolic. After all, 888 Technologies was not even an incorporated company yet, but forming a company was as easy as a few clicks, and she pondered its name. Triple 8 was considered a lucky number in China. It meant three times good fortune. Although confident in her business plan and her capability to execute it, she would take all the good luck she could get. In 1980, it was good luck for Bill Gates to receive a call from IBM looking for an operating system for their new personal computer. It was lucky IBM's first choice of partner negotiated badly such that IBM came back to Gates for a counterproposal.

Luckily, IBM did not insist on an exclusive agreement with Gates's fledgling company, Microsoft, and was fortunate that hardware, not software, soon became the commodity. Adding luck to Bill Gates's consummate skill and the compound multipliers of the technology valuation market, his wealth plateaued to just over $100 billion. Without such luck, Gates would have gone on to have made millions of dollars in any case, but not billions, and a billion made a Unicorn, and a Unicorn is exactly what Mae Li desired to create. That would show her father how remarkable the son he never had, had proved to be. Veracity was her brainchild and antithesis to Linkedin, where millions of professional profiles, backgrounds, and egos airbrushed to within an inch of their super-inflated business lives. An amorphous professional platform where personal statements replaced job titles along with politically correct value statements that, on the contrary, held no value. Mae Li considered the site a vast and nebulous spew of regurgitated press releases, company notifications, and righteous personal posts and shares. Announcements to connections which could not be more disinterested in the pile of grey, uninformative crap that expunged through the bowels of this giant living creature and shat out of each of its millions of profiled orifices. Some were bigger arseholes than others, serial posters, people who held several hundred or thousands of connections and collected them with a zeal that would match any other fanatic.

Having suffered its tragedy when attempting to build her network, Mae Li had the eureka moment of replacing it with something objective and candid, something that would strike terror into the hearts of the millions of psyches that hid behind the bullshit and bluster. The truth. A veracious portal where people could discover the reality regarding their colleagues or prospective employees.

The Linkedin description of an "Ambitious, talented and respected professional project manager, experienced working on large enterprise programs across retail and wholesale sectors" became replaced by Veracity with "Responsible for some large-scale blunders costing millions of pounds in time and budget; Has been warned on two occasions for invading the personal space of young female administrators; Suffers from halitosis and on occasions issues with personal hygiene." The list was endless, and skeletons had nowhere to hide at Veracity because no edited closets and manicured testimonials could be claimed by the recipient and posted by a friend. Instead, veracity-verified statements of fact helped professionals learn the truth about each other. Veracity enabled the dark web to come out into the light, a social site that nobody would admit to subscribing to but one that everybody would. HR departments would pour over such illicit details and revel in asking awkward questions to prospective applicants when it became apparent a prospective employer knows what happened back at the Travelodge after the last Christmas party. Veracity, morally bankrupt but financially worth billions. Mae Li smiled at the thought as she plotted a toned-down presentation and kept it subtle; using the correct language, the investors can work out the real intent and worth for themselves.

Spencer had closed the porn app and popped air pods into his ears. He toggled his mac book to reveal a logo design. The capitalized word "SHAGPAD" changed the right angle of the letter G into an arrow representing the male symbol. In contrast, the letter P became altered by the female character of a circle, which stemmed from a low inverted cross from its base. "Catchy, clever, and clear," he thought, gratified with his work. His air pods signified the next track shuffled, and something else clever and catchy rippled through his eardrums, and his fingers set to work, tapping lightly on the work surface while his right foot dabbed the floor. His cherry red Dr Martens made a satisfying clump on the hard laminate floor. A ripple of fingers started with his little finger becoming drum rolls and amplifying his forefinger. His left forefinger snapped the snare, and his right index finger's nail tapped the hi-hat against the hard desk surface. What started as a bit of light air-drumming slowly ascended into an audible syncopated rhythm, very well timed and equally annoying, particularly to Mae Li. Bom ta tap ta bom ta tap ta bom ta tap ta bom ta tap, with the four-finger ripple rolled every four taps performed at 75 beats per minute to synchronize to practically any upbeat dance track; however, in this case, BHS by Sleaford Mods.

Mae Li bit her lip and glanced at Spencer, whose head nodded as he played. She thought men could be so annoying, especially the boyish ones, which counted most of them. Most men never grew up, which explained a lot. It expounded a passion for football, drumkits, trainsets, motor cars, and anything that could move or they could move. They loved breasts, women dressed like girls, mum's roast dinner, anything electrical, anything digital, things that went fast, and best friends they could hug when alcohol relaxed a natural inhibitive state. Mae Li could go on, but Spencer personified her thoughts amply with his brown eyes softening innocently to the simple task of keeping time and the beat. Ordinarily, she would have found this irritating enough, but with the upcoming investor review on Friday, now was not the time to suffer fools for more than a moment.

"Stop drumming," she mouthed while waving her right hand across his peripheral vision. The communication attempt failed to register. Spencer had not noticed the signal. Keeping time to simple post-punk beats *and* completing some analysis on Excel was with as much as his brain could cope. Surjit became aware of the situation, as did Innocence, who sat to Spencer's right. Mae Li slunk down in her chair to offer her the leg length required to kick Spencer's shin from the heel of her boots. She calculated the most likely range and direction to score a direct hit, drew her leg back, and struck. "Ow, fuck me," Mae Li shrieked as her inside ankle caught the square angle of the inside table leg. The pain buzzed up her right leg numbing her thighs as it went.

"Take it easy," interjected Innocence looking puzzled, "What's up with you?"

"Him. The Duracell bunny over there," she seethed, poking a finger in Spencer's direction.

"Laying on a boat, well, what do you do" he sang under his breath, tapping some numbers into his spreadsheet. Innocence prodded his arm gently.

"What?" he asked loudly, the music dimming his auditory control.

"Stop singing and drumming," replied Innocence softly.

"What?" he shot back louder "I can't hear you."

"You're a fucking wanker", whispered Mae Li. Spencer sat upright and removed his air pods.

"Easy tiger," he smiled.

"See, you heard that, didn't you," said Mae Li, her arms folding.

"I didn't hear you. I could read your lips," Spencer replied.

"You can lip read, can you?" doubted Mae Li.

"Well, certain words and phrases, yes. I mean, "fucking wanker" is quite easy to grasp. It requires the hard consonants of F, K, ING, W, and another K with the softer vowels of U, I, A, and ER. Put together, and you get," and he mouthed pronouncedly "F-U-CK-ING-W-A-N-KER. It's one of the first things they teach deaf kids, "

"Really, and I thought they might start with thirsty, hungry, toilet, please and thank you, but oh no, according to you, it's "fucking wanker" and "what a twat" no doubt," smirked Mae LI sarcastically.

"Well, no, I was referring to the co-articulation of phonemes and visemes as expressed by the movement of tongue, teeth and lips and visualized by the recipient. You could be right, "fucking wanker" and "what a twat" is as good as a place to start as any, I suppose," he pondered and shot her another smile. Mae Li stared back at him; his eyes were dark and twinkling with mischief.

Mae Li turned to Innocence and exchanged empathic glances, their eyes rolling upwards with synchronized sighs. Surjit smiled nervously back at Spencer, whose attention had returned to modelling the numbers of daily room rentals required for him to surpass his first one, ten, and 100 million in pounds sterling currency. Spreadsheets made business seem so easy. Once you discovered a successful formula, it was simply a case of scaling up the numbers in the multiplier columns. The arithmetical procedures magicked terrific results in the column marked net profit. Who could fail to see the enormous potential that *Shagpad* offered investors? To Spencer, the investment opportunity was more philanthropy than a necessity to offer up a piece of this novel idea and business model. Sex had always sold, and property had always sold, but the two together had exclaimed Spencer, and you had pricks and mortar, the technological business equivalent of a racing certainty. He had contemplated "pricks and mortar" as the business name along with "Shag bnb," "Burple pricks," and countless other puns on already established enterprises. Still, litigation defence was a death curse to any fledgling tech company. Spencer had no funds to kick start the dream, and his only capital injection was five hundred pounds saved from various odd jobs to fund a cheap laptop.

Surjit multi-tasked during the morning between testing his app and watching the Mae Li and Spencer sideshow. At first, it was Spencer's *WhatsApp* texts that irritated her. His drumming accompaniment, followed by occasional vocal outbursts to whatever track he was listening to, and the heavy typing like somebody playing whack-a-mole with the keypads. Mae Li objected to it all. Spencer seemed unphased and angered her further with apologies of endearment. "Sorry baby," "Oh, ok,

Maisy," and to cap that, "I'm so sorry" sung like the chorus in Suedehead by Morrisey. An unamused Mae Li rejected each apology.

The testing part of Surjit's morning - his app's software element, as opposed to the distraction- went to schedule. Digamber had delivered some decent coding. Spanner was on track. On Friday afternoon, his piece de resistance demo was ready for the upcoming investor review. The panel could see how seamlessly and effortlessly a mobile user could manage the performance of their mobile devices, bypassing device and app factory settings and enabling selections to choose which apps consumed more available memory and power. Different spanner icons could tune various types of apps with additional layers of security. Imagine, at the fingertips of the world's 4 billion intelligent mobile devices, the capability to go beyond the device settings to fine-tune your mobile to perfect performance and security. A dollar per month per device, and he would need 4 million subscribers to annualize revenues of around $50m. 4 million subscribers was just 0.1% of the exponential tsunami of smartphones engulfing domestic markets globally. A $50m revenue achieved by a high-growth mobile technology justified a 20 times multiplier valuation on his business, a quick trade sale, and the result? A Unicorn. As predicted by Surjit's three-year business plan, a one billion dollar value company and by 28 years old, he could have anything he wanted. A wonderful house in the country – any country, a super yacht, a football team, a luxury villa in the Bahamas, a fast sports car, make that several fast sports cars, a mother proud of him and a wife?

Innocence ran through the gameplay again. Choose a cat or dog, and for Innocence, a cat. Choose a breed of cat. Innocence selected a sleek Russian blue with their namesake big blue eyes, accentuated by the cartoon character. Create a name for the cat, and she called it Benjy. Select a level, beginner, intermediate or advanced. She assumed new players would pick beginners and clicked the option. A high-pitched note signified the game was ready to start. Benjy had to navigate a world of pastel-coloured paths, flowers, trees, and skies, where mushrooms and toadstools were as large as a house because they were homes where elves and goblins lived. One belonged to Benjy, and he or she, hum that was something she needed to add, an option to select male or female. Or other. Would some players not want their cat, or dog, to identify with a male or female. Could a cat be transgender? Perhaps best to remove that option so Benjy could be whatever Innocence or game player A wanted them or it to be.

Benjy's task did not include sleeping for 15 hours each day, taking a shit in a sawdust tray by the backdoor, and disappearing at night to wreak havoc with the local wildlife population. It was to hunt and collect candies with different values according to their difficulty level and store them at home. There were obstacles to navigate, other cats to befriend or avoid, likewise dogs and other gameplay elements unlocked as the skill level increased, which Innocence had hoped would appeal to casual gamers anywhere and of all ages and genders. Casual games were played on smartphones or handheld game-oriented machines, where the object was to complete simple, menial tasks and pass the time. Lowly, minds became occupied since they were incapable of original thought to ponder the universe, its meaning, or anything between that and one's existence. Quite some gap thought Innocence, but fortunately, the banal and self-absorbed outnumbered the philosophers and dreamers on this planet. There was nothing wrong with this since every living organism contemplated no more than avoiding death, wondering where its nourishment was coming from and where it might next procreate, and this also applied to 99% of humans. Modern society had come to the point that such little time became consumed by activities that served the basic instincts of survival, sustenance, and procreation that other tasks needed to satisfy longer-lasting lives. Modern people required different things to do, given that philosophy, art, and the pursuit of knowledge were not for everybody.

   Innocence observed many men and women as children enjoyed playing football. By the time they reached adulthood, a few cunning ones had corralled it into a predominantly spectator sport where only the very few get to play for extreme riches for broadcasting to the very many. Most onlookers paid money to gambling companies through high-risk accumulative bets on outcomes and expensive club playing shirts replicating the teams they selected to support. The camaraderie once experienced through having fought and toiled to a physically draining result with ten other teammates against equally determined opposition was now felt by singing the same repetitive chorus of club songs throughout successive seasons with tens of thousands of like numb-minded victims. Even this supporter experience had become digitized, and that was not real. Life in the 21st Century Western world was not honest or sincere. Innocence had decided to exploit and create a short digital experience to consume otherwise precious minutes of a person's existence. They would spend hours gazing down at a screen, not up at life's vista, and try to win candies for their cat or dog, achieving a higher level of gameplay but, ultimately, a lower level of existence. But that was not Innocence's worry. She wanted a million casual gamers to her platform, which meant sponsors would line up eager to pay to advertise in the margins or obsessed to the extent that addicts would pay to download the next iteration of a popular title. The money would roll in, and Innocence could redirect that towards her passion, education for underprivileged children in Africa. Learning gave rise to intellect and an opportunity to consider and acquire the higher value things such as health, culture, and compassion. She had selected casual gaming as a means of siphoning resources from the economically advanced moronic masses to the underprivileged malnourished multitudes from her native continent. It was her plan, and she was sticking to it. She just needed Angel funding to get the project off the ground. The upcoming investor meeting on Friday was crucial to that and to all for which she dreamed.

Time ticked on across the table of dreams, the hourly room rental platform for illicit relationships, the honest, professional profile platform, the digital Swiss army knife for managing your mobile device, and the attention-sapping gameplay of puppies and kittens for people who needed to kill time and their self-respect. Today, this group shared just one table of dozens spread across the budget-priced floor of the Hive, where dreams and reality sadly managed to maintain a safe distance for most.

"Anybody hungry?" asked Spencer. The others raised their heads at the question, peering over laptop lids.

"I could eat something," admitted Surjit. "Me too," added Innocence.

"I'm ok, thank you, and will do my own thing anyway," asserted Mae Li.

"Then do you mind just keeping an eye on our kit and keeping our places?" asked Spencer ", just while we grab something for ten minutes," he was already rising from his chair while looking down at Mae Li.

"You can leave your stuff there, but I'm not responsible for it, OK?" she shrugged back.

"Cool, then we'll be back when we're full," smiled Spencer nodding to Surjit, who sat opposite.

"I'll wait until you are back," said Innocence "then maybe we could get a coffee or something," she suggested looking hopefully at Mae Li.

"Yeah, maybe, whatever," replied Mae Li.

Surjit stood adjacent to the much taller Spencer inside the elevator, and they descended alone before it slowed to collect a passenger on the second floor. A thick mop-haired white guy looking like Bradley Cooper, wearing a combat jacket and a canvas man bag slung across his right shoulder, stepped in to join them for the remaining two flights to the ground floor. The lift slowed within a few seconds, having just started its journey, with the numbered light indicating it was making a stop on the first floor.

"Lazy fuckers, one fucking floor?" exclaimed Spencer, tutting in the direction of Bradley Cooper with the man bag, hoping to garner some empathy for their unnecessary delay caused by somebody not walking down the final flight. But unfortunately, the retort was not reciprocated, and Bradley Cooper stepped out as the doors drew open to reveal nobody waiting to enter.

"Oops, that's pissed him off," remarked Spencer as the doors swung back shut. Surjit let out a cry of laughter. They arrived at the ground floor and walked out of the building.

"What do you fancy?" asked Spencer.

"I'm easy," replied Surjit knowing he was anything but when it came to food. He was vegan and very particular regarding its preparation, so he tended not to eat out much.

"Well, there's varying degrees of expense, usually corresponding to pretentiousness, but we don't want to go to that end of the scale. I occasionally have a pub lunch around the corner at the Britannia, but that's a no-go today. Monday's are too early in the week to get pissed, Tuesday maybe, but not Monday. There's a Chinese across the road, a bit pricey, but I usually end up wearing it, so probably not there or anything else, noodles and sauce. Finally, cracking bacon rolls down at the café by the underground station. I already have one; however, I could do another if you wanted?"

"No thanks, I'm fine. I just wanted to step out. You go for whatever you want. I'll just grab a coffee or on the way back," suggested Surjit, who did not want any complication of his veganism interrupting the novelty of going out to lunch with somebody else.

"Well, let's get a coffee at Starbucks around the corner, and I'll get a toastie," declared Spencer and spun on his heels as his thumb pointed the other way to the City Road branch.

"Sounds like a plan with proper preparation," smiled Surjit mimicking the conversation earlier that morning.

The branch was filling up, a busy queue had formed from the door to the counter, and a variety of people squashed into its small tables, designed for singles and pairs, the regular footfall for a city-based coffee outlet. Spencer picked out a ham and cheese toastie, a chocolate muffin the size of a cricket ball, and was ready to order his beverage. Surjit hastily snapped up a vegan chocolate bar and a banana, then held back to serve Spencer.

"Sorry for your wait," snapped the portly male assistant with a badge named Chris. He had a Latin appearance, chubby cheeks, a wispy black moustache, sweat glistening across his top lip, acne-scarred cheeks, and forehead.

"I'm cool with my weight, 6 foot 1 and 12 stone; I'd say you need to be sorry about yours judging by the sweat," replied Spencer. Customer-facing assistants did not appreciate sarcasm but less in busy stores with listening queues. But unfortunately, Spencer had mistaken the remark.

"Would you like that toasting?" retorted Chris ignoring the rude comment.

"It says Toastie on the wrapper," smiled Spencer, handing over the package.

"And to drink?" Chris asked Spencer.

At this point, the tall, suited man served in front of Spencer became more animated. "No Mochas? That's insane. I am in Starbucks, no chocolate powder at all?"

"If your definition of insanity is no chocolate sprinkles in your coffee, then I'm afraid it is," replied the young female assistant, half apologetic but with a sprinkling of sarcasm to replace the chocolate. It seemed infectious this lunchtime.

"We have called another store and will have some later," she added.

"That doesn't help me right now," objected the lanky customer.

"Sorry, I can offer you a grande latte for the price of a regular as an apology for ruining your day," the assistant smiled forcibly.

"Ok, it'll have to do, to go please," he added hurriedly,

"Your name please?"

"Humphreys"

"It'll be just a minute, please wait by the end of the counter, and the barista will call your name" she looked to Surjit "just that and to drink?" she asked as she scanned the chocolate and gave it back to him.

"A regular coffee with coconut or almond milk, please," he asked.

"Sure, that's £3.49 and your name, please? Ok, Surjit, wait at the end".

Chris returned from placing the sandwich in the grill and looked crossly at Spencer. "To drink?"

"I'll have a grand americano, please,"

"OK, £7.50 for it all, Milk with that Americano?"

"No thanks, just black, as an Americano should be, thanks,"

"And your name?" added Chris, who was ready and poised with his dark marker pen.

"My name is Mocha, same as the drink," Smiled Spencer, who waited with the others for somebody to call out his name. A few moments later, there was a call for Humphreys, who retrieved his large plastic cup without thanks and started towards the door.

"Mocha ready," called the Barista. Spencer thanked him as he took ownership of the piping hot drink and toastie already bagged. He turned and joined Surjit, who had collected his cup, and they walked towards the door. They bumped past an irate Humphreys on the way out, heading back towards the counter.

"I thought you were out of chocolate powder. I just heard a Mocha called for that guy over there," pointing towards Spencer, who had just left the store, laughing with Surjit.

They sat for lunch at the breakout area called the Honeycomb on the ground floor of the Hive. Spencer demolished the toasted sandwich in seconds while Surjit nibbled the banana back to its stalk, taking sips of his hot coffee.

"Where do you live?" asked Surjit.

"North Barnet, I share a flat with a mate, and you?" replied Spencer.

"Close to Elephant and Castle. I'm in between flats, so I live with my mum, but I'm moving out soon," nodded Surjit.

"Really, when and why?" asked Spencer.

"When you're 25 years old, you don't want to be living with your mum, do you? I'll move just as soon as I find somewhere, but I'm pretty focussed on my project right now," nodded Surjit.

"I'd say being home with your mum is pretty cool. Come and go when you please, always a dinner waiting for you whenever you get in, clothes and bedding washed and ironed, bathroom cleaned, home pretty much straightened out. Bung her 30 quid in rent once a week, then borrow it back Friday night. No, I'd say you're doing alright, Surjit, don't change that in a hurry. What are you working on?" asked Spencer, picking up on the second line of Surjit's previous answer.

"I've designed and developed a prototype mobile utility app, and I'm showing it to potential investors this Friday in consideration for funding," explained Surjit.

"No way sounds cool. The investors, they're not Angeltech are they?" smiled Spencer.

"Yeah, how did you know?" quizzed Surjit.

"I'm up in front of them on Friday, too. They are running quite a few slots this week".

"Really, what is your pitch?" asked Surjit.

"Business platform, connecting people and property," replied Spencer.

"Sounds brilliant. I'll be you get funded," added Surjit.

"And why do you think that?" asked Spencer.

"Because you are super cool and confident, I'd invest in you if I had any money," exclaimed Surjit.

"Ah, thanks, Bro, and me you too, you know, if I had plenty of money," lied Spencer, but he thought this young guy needed some confidence before the meeting Friday because he looked terrified about this. The coincidence bound them, and after talking over lunch, they took the stairs to the hot desk floor, walking over to where their laptops and bags were kept under supervision by Mae Li and Innocence.

"Hi guys, what did you eat?" asked Innocence.

"Chateaubriand with dauphinoise potatoes and seasonal vegetables, delicately matched with a bottle of Saint-Emilion, followed by a double espresso to keep us hard at work this afternoon," announced Spencer with a parodic French accent.

Innocence giggled "no, you didn't, did you?"

"Nah, a ham and cheese toasty for me, a banana for Surj, and two cups of coffee, courtesy of that Michelin-starred venue on City Road, Les Bucks du Star," chirped Spencer.

"Shall we go then?" asked Innocence looking across at Mae Li.

"If only for a break from him, sure fine," snapped Mae Li looking across at Spencer.

"I'll miss you too. Text me that you got there safely," Spencer replied. But unfortunately, there was no response from

Mae Li as she disappeared with Innocence across the work floor.

"Where to?" asked Innocence.

"Is there anything you can't or won't eat?" asked Mae Li leaving the Hive through the security gates.

"No, I love most things, but let's keep it light," replied Innocence.

"We'll go to Trade, it does cool sandwiches, brunches, and stuff, and it's just 5 minutes down Old Street," Mae Li's long legs strode off, strutting like a supermodel while Innocence tried to keep pace with a shorter, quicker stride. At the busy café, Mae Li selected the spare table by the window and sat down, shaking her long black hair loose and drawing in a deep breath. Innocence sat opposite her and surveyed the room.

"Do we go up to order, or will they serve us here?" asked the young African.

"I'll order from my phone, take a look at the menu and let me know what you would like?" said Mae, adjusting her make-up with a small mirror and lipstick. She was beautiful, thought Innocence, flawless complexion, and high cheekbones made many Chinese women look elegant despite their comparatively petite size. Mae li was much taller than Innocence, although her calf-length boots had 4 inches heels elevating her to 6 feet. The dark motorcycle leather trousers pulled tight across her shapely backside and thighs, a sight not unnoticed by Spencer and Surjit, although it was only the former who expected that he might see them peeled off onto his bedroom floor. Or hers, either way, worked for him.

"I don't know what to have. Hah, sourdough grilled cheese sandwiches, look at the selection Mae Li. And they make buttermilk pancakes. Pastrami sliced, and look at all these other sandwiches. Oh no, what to have? Look at the brunch options, chorizo chilli, and eggs! And the smoothies, oh my days. What will you have?" asked Innocence, her eyes wide like saucers.

"Salmon, avocados, and scrambled eggs on sourdough and a detox smoothie," replied Mae Li tapping the order into her phone.

"Can I have the same?" asked Innocence.

"Sure, I'll make that twice; anything else?" enquired Mae Li.

"No, I should not."

"But you will, I insist; what would you like?" smiled Mae Li.

"A salted caramel brownie, please; how much does mine come to?" Innocence reached for her purse.

"I'll get this. You can return the compliment another time," said Mae Li pushing Innocence's hand clasped purse back towards her pocket.

"I couldn't accept that," remarked Innocence.

"The food and drinks will be on their way, and I don't want to carry any cash, so we'll have no more discussion on the matter, so there. Anyway, please tell me, what are you working on?" Mae Li changed the subject.

"I have developed a casual game, mobile or handheld platform, it's at an early stage, and I am going to see if I can get funding to finish it and stay here." Innocence looked up as she spoke.

"Sounds exciting; from where will you attract finance? Have you received any investor interest yet?"

"Not yet, but I will present it to some investors this Friday. My first step is entrepreneur sponsorship for first-round funding, I hope." Innocence smacked her lips on the word hope.

"Is that by any chance the Angeltech investment group," suggested Mae Li softly.

"Yes, how do you know? Do you work for them?"

"No, sorry, I can't help you there; rather, coincidentally, I'm presenting to them for funding for my project, too," said Mae Li.

"Oh, that's scary, wow. When is your meeting?"

"Mine is also this Friday, in the morning, 9 o'clock."

"What are you pitching?" asked Innocence. She hoped it was not a casual game because Mae Li looked and sounded so composed and professional.

"It is a social media platform for professionals," replied Mae li.

"Like Linkedin?"

"No, I don't, and this is quite the opposite of Linkedin," smiled Mae Li wryly.

"Do you live in London?" asked Innocence,

"Yes, not too far away, near the University of London, but I drive in on my motorcycle, it's only 5 minutes door to door, and it is easy to get around town without a tuber,"

"Tuber?" puzzled Innocence.

"Tube or Uber," replied Mae Li flatly, to which Innocence nodded in acknowledgement. "And where do you live?" added Mae Li.

"Dalston. I live with my elder sister, quite close to the station. I walk to and from the Hive each day, and it's two miles each way or about 400 calories. That equates to two free, small bars of chocolate every day, or four for two as I prefer to see it." Innocence grinned nervously back across at Mae Li, who sat poker-faced. She did not consider that Innocence needed to worry about calorific balance. Sure, she was a fuller figure, but she was pretty, and her form suited her. So, innocence changed the direction of the conversation. "Surjit and Spencer seem nice enough boys, don't they?"

"Nice enough "boys," indeed. Surjit is not very experienced around women, is he? Spencer, he is so immature, don't you think?"

"I'm not an experienced girl to judge males, so I'm not going to comment too far, but Spencer seems sincere and friendly if a little distracted at times," she giggled, thinking about him that morning.

"Man cubs, the pair of them, the only difference is that one knows it and the other doesn't. Fortunately, we will only be sharing desk space with them for one day, or I'd end up killing him," and Mae Li gritted her teeth but then smiled back at Innocence. "Innocence. Such a sweet name. What is the story?"

"There are many Zulu names for the English adjective Innocence or sweetness, but my mother could not choose, so she said I'd keep with Innocence, and so Innocence I became. How about your name Mae Li? What does this mean?"

"It's Mandarin for - don't fuck with this bitch", smiled Mae Li slyly. Innocence smiled nervously and looked out the window to avoid constant eye contact. The traffic sauntered past with its ever-present drone while pedestrians kept up an endless array of faces, figures, and forms. London was a people watcher's paradise, with patio coffee bars at mainline railway stations the best vantage point. Trays, dishes, and glasses clattered and chinked as background accompaniment to the din of chatter from which the food eventually arrived. Innocence dug hungrily into the eggs, salmon, and smashed avocado while Mae Li carefully picked the protein items, only taking a few small bites from the toast between sips of the smoothie. Their conversation turned to how they had come to London to study from thousands of miles apart and how they were sharing lunch ahead of meetings with the same investment body that could dramatically change their futures. Mae Li was sent by her father to study business and economics at UCL and to further his connection with London and Europe. Innocence had won a scholarship to the London School of Oriental and African Studies from her college in Johannesburg to study Anthropology. However, they both needed sponsorship from Angeltech or any other government-approved business endorsing body to remain in the UK to qualify for start-up entrepreneur visas beyond the end of the year. Mae Li, driven by a desire to be independent and respected as a woman by her father or any man, Innocence by the urge to make change for so many less fortunate youngsters she had left behind in South Africa. The last blobs of the detox smoothie slipped down effortlessly before Innocence pocketed her salted caramel brownie to be consumed later with her penchant for weak, milky tea; An early afternoon brew now beckoned.

"Ladies, how was lunch?" enquired Spencer as Mae Li and Innocence took their seats adjacent to Spencer and Surjit.

"Very healthy, nutritious, and delicious," replied Innocence pleasingly.

"Two large kebabs with fries then, was it?" chirped Spencer.

"With lots of chilli sauce and no salad," added Surjit.

"Are we that predictable" sighed Mae Li. Spencer looked at Surjit, offering him the opportunity to retort. But, instead, Surjit's smile turned to anguish as he sought a witty reply. His forefinger half pointed as if to stab home the remark but then wilted as nothing came from his lips.

"Erm, good, good," he said finally and buried his head, furrowing his brow as if something important had appeared in his inbox. Spencer could not leave that comment hanging.

"No, but the sauce on the corners of your mouth gave it away," quipped Spencer with that glint in his eye, "You've just got a little more on your chin too, at least I think that's a sauce, here you go" and he handed Mae Li a tissue. She looked back at him disdainfully, folded it, and pursed her lips across it, and their faint outline held on to the tissue, becoming apparent as she unfolded it. Then, finally, she handed it back to Spencer, "better?"

"You have no idea what I'm going to do with this," he chuckled, taking back the material carefully and placing it in his bag.

"Oh, but I do, she replied, and that's as close as you will ever get to the real thing," her smile turning to a frown, "Now, please, let's get back to business, shall we?" and she patronized the words "shall we" while giving a sharp glance to Spencer and Surjit to her side before clearing her throat. Her body language was thus clear; playtime was over.

Spencer looked where the girl with the blue beret had been peeking at him. He stared across and waited to smile. She glanced through and recoiled when their eyes met unexpectedly before slowly looking back at him. He was still transfixed by the smile and darted his eyes to the water cooler and machine coffee breakout area. He rose from his seat and strolled towards the machines taking his spent coffee cup with him. A quick splash from the taps and a couple of shakes, and it was ready for a top-up, not that he wanted another coffee, just a distraction. He selected espresso from the display and waited for the short jet of hot coffee to spurt into his cup. Just what was on his mind, he thought.

"All that porn worn you out, has it, in need of a pick-up?" the blue beret voice said.

"I don't watch porn, I do porn, and it never wears me out, not that I've been told in any case," he replied.

"Perhaps people need to be honest with you then", she teased.

"What time are you leaving this place later?" said Spencer.

"Half five, not that's any of your business?"

"Well, at half-past five, I'm going to take you around the corner for a drink,"

"No, you won't."

"Then I'm going to buy you another one,"

"No, you won't."

"Then I'm taking you back to my flat,"

"No, you won't."

"And I'm going to undress you slowly while kissing every part of your body,"

"No, you won't," Holly's eyes were a mix of anger and intrigue. Spencer leaned forward to whisper something in her left ear.

"Then I'm going to take you into bed and fuck your brains out,"

"No, you won't," the "no" was accentuated.

"And I won't wear a condom," he hissed.

"Yes, you will," she snapped back. The deal was sealed as Spencer took her number, turned on his heels, and hiked back to his chair. Holly took some quick sips of her coffee and did likewise.

Mae Li looked across; having noticed the exchange, she felt a slight pang of jealousy and anger for feeling so. Surjit could see the brief encounter and wonder what magic words Spencer could weave such a spell on young women. But, of course, there was no magic, just an illusion and Holly was happy to be knowingly led on that this fit young guy could make her feel good like when a magician asks you to place a card back in the pack, knowing he was going to trick you and it was harmless fun. Whether or not Spencer could pick the right card was down to him, but she thought he was cute enough to be given a try, or maybe several.

The afternoon meandered on, and as it did, the desks began to empty, at first at a trickle but then, by 4 o'clock, there were as many empty chairs as occupants. For the next hour, more chairs screeched back across the wood-panelled floor, laptops snapped shut, and bags zipped closed with a flourish before more deserters trooped towards the lifts and stairs. The day's fight surrendered until later that evening or tomorrow. By 5 o'clock, Spencer had finished internet surfing for the past two hours, Surjit was tired from code testing, Mae Li was in dan-ger of over-complicating her presentation, and Innocence had finished the Brownie with a cup of tea.

Spencer's phone buzzed in his pocket,

17.01 CHANTELLE	*How are you, Spenny xxx?*
17.01 SPEN	*Cool but working late.*
17.02 CHANTELLE	*All work and no play? 2nite? Xxx*

"Fuck, that was creepy," he thought,

17.02 SPEN	*Yeah, but it will be worth it when I'm loaded.*
17.03 CHANTELLE	*Hope so call me later, luv u xxxxxxx*
17.03 SPEN	*OK, back to the grindstone, bye x*

"Anyone fancy a pint?" he suggested.

"No thank you, and it is Monday", replied Mae Li.

"Then let's celebrate; that's the first day of the week out of the way, all downhill from now", pleaded Spencer, who did not fancy sitting in the pub alone for an hour and a half.

"I don't drink alcohol. But I could have an orange juice," admitted Surjit.

"That's the spirit, or they serve no alcohol, beers, and wine, you know," said Spencer, galvanizing support, and he looked at Innocent.

"Come on, I'm buying", he tempted. But, instead, Innocence looked across at Mae Li.

"We could just have one drink," she said, looking hopefully, and the cracks had appeared in her defence. But instead, they all looked at Mae Li.

"Well, OK, but I'm driving, so just one then, and no alcohol for me", she snapped.

"Looks like a cheap round; then come on, I know this great little boozer round the corner from here," and Spencer rose from his seat, packed up his MacBook, squeezed back his shoulder blades, and rolled his head, loosening his neck as if preparing for a heavy weight lift and then popped his rucksack across his shoulders. The others followed suit, minus the shoulder stretching and head-rolling, and they made their way to the stairwell.

"Ladies first", declared Surjit as he approached the doorway first and held open the door for Innocence and Mae li.

"Don't be starting with this gender stereotype bullshit?" said Mae Li. "I think Innocence and I are more capable of pushing open a fire door and far more likely to succeed if it was any heavier." Surjit was mortified. How could he get something as simple as a common courtesy so wrong? Perhaps he should not have called them ladies or implied they were too weak to push open the door themselves? Still, he had said "ladies first", suggesting he thought ladies should exit a building first. Wasn't that what they once called chivalry, but chivalry in London in 2016 was long dead. It was every man, or rather, every "person" for himself, or rather, "themselves".

"Sorry" in a defeated sort of way was all he could muster in response. Mae Li felt slightly regretful for her comment; after all, Surjit struggled with the complexities of socially interacting with women in a world of ambiguities and contradictions. Social etiquette was changing faster than fashion and with little sympathy for anybody caught in its wake. If to prove the point, Innocence politely uttered "thank you" as she stepped past, and Surjit felt a mixture of dismissal and confusion. Best for him to stay quiet, let Spencer do that talking and see where this one drink with new friends took him. Friends? No, it was too early to call them friends. Acquaintances was a more accurate description, but then there was hope.

The Old Fountain, with its glossy brown tiled exterior ground floor walls, stood towards the Old Street end of Baldwin Street. It was a traditional City pub, with several ale pumps, a glass-fronted food serving counter by the stained-glass front door, and three floors of dark wooden chairs and tables that led to a closed rooftop garden, given it was both early in the week and just turned Spring. One small group sat in the centre of the ground floor bar chatting whilst a few individuals sat at the peripheral tables, each taking the inside seat looking out, hunched over the hidden screens of their laptops and phones, nursing a quiet Monday night pint.

The front door flew open, and Spencer strode purposely, with his newly found posse in short tow. He walked directly to the bar and drummed the counter with a crescendo that irritated the thin, pony-tailed guy behind the bar, who raised his eyebrows and muttered, "What would Sir's pleasure be?" to which Spencer thought the aptest reply to be, "football and fanny" but for once caution got the better of him, and instead he replied,

"A pint of Pride, please". With one hand, the bartender promptly produced a pint glass with the name Fullers London Pride branded across the exterior, and with the other, he gripped the pump handle, ready to pour. No sooner had he squeezed the handle than Spencer changed his mind.

"No, I won't; I'll have a Camden Town pale ale".

The bartender sucked in hard through his nostrils and replaced the glass with another with matching branding. He headed towards the appropriate pump before being stopped in his tracks.

"Nope, changed my mind", declared Spencer. "I'll have a Redemption White IPA".

The bar guy turned and replaced the Camden Town pale ale glass, stooped to collect one that read Redemption, and paused as he searched for the logo.

"I don't think I've got a clean Redemption pot. Do you mind if I use something else?" the bartender asked,

"Provided it holds a pint and I can hold it, I don't give a fuck mate", smiled Spencer turning to his guests and raising his eyebrows with an ironic grin. "Reminds me of a woman who stood at a bar, and the fella beside her says I'd like to fill your fanny with ale and drink the lot. The woman says, how dare you, I'm going to tell my husband which she did, and she says to her husband, so, what are you going to do about it? He replied, "nothing; if you think I'm going to have a go at a bloke who can drink 16 pints of draught ale, think again," He looked around at Surj, who was suppressing a giggle.

"I don't get it", replied Innocence.

"Let me explain, the guy…" said Spencer before Mae Li interrupted him.

"Just don't bother Spencer and keep your misogynistic jokes to yourself."

"They're not misogynistic", declared Spencer. I tell gags about everybody, men, women, gay, straight, black, white.."

"Then just don't", snapped Mae Li.

"Anything else?" sighed the bar guy.

"Well, I know the one about a fella who has a crocodile and walks into a bar, and he says".

"He means anything else to drink, not any other of your pathetic jokes", interrupted Mae Li. "I'll have a lime soda, Innocence?"

"A dry white wine spritzer, please", replied Innocence, who had already calculated the calories, 120 and another kilometre to add to the walk back home. Next, the attention turned to Surjit.

"Erm, a shandy?" he answered hesitantly, sounding unassured. Of course, it contained alcohol, but he wanted to hold a pint glass with Spencer, and indeed he could manage a shandy, thought Surjit.

"Beer or lager", asked the bar guy.

"Erm, no, just a shandy, please."

"I meant beer or lager in your shandy?" added the bar guy whose fingers started to wag impatiently on the empty glass he'd produced.

"What's the difference," asked Surjit.

"One's made with beer, and one's made with lager", sighed the bar guy drily.

"For fucks sake, go with lager Surj. We'll be here all night, and I've got to see a man about a dog later," piped Spencer smiling, and the others, including the bartender, glared ironically at each other.

The drinks were poured, Spencer flashed his card at the reader and then suggested they occupy a table centrally set in the front bar, allowing Spencer to spot the blue beret when she came in; there was no "if" about it.

"Ok guys, what are you working on?" enquired Mae Li, who shot the boys a glance and a raised eyebrow smile each.

"You go first", suggested Surjit to Spencer; it would deflect his attention, and hopefully, the conversation would go down a rabbit hole, avoiding the need for him to explain his project.

"Tinder, Grinder, Match, e harmony, our time for the over 50's for fuck sake, all of these apps connect people who want one thing in common?" Spencer opened the palms of his hands and hunched his shoulders as if asking a question.

"Love?" replied Innocence.

"Love? If you are referring to the act of fornication, physical arousal for personal or mutual, if that's your thing, pleasure, then yes. Sex sells. I mean, think of all those dating apps; they are all about 100% fuck and no commitment. They serve one of mankind's primal needs, to fornicate, procreate, fuck, frig, shag, shaft, screw, score, bonk, bang, poke, pork, hump, bed, jab, lay...." Spencer paused for breath,

"grind", suggested Surjit, who then gulped his shandy; what had he said aloud?

"Easy tiger", smiled Spencer, who looked across at Mae Li, who was poking her tongue down and playing with the straw in her drink before letting it bob up and popping it into her pouting mouth. The teasing display was not lost on Spencer.

"There are more words to describe sex in the English language than Eskimos have for snow", exclaimed Spencer.

"Yeah, well, I think we just heard most of them," Mae Li remarked dryly. "Grrrrinding", she growled, glaring at Surjit, who had seemingly blushed despite his acorn skin colour.

"No, you haven't. There's having it off, copping off, getting laid," continued Spencer.

"We've heard enough; where is all this going? What's your plan and try to get to the point?" huffed Mae Li.

"My point is that there are now millions of people meeting up for social interaction without, in most cases, a discrete location to socially interact, if you get my drift. Some apps allow people to rent out their homes, Airbnb, daily. People meeting up to socially interact for an hour don't need somewhere provided for a day. They need somewhere provided for an hour and priced as such. That's where Shagpad comes in," and Spencer glanced furtively at the other three sat at the table and sat back with his arms folded.

"Shagpad? Really?" uttered Innocence. "You make it sound like a cheap illicit place for sexual demeanours."

"That's because it fucking well is", whispered Spencer. "People can't use their own homes, and even Travelodge in Barnsley is 39 quid for a night. That's a lot of money in Barnsley when you only want a ten-minute bunk-up. Bunk up, there, that's another one!"

"So, rent your rooms out by the hour like a cheap knocking shop. Convert your home into a brothel," surmised Mae li.

"Exactly. Supply meets demand. Some people need somewhere to socially interact, some people need to supplement their income, sweat their assets, so to speak," declared Spencer like a magician revealing the hidden card.

"A lot of sweaty assets, yuk", replied Mae Li. "How classy. Why did I think that would be something you would think up?"

"Get over yourself. It's business. Do you know how much porn is worth? Billions of dollars, no, nobody knows how much, but if people can meet up somewhere for ten pounds an hour and my platform rakes in a 20% commission, that's two pounds per fuck, sorry Innocence, social interaction. So given there must be thousands of these each day, that's a lot of two pounds, add it all up, and it is a few million a year for the UK alone and then when I go global, that's a lot of Euros, dollars, and Yen," Spencer sat back, raised his pint and took a large swig.

"Great idea! It just needs another name," quipped Innocence.

"Let's just meet", sang Surjit, copying the jingle from the online food delivery service of a similar name.

"Love it", shot back Spencer and jabbed the idea into the notepad of his mobile.

Mae Li laughed, "what's your idea Surjit? What great plan are you working on?"

"Me?" Surjit cleared his throat. "It's a bit techy, but in layman's terms, it is a utility for optimizing the performance of a mobile's OS. If you download the utility, it runs some code that will turbocharge your mobile performance, like gaming or any app requiring high system execution. It utilizes a proxy .exe file that engages the kernel and replicates commands to trigger quantum-like instructions without impacting the integrity of the core processor." Surjit looked up, and the others nodded back at him.

"Sounds amazing", chirped Innocence.

"Yeah, it does. But, would it invalidate the phone's warranty?" asked Mae li.

"What? How do you mean?" asked Surjit, panicking.

"Running third party code in an executed instruction usually invalidates warranty, a bit like turbocharging a car engine will invalidate a vehicle's warranty because car parts aren't designed to handle higher performance. I guess you've looked into that and have got that covered" Mae Li smiled.

"Yeah, I've got my lawyers looking into that. I think we're cool that one," lied Surjit whilst simultaneously crying "SHIT" inside his head. He could no more manage a poker face than drink eight pints of his shandy, and his face sank as he nervously drew the frothy pint to his lips, his hand shaking slightly.

"So, how are you going to get rich?" countered Spencer nodding towards Mae Li, part in courtesy for her turn and part to protect his shy young protégé from further punishment, who looked as if he had been floored onto the canvas and had just soiled his boxers.

"Tell me, do you use Linkedin?" asked Mae li.

"Erm, sometimes", replied Spencer.

"What do you think of it?" snapped Mae Li.

"Fucking tragic", batted Spencer straight back.

"Any why is that?" followed Mae Li.

"So full of Bullshit. It is a big job board full of the biggest load of self-righteous, lying tosspots. It makes me sick I can't look at it," shrugged Spencer smacking lips after another heavy swig.

"Maybe I got you wrong, but I'm beginning to like you, not much, but more than I did a minute ago", exclaimed Mae Li.

"Give it time, and you'll fall in love with me," laughed Spencer.

"I don't think either of us could live that long, " replied Mae Li before continuing. "I am developing a professional platform that will enable people to rate colleagues truthfully and with transparency that will render Linkedin irrelevant, obsolete and transfer much of that revenue to my business." She tilted her head and smiled. "I can't say any more than that, or I'd have to kill you" she looked across at the two men who synchronously picked up their drinks.

"What's your story, Innocence," asked Surjit.

"Mine is not quite so ambitious or hard-hitting as you guys. I have developed a mobile platform casual game based on cats, dogs and chocolate. People either like cats or dogs, and everybody loves chocolate."

"I don't particularly. I can take it or leave it," replied Spencer.

"Me too," added Surjit.

"Oh, but you love dogs, don't you" smiled Innocence, referring to Daisy, Spencer's mother's Rottweiler. Spencer smiled and nodded in affirmation, his eyes darting towards the door.

"I don't particularly like cats or dogs either," remarked Surjit.

"That's because you're a propellor head", laughed Spencer elbowing his side "both Surjit and I have got investor meetings with Angeltech at their office in Old Street this week, on Friday, the same day.

"Get lost. That's amazing, so have we," replied Innocence, and Mae li nodded in unison.

"Fuck off", replied Spencer.

"Straight up, we both found out at lunch; how ridiculous is that" laughed Innocence. "I have 9 o'clock, and Mae Li is at 11."

"I'm in after you at 10.00", added Surjit,

"I've got 08.00", declared Spencer.

"Well, I'm just glad I'm following you", laughed Mae Li. "Following *Shagpad*, my business is going to sing.

"Same format? 60 minutes total, 30 minutes pitch, and 30 minutes questions?" asked Innocence. Surjit replied enthusiastically.

"Yeah, if they think it has potential, you get a call back for an hour next week. Correct?" Everybody agreed.

"Let's meet in here Friday lunchtime, and we can toast our success," piped Spencer,

"Or lick our wounds," said Surjit, downbeat, still dwelling on the legal loophole swallowing up his strategy. Perhaps he could postpone the meeting and ask for an extension.

"You'll be fine; I think they'll love your idea", smiled Innocence, "that's fine by me. I could do with a drink by then,"

"Ok, with me too, if only to hear what they think of Shagpad," tutted Mae li.

"Friday midday, first round on me…again," snapped Spencer, jabbing his empty pint glass on the table. Its provocative display was not lost on Mae Li. "Fancy another before I GO?"

she asked him. The clunking sound of the door opening coursed across the other groups' feint mutterings, and Mae Li instinctively turned her head towards it. Holly, the girl with the blue beret, stepped in tentatively to survey the occupants. "Oh, what a shame you won't have time", she added, having noted the earlier liaison at the kitchen breakout in the Hive.

"No, I've got to see a man about a dog", replied Spencer ascending from his seat. "Maybe see you guys tomorrow?" he asked.

"Maybe", replied Mae Li nonchalantly.

"I'll be there", affirmed Innocence.

"Me too," added Surjit with enthusiasm.

Spencer walked towards the bar and could be heard asking the blue beret girl, "what can I get you?" as the others finished their drinks, Mae Li snapped at Surjit, "finish your drink then, we're off,"

Surjit did not want to be seen left wanting and downed his nearly full pint and bashed the empty glass on the table in triumph. Mae Li could not have been less impressed, and for one terrifying moment, Surjit thought the pint might head back up and projectile vomited the two girls rising from their seats. He felt the uneasy stick settle into his cramped stomach before heading to the door, glad to be the last to leave so that the charade of chivalry could be omitted from the complicated process of simply leaving a building.

"You can get me laid" was the brief and direct answer to Spencer's question. So they left without the social formalities of having a drink and getting to know one another for the informality of taking an Uber taxi straight over to Holly's flat. Her home was on the second floor of a converted Regency townhouse in Primrose Hill.

"Nice drum", extolled Spencer having strode into the high ceiling lounge room; soft cushions and throws adorned the two settees that sat perpendicular in arrangement, each affording forty-five degrees view of that large TV screen straddling the corner. Fashionable prints hung from the white-washed walls, one depicting an ancient Greek figure. Adonis stood naked, holding a horn in his right hand, a scroll in his left, while a dog and a wild hog knelt at either side. "Well, I can at least top that," thought Spencer glancing at the small flaccid penis perched aloft, a small scrotum in opposite scale to the prominent figure that stood proud, unjustly so, he thought.

"Drum?" whispered Holly inquisitively. "Drum pad. Flat," replied Spencer, "Looks like he is ready to blow his horn," nodded Spencer towards the print of the figure he had observed.

"And I'm about to blow yours", smiled Holly, pulling Spencer towards her bedroom door that led from the main room. Spencer was tall, dark and handsome as would describe a cliched hero of a Mills and Boon romance or a Barbara Cartland saga, but even by his prolific standards, this embrace was as forward as it got, and on a Monday night too. Depending on her appetite, he might be able to get the job done and still make the second half of Monday night football and a ready meal cremated by Chantelle. Spencer could be "up for her" too, following a Sainsbury's Lasagne scraped and consumed from the sides of the plastic tray. "Let's just see how this plays out," he thought, "One game at a time", to repeat an old chestnut trotted out by football team managers setting no future expectations other than focussing on the match at hand.

Holly's bedroom was distinctly female, bed made, white sheets, pillows, and duvet neatly palmed across the surface of the double queen-sized bed. The dressing table by the panelled window was neatly attired with bottles, brushes, and makeup pots aligned in ascending order. A fitted double wardrobe lined up parallel with the far side of the bed and a small table perched next to the bed head, a soft pink pastel colour that matched the carpet. Not that Spencer noticed or cared, but Holly was neat, tidy, and ordered, everything that he was not, and she liked control, as he was about to find out. She stood opposite him, undoing her skirt, which dropped to the floor and then pulled off her top, which left her standing in heels and matching black underwear. She unbuttoned his black shirt and pulled it back off his shoulders. His muscles were taut with defined lines, his low body fat reflecting a well-worked torso. She cheekily pinched his nipple as her hand drew across the surface of his chest. He smiled to conceal that it hurt; her nail caught it, and the others in her delicate fingers were sharp and scratching at his back. Fuck, it was like patting next door's cat, claws in his back pulling at the skin like they do when being stroked and purring. Her tongue flickered in and out of his mouth and ears, fuck not his nose, he thought as he sniffed hard, his hay fever still evident through laboured breathing. He felt her hands unbutton his jeans and run the zip down his fly as she smiled and flashed her eyes. Spencer's reciprocal smile turned to terror as the zip snagged his foreskin protruding from the open fly of his boxer shorts.

"Ouch! Fuck. Stop" he screamed, turning away in a judder. His mouth hung open while he stood paralyzed on the spot.

"What is it?" demanded Holly, looking distressed but not as much as Spencer's.

"You've got my cock caught in the zip", he shuddered.

"Let me see," she said, dropping to her knees and peering at his groin. Then, she pulled at his jeans to gain a clearer view.

"No", he screamed in a high-pitched falsetto that hung on the letter o. "Don't touch anything; the skin on my shaft has caught in the zip, just a fucking minute", he shook.

"I was trying to help", she snapped back.

"Well, fucking don't, leave it. You've already done enough. But, shit, it fucking hurts, fuck, fuck, fuck," Spencer grimaced through gritted teeth. "Let me try and release it," and Spencer held the zip and started to pull gently at the loose skin that had immersed itself in the runner. The application of the metal upon his foreskin meant it had swelled and become painfully lodged into the slider.

"I'll get some cold water and some oil," said Holly standing and starting towards the door.

"I'm not thirsty", he replied in a self-deprecating attempt at humour.

"It'll reduce the swelling, and perhaps it'll come loose." She replied, leaving the room. Spencer looked down at his predicament, his cock snared in the zip, still in his pants but the exposed part caught by the fly opening of the shorts. "Who the fuck designed underpants with a fucking fly" he uttered under muted breath. Not another man, that was for sure. This was an accident waiting to happen, he thought. Not to a male who knows to be careful unzipping his fly and retrieving the old man for a piss or a wank or, if you are lucky, a blow job, but to a woman of no experience or empathy. Well, it was as clumsy as a teenager fumbling at a bra clasp for the first time. Only a poor girl's skin between the shoulder blades could not be as sensitive as a man's penis, or at least not the soft skin that encased it.

"Fuck romance or the passion of the moment," Spencer thought. "Message to self; never let a woman undo your fly when your cock is already excited. You are not in a rational state to be running a risk assessment whether she has the skill or patience to release the Kraken, injury-free."

It was as if Holly had the skill of a surgeon attempting micro-surgery wearing boxing gloves. But, speaking of micro-surgery, what if he needed it? What if his cock tore being removed and stitches were required? Holly returned to the room holding a glass of water, a towel, some eyebrow tweezers, and a small bottle of olive oil.

"What if it bleeds and I need stitches?" posed Spencer.

"Let's hope they have a micro-surgery team on standby at the Royal Free", she teased.

"But if I get a hard-on, it'll burst the stitches", he pleaded. "I can't go a day or two without a hard-on. I can't go an hour or more without an erection." Spencer looked terrified.

"Let me see what I can do?" she sighed and knelt before him. The sight of a fit young lady in bra, heels, and knickers, on her knees in front of him with her soft hair pulled from her ears, applying oil to his prick was not lost on Spencer, and he felt his member stiffen again. The pain intensified.

"You are going to have to stop", he stammered.

"Why is the thought of me using tweezers upsetting you?" she asked.

"No, you are turning me on. That is what's hurting," Spencer replied frustratedly.

"Men are so fucked up", she exclaimed, rising to her feet and then walking away. "It is probably best you try and retrieve yourself; I'll get some coffee, use the water to cool it down, the oil to lubricate it, and the tweezers if they help, and good luck" she shrugged and left the kitchen for caffeine. He turned and caught his reflection in the dressing table mirror, the angle humiliatingly upturned so he could appreciate what a drained man looked like. One stood in the bedroom of a girl he'd barely known, with skin from the shaft of his dick lodged in the zip runner of his jeans. Fuck corporal punishment; he thought he could never do that shit for fun. Those who did were more fucked up than he was. His phone rang. For shit's sake, it hadn't been switched to silent. He retrieved the item delicately from his pocket and looked at the screen. "Chantelle" flashed in beat with the tune and then died as he flicked the screen to silent. With his hands shaking, he dabbed more cold water onto the affected area and then applied the oil as gently as he had ever mustered when managing his prick. He closed his eyes and bit his lip. Following a short tug and a sharp scratch, his phallus fell limply free from the metal. The skin was bruised but not bleeding, sore but still playable. With the fickleness possessed like a predator, the past travails were immediately forgotten, and he looked forward again to the impending action with Holly.

The small bar had a pink neon sign over it, "Bar", it said as if anybody could be so stupid as to mistake the arrangement of bottles placed within it and the stack of assorted glasses as anything but that. A disinterested-looking girl was topping up an overpriced pint of lager to the rim of the glass before taking payment and handing it to a mid-thirties man. He had fairish receding hair, a boyish ruddy complexion, and rounded steel-framed glasses. He wore a waistcoat, too small for his advancing frame. It probably fitted when he had bought it. He beaked his neck forward like a pigeon mid-stride to take a sip, lowering the liquid from the top of the glass and the likelihood of it spilling before he took up his seat close to the action. Several other men gawped at the raised platform upon which a scantily clad girl performed acrobatics whilst holding on to a vertical pole. Her legs extended up and around the bar, the taut gusset of her thong pulled tighter with retreating success covering modesty if she had cared for any given her performance. Her shoes were opaque, standard fare for pole dancing as Mae Li had observed who stood to the rear of the stage, waiting in the wings.

"Give it up for Mandy", enthused the announcer as the display concluded. Mandy smiled in acknowledgement whilst adjusting the crotch of her attire, forgetting her artistic integrity, but this wasn't the Olympic finals. The small gathering of men sat and spread evenly around the podium and clapped politely. Then, the music changed, "When doves cry" by Prince, released fifteen years before the advancing dancer was born, emitted loudly from the speakers suspended from the black ceiling. A wolf whistle peeped from the recently seated, plump, balding customer, which raised an eyebrow from the hefty gentleman standing discretely offstage and wearing a tight black t-shirt with the word "Security" written across it. He twitched his biceps in a reflexed response but stood them down immediately. It was early; enthusiasm did not likely need pacifying, particularly on a Monday evening.

"Here she comes, putting the east in "feast". It's Chi-Chi," announced the compere. Mae Li strutted forward and began her routine with a handstand which enabled her long legs to envelop the pole, grip it and pull her up with the agility and ease of a panther. She wore silver hot pants that inevitably rode up her backside, and her sheer bra worked hard to contain her breasts. The flash of the silver outfit sparkled from the lights and the disco ball that spun above the room. This was cheesy, but cheese is a commodity, and cheese sells. In a country where most people favoured medium matured Cathedral City cheddar rather than more substantial types, spangly silver sirens on a pole worked for this club, and it did not matter for Mae Li. She was not here for the money, although she could clear four hundred pounds cash after expenses later in the week. But she did not work later in the week. It was too busy and full of drunken pervs who had convinced the offer of more cash was enough for her to want to meet later to have sex with them. Either that or they were good guys, dragged along against their will, and wanted to meet later to ensure she got safely home. She could knock any one of them out, cold, and she knew it. She worked Mondays and Tuesdays, it was quieter, and she got paid for keeping fit. She enjoyed teasing these sad little men who giggled like schoolboys or frowned, attempting to be mysterious. They were both uninhibited by a fair dose of alcohol and a distorted self-orientation from the male mirror that never told the truth. She worked with four other girls, each taking a two-track set for about 10 minutes, and a three-hour shift with private dances meant she danced a dozen times for a night's work. This amounted to an hour she enjoyed and was paid between one and two hundred pounds. The money was insignificant, her father being one of China's wealthy exporters. Mae LI worked the pole with deft skill, never smiling as the other girls did; she held the same contemptuous stare that the customers could mistake for smouldering, pent-up desire. It was anything but that. She carried on, spinning around the pole with the power and poise of a circus acrobat.

Within a couple of hundred seconds, Prince petered out. Her second and final song, pattered in "Addicted to Love" by Robert Palmer, started up. A classic from the 80's announcing its arrival with the bass drum and open hi-hat combining and offset against a tight ambient snare across four opening bars before the keyboards blasted in. Anybody that skipped to this from that era with big hair and voluminous clothing would know it instantly. Sadly, some punters did, and the bespectacled balding bloke clapped and cheered. He was on his second pint, the one from which you got you a taste and were either going to get pissed or be left hanging. Mae Li shot him a momentary glance. His hands were clasped and wringing, like a miser, thinking about the cash hidden under the floorboards, his tongue visible as it flicked out like a lizard as he took another gulp of the pricey beer. Mae Li focussed on the music and danced on, oblivious to the base thoughts and moronic stares.

Innocence placed the tomato on the chopping board and, with a firm grip on the slippery skin, sliced with the serrated knife placing the contents on her plate. The remains of a supermarket salad bag had been scattered around a chicken breast portion upon which the tomato pieces lay. She applied a generous squirt of salad cream in a zigzag formation across the food. The bottle was near empty and made a noise like a wet fart as it strained to emit its last contents. She smiled, thinking of Surjit and his embarrassing faux pas leading to the group meeting for a quick drink. There was the prospect of another at the end of the week after the presentations had been delivered. The chicken salad, all 600 calories, was nearly ready for eating, just the last ingredient needed to be added for it to be complete. She stooped to open the oven door, and a gust of smoke billowed across her face as she pulled the tray from the hot furnace. A generous portion of gourmet oven chips was shuffled over the salad and cream, and the door closed deftly with her heel as she turned away to carry supper to the table.

"Voila, chicken salad, and a few chips on the side, " she declared, smiling at her sister, who sat opposite her laptop open and looked non-plussed.

"If that's a few chips on the side, then you'd need a serving plate for a full-sized portion", replied Agnes.

"I didn't use the whole packet", appealed Innocence.

"No, not the whole packet, just all of the contents inside the packet", teased Agnes, drawing her coffee to her mouth. Her eyes flashed bigger over the cup at Innocence, laying more bait.

"There's a portion left in the bag," uttered Innocence clumsily, cradling a hot chip in her mouth.

"There are four leftovers in the bag. So why bother? You might as well eat them all?" laughed Agnes.

"Why bother indeed?" thought Innocence. Why was counting calories so hard? It was like counting cash when you had none. She never had enough money and certainly never had enough calories. What would she wish for if she were given just one? Ten thousand pounds, every day for the rest of her life, or ten thousand calories to be consumed how she wished, with not one of them counting to her bottom line, no pun intended. It would be the calories every time. Of what use could ten thousand pounds every day become? Buying a car every week meant nothing to her. Fancy holidays, clothes, and a bright place to live? None of it was worth a jot if she could not enjoy what she wanted, to eat and as much of it as she wanted to. It was not where she ate and who she ate with mattered to her. She was happy with her sister, a man one day who loved her and she, him, and with kids too, but to start and end each day with chocolate, and fill it with patisseries, cheese and milkshakes, and not be unhappy with its effect, that was being rich. She looked down at the plate and felt depressed. Why couldn't salad taste good? Even with salad cream, it sucked. It was a nice crunch and added bite, but only if accompanied by something like a big fat juicy burger in a brioche bun or buttermilk battered fried chicken dripping with fried onions. Sugar rush would be her passport to enough money to enable her to invest in the product development of the world's first fast-food chain that never put a pound on you, not an inch. Now that was an idea that would be worth a fortune, a guaranteed Unicorn.

That evening, the Northern Line was quieter than in the reverse direction earlier that morning. Surjit found a seat at Old Street Station, and the train soon tugged at the powerline, thundering towards Elephant and Castle. Surjit held his head a little higher on the return journey. If that were what a whole pint of lager shandy could do to his self-esteem, perhaps his teetotal formative years had been mistaken, placing his physical health ahead of his mental wellbeing. Dutch Courage, he had heard it called, intoxication to engender bravery. However, the Jenever gin that Dutch soldiers of the 17th Century drank before fighting the English offered a 40% proof boost which was somewhat more potent than the 2% provided by Surjit's pint.

Nevertheless, it had encouraged him as much as Spencer's slap on the back and "later mate" comment as he departed and strolled into the direction of the girl with the blue beret who Surjit had noticed in the office earlier and who had coincidentally appeared at the pub. "Mate", yes, he would be Spencer's mate. Spencer exuded confidence, which would rub off on Surjit, and before long, who knows, by the end of the summer perhaps, Surjit would walk with a swagger, wearing a distressed leather jacket, ripped skinny jeans, and muscle t-shirt, and scuffed tan boots. Surjit crossed his arms and felt his biceps beneath his cotton shirt. Perhaps the muscle t-shirt could wait whilst he did something about his arms, which wore the circumference of a child. There were tablets that he had read about that could provide a boost. He was thinking about booze and pills; it was only Monday evening. Where could this week lead? Surjit smiled and then felt a slight discomfort under his scrotum. The feeling became heavier as the train sat back, and his seat bumped across the stiff suspension of the ageing rolling stock that vibrated across the uneven tracks that dipped under the Thames for London Bridge, the next stop. Alcohol might boost courage, but in the form of a pint of beer on Surjit's compact bladder, the additional effect was that he was going to piss himself unless he could get off at the next stop and find a convenience within a few minutes of the exit doors. The tidewaters rose inside his pelvis like a balloon filling with water, and sitting soon became uncomfortable. Surjit stood and was relieved to discover this miraculously improved capacity meaning perhaps the need for an emergency stop receded. That, however, was before another unscheduled interruption of a different kind. The train shuddered to a halt. Surjit's heart sank whilst reminding himself of the adage, shit happens. Given the circumstances, it is not the best analogy, but at least that was not a direct comparative predicament he was in. It would only be a few minutes for the delay, not uncommon under the Thames as clearance on the other side was sought from heavy traffic. The seconds slowed until it felt that time had stood still. The most sought-after conundrum of space-time physics to confound the greatest mathematical minds of the centuries unlocked. The simple predicament of desperately needing to urinate when incarcerated inside a public vehicle with dozens of strangers with no means of leaving because of being stuck in a tunnel several yards underneath the main river that bisected one of the world's greatest cities. Time stood still.

By the time the train and Surjit in it had surfaced on the south bank of the Thames, over ten minutes had elapsed, and he had become more desperate. Finally, the doors pulled open, and Surjit bundled out onto the platform, bandy-legged, feeling like he'd had a bowling ball sown into his scrotum. He swung his legs deliberately wider and winced with each step as he drew closer to the actions that led to the escalators. London Bridge underground station boasted many facilities. You could buy a ticket, buy Euros, redeem cash, make a fixed-line phone call, receive an adequate WIFI signal and take an escalator either up or down, from or to the platforms, but you could not take a piss. That was taking the piss, thought Surjit ironically, and with a pained smile on his face as he had felt that he had thought of something reasonably witty and was just a little vexed there was nobody he could recount it to, maybe save it for later. He shuffled to the escalator and bit his lip as he stepped gingerly onto its moving surface, and slowly rather too much so, he began to rise from the catacombs. This was agonizingly slow, the adverts passing by with too much time, enough time to not only look at them but read them, and probably the reason for dictating the speed more than any regard for health and safety. Then, at last, he sensed daylight and the gates ahead, a passport to freedom and a location from which he could discharge this gathering ball of urine pressing hard against his urethra. A flash of his card at the gates and he was out into the dimming light of the early evening April sky turning sharply to his left and stepping like a penguin the thirty yards to the archway that ran to the Kings Arms. Surjit had not visited a pub in 30 months but was about to call in his second on the same day, pushing his way into the green doors and surveying the homely layout for a clear sign of his salvation.

"Which way are the toilets please?" he pleaded to an early evening punter stood with a pint surveying the Monday curry club menu.

"Round the corner of the bar, mate," came the reply to which Surjit could not muster the strength to utter thanks. Every ounce and jot of his energy was focussed on his legs, propelling his body to a urinal before they became the wet, warm victim of a burst bladder. His feet were turning inside uncomfortably, each step an excruciating twist on a sensitive part of the internal anatomy he never knew existed until now. Finally, he pushed the door marked "Gents" and stepped into a small bathroom with two small porcelain urinals. Both were occupied. A guy stood to attention, his head held aloft as if in prayer, the other with an elbow against the wall, his head cushioned into his supporting arm. "Try the cubicle," thought

Surjit charging at the door like a copper from the Sweeney, and fortunately, no occupant was sitting on the other side of the door or worse, still bent over dealing with the paperwork.

Surjit fumbled at his trousers, letting them and the pants he pulled at in unison drop without a care if the floor was clean or not. The strain to pee when his bladder was so tight was intense, and he wondered if he would ever feel the sweet release of pressurised urine against the water below. He looked down, and something unpleasant bobbed up in the bowl, looking back at him. The pan was old, in need of brushwork, and had seen as much traffic as the famous bridge that arced across the river only yards away.

"Filthy fucking London," he swore, and another first for Surjit, who rarely cursed. He flushed the toilet and winced as his fingers depressed the lever to enable the motion. One pint, two pubs, and a fuck, if sadly, the latter applied to only the word, and at last, the slow dribble from his penis tinkled onto the flowing rush of water that foamed around the dirty bowl. It was disgusting, but it was beautiful, and he could do no more than letting out the relieved cry of a desperate and frantic man who had found the epiphany. The jet accelerated, and the beginning of the monsoon started with a single drop, at first a trickle before becoming a gush. He moaned another sigh of relief when suddenly the jet overcame his control. He fumbled his whiplashed appendage such that the resultant down-blast missed the open rim of the pan and instead directed straight into the vulnerable gape of his trousers and pants that lay open and exposed below his knees.

"Oh, Fuck," he screamed. He had sworn again.

TUESDAY

Innocence stood in front of the panel, who were seated in a variety of armchairs. Three men and two women listened impatiently to her presentation, legs were crossed and uncrossed, and pencils twiddled and sucked. The man sat to her left folded his arms, and the woman to his right sat motionless, sucking her mouth tight like she was retrieving some part of her breakfast from a gap in her molars. Innocence felt the slightest cold sweat trickle down her back behind her overheated neck. Why had she fastened her shirt so tightly up under her chin? Why wear a formal blouse at all? It was not as if the panel would invest in her addictive, casual game based on her sense of dress? She cleared her throat and concluded the opening pitch,

"Sugar Rush, a casual game, so addictive you become a casual…ty." And she over-accentuated the pun. She smiled nervously and waited for the oncoming questions. Peter Jones was the first to respond.

"You are asking for £50,000, yet you only offer 10% of the business. This means you value your business at £500,000, which is ludicrous. So I'm out, you have no customers, you haven't launched, you have no test cases; no further discussion is needed."

Deborah Meaden was the next dragon to speak up,

"I hate games full stop. Pocket games, board games, computer games, play station games, ball games, card games, table games, outdoor games, indoor games, playing games, it's all a waste of time. So, I'm not interested either; I'm out too." This was becoming the fastest rejection recorded during the 17 series that Dragon's Den had run.

"Why will people download your game instead of the tens of thousands already in the market?" asked Theo Paphitis.

"Erm, research has shown that 60% of people identify with games that represent something important to their life, and pets, particularly cats and dogs, are essential to people worldwide," she replied hesitantly.

"They're not important to me, but maybe I'm in the 40% who would agree. So I suggest you go and find somebody in the 60% to invest because I'm not, I'm out." He snapped his book shut and crossed his arms. Innocence looked across at Sara Davies and hoped for something more sympathetic.

"Well, I think you've got a big fat arse, and so on that basis alone, I'm out", she yelled.

Innocence's heart sank, she felt humiliated, and the dragons laughed at Sara's comment. There was no point even listening to Tej Lalvani, the remaining dragon. He was crying with laughter, pointing towards her lower half. The laughter grew to a reverberating cacophony, and Innocence started to cry.

"Big fat arse, big fat arse, you've got no chance, cos you've got a big fat arse", they all sang in a chorus.

Innocence opened her eyes and blinked, staring at the white paint crumbling from her bedroom ceiling. The relief consumed her, like that missed deadline nightmare everybody has tossed and slept through, exams not revised for, speeches not rehearsed, or any other such unprepared common life occurrence that Spencer winged his way around. The respite came compassionately with each blink of her eyes, still calibrating focus and with each expelled breath that was deep and laboured. Without recounting that nightmare, Innocence could never watch an episode of her favourite TV show again. She reached for her phone, dabbed the screen, and the display lit up, 5.45 a.m. She might as well get up 45 minutes before the alarm triggered, but she could not sleep now, not after that traumatic experience. It was time to break into the bank.

Across town to the northwest in Croxley Green, Chantelle reached out for Spencer and felt the vacuous space of the empty half of a double bed. She had expected to touch the reassuring warmth of her fiancé, even if it was typically his long hair across the back of his shoulders, but there was just a cold flat undisturbed sheet. And then she immediately remembered he had not come over to her home last night, he had said he had something to finish, and it would take all evening. The burned, pre-packed lasagne had gone uneaten and lay in the baking tray downstairs. Terry, her father, would eat it cold in a sandwich with ketchup. He ate everything with ketchup, and it had to be Daddy's sauce, splashed with such abandonment that whatever he ate resembled roadkill.

Surjit was out of bed much earlier than usual, his phone's alarm waking him just before 6 a.m. Following a short shower, he selected new pants, unusual for a Tuesday but following his accident, and a pair of jeans, his trousers, and Monday's pants were in the washing basket. He threw some jackets into a sports holdall, picked up his laptop bag, and tore down the stairs. There was no time for breakfast before he hurried out of the front door and into the brisk morning air, tainted by the whiff of diesel and petrol fumes of the ever-present inner London traffic. He skipped nimbly towards the underground station at Elephant and Castle before flashing his card at the machines guarding the entrance and descending into its groggy bowels. The arriving train doors clattered open as he stepped into the car. He was immediately reminded of the previous evening's nightmare when he had strained so hard to avoid urinating into his trousers only to fail at the last hurdle.

An unfortunate and distressing ending when all had seemed to be saved. Life was one long lesson. Don't count your chickens before they hatch. Pride comes before a fall, and don't leave your penis uncontrolled when releasing a solid jet of lager shandy from a distressed bladder. At this time of the morning, he could select a seat, all of them looking grubby from the collective wear of tens of thousands of collective arses slumped upon the coarse cloth fabric each week. It was best not to think about that, so Surjit focussed on getting to the Hive before seven o'clock at a point that the hot desk floor was under-consumed. The journey under and across the Thames was quicker than his usual train, with fewer passengers bustling in and out for position, taking up precious time. He was soon at Old Street station, bouncing up the steps to the surface and the remaining short walk, which he traversed quickly before pushing himself through the Hive's front swing doors. As he arrived on the fifth floor, he glanced across the four seats centrally placed where he had sat with the others the day before. They were unoccupied, and his heart gladdened. Shuffling quickly across and around other desks, some already possessed by early adopters, he sat at the seat where he had unceremoniously announced himself to the others. He pulled three jackets from the holdall he had placed on the table. He cloaked each chair with a coat and claimed the workspaces with the equivalent authority of beach towels on sun loungers around busy pools. He would have set three extra laptops to complete the effect, but the jackets had to suffice. He would guard the places and announce to any enquiring occupiers that his "friends" had just stepped out for breakfast and would be returning shortly. Surjit sat down, opened his Mac, and peered over the lid with the attentive surveillance of a meerkat.

Mae Li sat at her breakfast bar and scooped the last of the plain yoghurt from her bowl, where it had cradled muesli and fruit moments before. Two large screen TVs aired synchronously across the clean and spacious open planned kitchen and living room, CNN piping out from one, whilst the Chinese Daily News broadcast from the other. Her phone buzzed. It was her father, he always called in the morning before eight, and she ignored it, as she often did. She'd return the call later when she felt at least some blemish of positivity and hope. He darkened her heart with his rhetorical questions and rational commentary. The calls were annoying and demotivating, the worst part being that she knew them to be sensible and correct. She slid off the breakfast bar stool, stepped into her boots that significantly elevated her height, collected her helmet, keys, and bag, and slammed the front door to head down to the garage below. Once astride the big bike, within minutes, she was purring down the Gray's Inn Road, lifting a gloved finger to any vexed van or irate Uber driver as she flew by.

Spencer awoke, yawned, opened his dark brown eyes, squinted, and realized he was back in his bed in the flat in Barnet. It had been late when he left Holly, having been called back under the covers for two encores. Since he was spent, the prospect of pleasuring Chantelle in exchange for an overcooked supermarket Lasagne was not worth the trouble to transport himself the additional few miles. He surveyed the room briefly, and a Chelsea scarf and shirt adorned the wardrobe doors under which his jeans, jacket, and shirt had been tossed. A blue curtain drew flimsily across the single ground-floor window, letting in the light that had been enough to stir him from dreams he could never remember. He instinctively became aware of the hard-on in his Chelsea patterned pyjama bottoms, and his right hand slid inside to grip his shaft. Fuck, this was hard; why was it not this stiff last night with Holly? It was as hard and long as a flagpole. OK, maybe a slight exaggeration, but all the same, it could poke holes in a cheap door. He'd better not let it go to waste, and he closed his eyes, thinking of Holly's tits rubbing against his face whilst his hand worked up and down his morning glory. He was suitably aroused, and the job would be short as he quickly came to the vinegar strokes, and then the bedroom door flew open.

"Have you got any deodorant, Spencer? Whoa, finishing a breakfast roll, are you?"

"Fuck me, Will, knock on the fucking door next time, and I'll put the handbrake on. I could have had someone in here," gasped Spencer, "It's on the table over there, and buy your fucking own."

"Sorry, won't be a moment, and you never bring company back, always shag them at their place, frightened they might come back here again, not that they'd want further punishment. I'll let you get back to the old five-knuckle shuffle," laughed Will, his tall flatmate rushing to be first to the office at the estate agents and retrieving the spray for a Frenchman's bath.

"Forget it; the moment's lost. I'm getting up. I need a cup of tea and a dump", groaned Spencer kicking back the Chelsea F.C printed duvet cover from his bed, his long legs spreadeagled as he rose from his pit. He stood and scratched his nuts, then ruffled his hair and another tug at his crotch again to fetch the pyjama bottoms from his arse cheeks. Who could deny man had not ascended from apes?

Surjit's eyes widened as he spotted the girl wearing motorcycle leather stride into the hall. He observed her hoping she would look across and see him, his arm twitching nervously, ready to jerk up and catch her attention. He called out but hesitated at the last second and only mouthed the words, "Hey, Mae Li, over here".

She came across an empty spot. There were a few more this morning. The second day of the week had claimed a few no-shows and later comers, after which there'd be a torrent by Friday. Before she had a chance to place her bag on the empty desk, Surjit croaked her name across the hall in that loud whisper format, the type that is normal audible levels, neither a cry nor a hushed tone. She did not respond, and her arm swung her bag from her shoulder to land on the target. This was enough. Surjit pinched his fingers inside his gaping mouth and piped a short, sharp whistle across the floor. He'd underestimated the strength and force of the blast, and it shrilled across the floor like a shepherd calling a collie. Mae Li looked up and across, as did the other thirty-two people sitting across the myriad of desks.

"Sorry, Hi, over here, I've saved you a desk," husked Surjit in the same semi-shout, hushed tones but audible enough for Mae Li to hear and the others. Mae Li was too confident to be embarrassed, but she was visibly annoyed as she strutted over to Surjit.

"This is not school, Surjit, and never whistle at me again. So you think I'm your sheepdog you can direct left, right, and backward?" she hissed.

"They don't go backward. Just left, right forward, and stop," remarked Surjit, unable to let any incorrect statement go.

"I don't care if they go head over fucking heels, do not whistle at me again, understood?" she raged.

"Understood", replied Surjit submissively. He looked down at his laptop, beaten. Then, just as he thought she was walking away, he heard the clump of her bag on the desk, and she sat at the place she had sat the day earlier, diagonally to him, when the four of them had met. Surjit glanced over and caught her eye, glaring back, then nervously glanced back at his screen, furrowing his brow, pretending to concentrate. A moment later, his eyes were furtively surveying the landing by the stairs and lifts, which he could see by the glass panelling. Where was the long-legged swagger of Spencer or the jaunty bounce of Innocence? His wait was not to be kept lingering as Innocence bounced into the hall holding a cup, undoubtedly weak milky tea, and looked across the aisle to choose a space to dunk a Galaxy ripple before starting work. This time Surjit's hand shot up enthusiastically, just as it had in the classroom more than ten years ago, eager to answer the teacher's question. He flapped and waved until it caught her attention. Innocence squinted, recognized Surjit, and smiled joyfully, the dark chestnut hue of her cheeks accentuating beautiful white teeth. She waved appreciatively back with her unoccupied arm and headed towards the table. Two down, one to go, he thought.

"Good morning, Surjit, Mae Li. How are you both?" asked Innocence.

"Great, thanks. I thought I'd save us a seat; it can get busy, can't it" nodded Surjit.

"That's very thoughtful of you," replied Innocence, looking across Mae Li. Her beaming smile could not be ignored.

"Hi babe, how are you doing, OK?" acknowledged Mae Li.

"Yeah, everything is cool. I was up much earlier this morning," sighed Innocence thinking back to the horrifying experience in the Dragon's den. She'd been cursed by the lady mirror and selected a loose skirt to wear to hide her backside. The dragons were correct. It was too big, but what could she do? She was one small Cadbury's bar on the day already, consumed after her dreadful dream, and ready to unwrap a Galaxy Ripple and dip it into the hot chocolate. She'd skip lunch and go for a walk instead. That was 600 calories saved on the lunch, and 200 extra calories from the walk, meaning 800 calories spare, so the Ripple at around 600 calories was OK, which left at least 200 calories left over. She'd have a banana from the fruit bowl, brought out during the mid-morning to keep her energy levels high enough for the walk following a hard slog at the keyboard. The investor meeting was less than four days away. Satisfied by the calorific equilibrium being met, she peeled back the chocolate bar wrapper and dipped the smooth, nobbily brown end into the hot bubbly liquid, and soon the world was a much better place to be.

Where was he? This morning dragged on slowly for Surjit. An hour had dawdled since Innocence slurped back the last of her drink, and Surjit felt a pang of hunger as he noticed the fruit bowl delivered. Innocence scampered over to claim a banana, the highest value fruit in the basket and usually the first to go. Surjit could not risk leaving his seat and missing Spencer. Only the thought of an accident of the type he had suffered the previous evening would tempt Surjit from his position, and having consumed no liquids since he was confident he could sit it out until lunchtime. By that time, it would be evident Spencer might not be showing up.

Surjit noticed that to his left, the girl who wore the blue beret and the one Spencer had met in the pub arrived at the desk where she had sat yesterday. Although she stood a long time arranging her bag, hair, and disrobing before sitting, it seemed clear she was standing surveying the room with as keen an interest in Spencer's whereabouts as Surjit.

"I've got to spot him, " thought Surjit, who considered Spencer understood how to attract women, engage them, and talk to them. Surjit studied many self-help books that conveyed the importance of finding mentors and people who can help you achieve your goals. Spencer would be his guru, a teacher that could navigate the most complex puzzle that had baffled Surjit, women and how to attract them. Surjit was glad that the doors were situated behind her, and unless she could rotate her neck like an owl, she would be unable to see Spencer saunter in before Surjit swooped.

Spencer Churchill swaggered to the High Barnet underground station with his bowels and a mug of steaming hot tea emptied with the same clothes draped on his body the previous day. Surjit was on the lookout for him with the alarm of a mother hen that had lost a chick. If Surjit could have clucked, strutted, and flapped his feathers across the fifth floor, hot desk section of the Hive that morning, he would. But instead, he had to dispel his anxiety with sharp inhalations and exhalations of breath through his nose, each one controlling his rising nerves. And then he appeared, the long, ruffled shoulder-length hair, the black leather jacket with his bag slung over his shoulder, the walk that played out Tony Manero's last line in the film "Staying Alive", "you know what I wanna do? Strut."

Spencer shimmied between the aisles of tables and headed towards Surjit, who had stood up, sadly with little added effect to his overall head height. Surjit, now on tiptoes, smiled and beckoned Spencer forward to the chair bedecked with his light rain jacket that he had reserved for him.

"Oh, cheers, man, nice one, alright, girls", smiled Spencer swinging his bag around and onto the table and missing Mae Li's left shoulder in the process by centimetres.

"Good morning, Spencer," ushered Innocence cheerily.

"Good afternoon, lover boy", smirked Mae li, emphasizing "afternoon", having noticed that the time had just passed noon.

"I'm just a good old-fashioned, lover boy", sang Spencer mimicking Freddie Mercury and then twitched his upper cheek, not quite a wink, but dangerously close to being one. Mae Li huffed and returned her attention to her document.

"You're late. Where have you been?" laughed Surjit nervously. Spencer's brow furrowed.

"Late? Late for what? The great thing about this gig is you don't have to be anywhere, anytime, for anybody."

"Except for Friday morning", replied Surjit. "We all need to be on time at the same place for the investment board, don't we" he whispered, his eyes darting between the other three. "We're all in it together", he laughed sympathetically, trying to garner camaraderie.

"Except *we* are not", replied Mae Li swiftly.

"I just meant we are in the same boat", he shot back hesitantly.

"Er, no. Same destination, different boats. Mine is watertight. How about yours and that dodgy third-party warranty disclaimer," hissed Mae Li; Spencer had set her hackles off.

"I'm working on that, " lied Surjit, his heart skipping when he remembered this was still an outstanding item he had no time to negate before Friday.

"If you're taking on water, I'll bail you out, buddy", smiled Spencer diffusing the tension. "Climb aboard my carrier, dry out and fly some jets with me" Spencer's flat hand takes off, heading upwards confidently. "Did he mean it?" thought Surjit. The conversation fell silent for a moment. Spencer flipped his cheap laptop open, yawned loudly, and slunk down in his chair. He felt the buzz of his vibrating phone in his trouser pocket and retrieved it to scan the alert as if he did not know who he knew it would be. Chantelle was shopping in Watford's harlequin centre during her lunch break from being a receptionist at a busy town centre dentistry. She had grabbed a meal deal at Boots, a wholemeal sandwich with salmon and avocado, a raspberry juice drink, and a fruit and nut muesli bar. The troika of starch, fructose, and proteins was full of sugars of a sort, but Chantelle thought it healthy. 54 minutes remained before she was due back, checking people in, arranging and rearranging appointments and processing thousands of pounds of daily payments. Business from North Hertfordshire's gnashers treated the senior partner dentist to a Jaguar leased car changed every three years and a side interest in younger women through sugardaddy.com, which he changed every three weeks. The irony of one form of filling sustaining the other was not lost on him; neither was the need for a hygiene check-up every six months. Chantelle wandered through the soulless town square and past McDonald's, where processed bread, cheese, and a variety of beef McMeals were still preferred to McSalads and healthy McWraps and where desperate people took a McShit. She'd messaged him to tell him about her lunch, partly from the delusion that without such an update, Spencer would have been beside himself with worry and partly because she needed to. All that, except nobody deludes themselves about anything, deep down, there is a rational, curmudgeonly part of you, a cynical troll that tells you exactly as it is, if only you want to listen. Sat beside the gloomy imp is the opposite to it, the cheery voice, daring you that miracles don't only happen at Christmas but in Watford too. Dreams could come true, just like nightmares. The question was, who really were you? Who judged these twin genies, each with polarised views on opposite sides of the spectrum? Or was the judge another pair of twins with dissenting voices towards their opposite number? How far did it all play out? Was there an eternity of opposed beings, to the point where no truth could be drawn? If you wanted to think that deeply or were capable of such profundity, fortunately, Chantelle was not. She bobbed happily on the surface at the shallow end, preferring to float on the hopefulness of the cheerful inner voice and her cheery outlook. Everything would be ok, and if not, she was not prepared to drift off to the deep end and risk drowning to find out why? Spencer did not respond to her message; therefore, he must be busy, and not that he couldn't give a toss. Stay where your feet can touch the floor, Chantelle, or if not, hold on to the side.

"Anyone hungry?" posed Spencer calmly without looking up from his screen. He was immersed in a new dating site for transgender people. Indeed, they'd want privacy and somewhere local to hook up. He'd add it to the hundreds he'd identified as targets for Shagpad to advertise, maybe cross-promote if you'd pardon the pun. Ads targeting specific locations could offer two consenting "Shemales" or "Transmen" a clean and affordable bedroom in a respectable semi to change and dress up or strap on for an hour in Macclesfield for twenty quid. Cheaper than the Premier Inn by Tytherington business park, depending on the date. "Strapped for cash? " Check Out Shagpad," thought Spencer was thinking about a picture of a unisex harness device under the Shagpad logo, clever and straight to the point, just like a dildo.

Mae Li looked around at him, "You have only just arrived here, babe."

"I didn't have breakfast," Spencer replied.

"You probably weren't up early enough for breakfast," suggested Innocence.

"Oh, I was up alright?" smiled Spencer nodding at Surjit.

"Up at the crack of dawn?" replied Innocence, jauntily.

"Yeah, I was, but her name's Holly, not Dawn", replied Spencer deadpan. Innocence and Surjit looked puzzled whilst Mae Li sighed.

"Look, I'm famished. Are you ready for a break, guys?" asked Spencer, closing his laptop.

"Yes, me too. Sounds like a good idea," chipped in Surjit. His early morning hiatus to the Hive meant he'd skipped his mother's breakfast paratha, which was delicious and sacrificed to snag the table and chairs. Nevertheless, it had been worth the risk and was about to pay off as he closed the lid to his machine.

"We'd better stay here and mind your stuff then", added Innocence.

"Nah, come on, the afternoons are quieter. So there'll be space, just maybe not together", replied Spencer standing and stretching.

"I've got some spare bags and clothing; these will do," Surjit replied, applying his additional clothing and bags to the seats as they became unoccupied.

"It's strictly against the building's policy", observed Mae Li. "You'll get us into trouble,"

"Only if you leave them unattended for longer than it takes to go to the loo or get a coffee," replied Innocence.

"Coffee queues are a nightmare at lunchtime, and so are the cubicles, so we will be fine," assured Spencer, turning towards the doors less than ten minutes since he brushed through them.

Surjit headed to the doors. But, he did not want to get caught up in any social dilemma extending doors open for Mae Li. So all four stood at the lift doors, and they soon swished open and moments later were stood on Old Street contemplating a venue for lunch.

"There's a "Spoons" across the road, pie and a pint cheap, plus we get to laugh at the pissheads who have been on it since breakfast", chimed Spencer.

"There is no fucking way. I'm going into a Wetherspoons pub, babe," protested Mae li. "Carpets that make you feel sick and a ready meal menu, I don't think so!"

"The food is served quickly, freshly microwaved, and cheap," appealed Spencer.

"Gets my vote," added Surjit supporting his newfound mentor. Then, the three of them looked at Innocence.

"Don't ask me to decide, I mean, I'm OK, but if Mae Li isn't", she stammered.

"Three to one majority verdict, the Spoons it is, but the clear winner is democracy", barked Spencer triumphantly and turned on his heels like a sergeant major.

"Oh my God, and another new low for me, lunch at JD Wetherspoons, this week keeps getting better and better," said Mae Li, ironically, and she unfolded her arms to follow in step with the others. They crossed the road and walked further west by a few hundred yards to the corner pub with the Masque Haunt's aquamarine signage. It had just gone midday, but several tables were occupied already, some by customers who had already enjoyed more than a few ales as judged by the empty glasses that had totted up. In strode a tall young man with long raven hair and a black leather jacket and ripped skinny jeans; a young black lady with a loose-fitting skirt and a pink t-shirt with a logo that emblazed "Sugar Rush" across her ample chest; a young Chinese lady in sunglasses with nu-buck tan leather trousers a matching jacket cloaking a black vest; and a shorter young man of Asian heritage in Marks and Spencer dark jeans and navy V-neck sweater under which was a white shirt with the collars protruding out. They looked like a racist joke by any fat male comedian from the 1970s. Still, they were four young entrepreneurs of 2016, two British, two not, hungry for success, life-changing wealth, and in Spencer's case, a quarter-pound burger topped with bacon, cheese, and onion rings, a side of chips washed down with a pint of cold lager, or maybe two.

"This will do," remarked Spencer pointing at the empty table by the window with the four seats arranged two by two opposite each other, just like the other 20 tables that formed the group at this side of the bar.

"I'll have a window seat; the views are to die for," said Mae Li pulling up a chair and glancing at the traffic from Bunhill Row into Old Street.

"Then, you can sit and look at me instead," smiled Spencer pulling up the seat opposite her.

"Oh great, I think I prefer to look at the traffic babes," Mae Li retorted with an ironic smile.

"An Aisle seat for me, easier to get up for the loo without waking anybody," added Surjit, sitting next to Spencer.

"Wow, the menu is very extensive," remarked Innocence holding the large A3-sized folded laminate showcasing a variety of pub grub. It displayed curries to steaks, British classics to pizzas, burgers, sandwiches, wraps, and all available with a choice of chips, chunky, fries or sweet potato with the skin on, and salad or both.

"The chef comes highly recommended," advised Spencer,

"Oh really," remarked Innocence.

"Yes, the things he can do with a microwave are legendary, a very innovative minimalist approach to western culinary classics. Oh yes, the master and originator of the rip, bang, and ping method. Rip goes the plastic wrapper, bang goes the tray into the oven, and ping goes the timer three minutes later when it's heated through. His deep fat frying skills? Not so much Heston Blumenthal, more Heston Services, triple cooked chips because leftovers get thrown back in! All this on nine quid an hour, including two fag breaks. Still, you can't go wrong, can you for an eight-quid lunch that includes a pint of lager, can you?"

"I'd say you could. You're not selling it to me, Spencer babe," sighed Mae Li.

"There are plenty of choices, look", chirped Surjit optimistically. "Vegan, vegetarian, pescatarian"

"And Octagenarian, look at that list of mush. You don't need teeth, they just give you a bowl of stodge, a bib, and a big spoon," pointed Mae Li to the British classics selection that included shepherd's pie, macaroni cheese, sausage, and mash and pie and mash.

"You'd need teeth for sausages," remarked Innocence.

"Not here, you don't; these bangers are about as firm as Surj's flaccid cock," smiled Spencer.

"Sausage or chipolata?" laughed Mae Li.

"Maybe cocktail, and no chance of any of them passing a woman's lips", added Spencer, half winking at Surjit and Mae Li guffawed, then straightened her look.

"Hey, will you leave my flaccid cock alone" piped up Surjit loudly, not noticing the young lady approaching with the apron and badge?

"Can I wipe the table down, please, and when you are ready to order, go to the bar and remember your table number," she looked non-plussed and gave the table a half-hearted wave of her cloth across the heavily scratched surface. All eyes were on Surjit, who had closed his in embarrassment, waiting for the girl to depart. She took what seemed like minutes to perform the task in a few seconds before she was off to deposit the same dirty wet cloth across the neighbouring table for the same swipe exerted with the same level of enthusiasm.

"You do have a way with words and attracting attention," giggled Innocence, trying to suppress any laughter further before squealing again. Surjit drew his breath in and the menu closer to his face. He was not yet ready to take this into his short stride. Instead, his eyes darted across the options before settling upon the vegetarian soup and roll.

"I'll have the soup, no drink," he declared, not daring to order another shandy. Besides, a combined 2 per cent proof was enough to make him sleepy for the afternoon when there was still more work on "Spanner", his mobile performance utility app.

"Full house Burger and a lager for me", added Spencer,

Innocence faced a dilemma. Spencer's choice sounded attractive, but at 1200 calories, that would mean a diversionary route, the long way home and another half an hour on her journey to burn the extra fuel. Or, she could have the Spicy Cajun chicken wrap, forego the chips, and have an ice cream sundae which looked tempting, judging by the picture on the reverse of the menu.

"Come back to me," she said, buying a moment more deliberation whilst she weighed the food and the odds.

"I'll have the salmon fillet and salad and mineral water," said Mae Li attempting to close the menu. Still, the plastic was sufficiently strong and was annoyingly permanently ajar at 60 degrees. So the three who had chosen their selections waited for Innocence, who pretended to thumb up the page again.

"Erm, erm, erm", she deliberated.

"No pressure, it's a big decision. Will you take the money or gamble for a go at the jackpot" whispered Spencer.

"No, I don't want a jacket potato", replied Innocence, her eyes fixed, and her ears were not listening; her brain was still reckoning the outcome. The others tittered.

"Go with your gut," suggested Surjit. She heard the last word and responded defiantly.

"What about my gut? I'm feeling a little bloated today. I don't remark about your body; you mind your own business," snapped Innocence.

"I meant to have what you fancy; your gut feels," protested Surjit. It seemed he could not say or do anything to women who were not misconstrued and wrong.

"I'll have the same as Mae Li", sighed Innocence. "With chips, onion rings, and a diet coke".

Mae Li reached inside her jacket pocket, "I'll get this,"

"No, you bought lunch yesterday; please, my turn", interrupted Innocence, reaching for her bag and producing her purse.

"No, honestly, I've got some cash I picked up last night that I want rid of," and she took the role of brown notes from inside her leather jacket pocket and peeled a couple off and handed it to Spencer, "Here you go Mr Churchill, make yourself useful" and she nodded towards the bar.

"Look at all that paper, fuck, are you dealing drugs?" exclaimed Spencer, eyeing the bundle from which she'd pulled two crisp twenty pounds notes.

"No, but cash is king in any business, particularly this one", she replied. Surjit thought hard and then blurted his question, "You're not a prostitute, are you?"

Mae Li turned and looked back at him open-mouthed. He dug the hole a little deeper, "I meant, you know, a high class one, expensive, you know, I mean, you know, an escort lady, er, you know what I mean,"

"I'm not a hooker, escort, or whatever you are trying to say, Surjit, but I dance for cash," she replied.

"You mean lap dancing or pole dancing?" asked Surjit.

"No, Morris dancing, what the fuck do you think she means" laughed Spencer breaking the tension.

"Where do you dance, and how much do they pay?" asked Innocence.

"At a club not that far from here, I get twenty pounds for a private dance, and numerous five pounds notes tucked in my pants if I'm on the stage or the pole; it's always a fucking fiver. It's the cheapest paper currency, babe," replied Mae li.

"When did you start doing this?" Innocence leaned forward with interest.

"During my time at University, I got asked by some guy, and I thought why not? I get paid to keep fit, and there is no touching by the creeps who hang out there, so easy money,"

"So, I wonder what the University of London thought when you paid your tuition fees with a carrier bag of five pounds notes," laughed Spencer.

"I don't need the cash, my father is incredibly wealthy, and I am lucky to have my own flat with cash in the bank," Mae Li sat back and thought pensively.

"So why do you do it?" posed Innocence, asking the same question Mae li often asked herself. Mae Li looked back as if she were pondering her answer, but she already knew that.

"Because I'm greedy, I enjoy it, and I love being in control of weak, willed men", and she looked across at Spencer as she uttered her words slowly and deliberately.

"Now go and order the food because I'm not downloading the fucking Wetherspoons app," Surjit and Innocence darted looks at Spencer.

"I'll keep the change then, service charge," smiled Spencer taking the money, and he jumped up from his seat and shimmied towards the bar, his feet skipping boyishly yet gracefully.

The bar had filled with more punters, pints, and wine glasses bedecked most tables and were necked with speed. As the food was hurried out, everything moved fast around Tech City. Some of the earlier customers drank at a more leisurely pace. These consultants and contractors believed they were still a part of the city and its business if they sat looking at phones and laptops. Still, they were on the outside looking in. They were trying to look busy but were instead sinking into an alcoholic, unemployed malaise of cheap Marston's bitter or Foster's lager or whatever the £1.99 a pint offer was for that week. Were any so desperate to keep up appearances to fake a conversation on the mobile? No, nobody cared here, at least not after the third pint. Who were you trying to impress?

Not the other professional drinkers occupying tables for four with their coats spread out across ownerless chairs like Surjit had done that morning at the Hive, but then, at last, he knew they'd become occupied. These people faced the occupational hazard of taking a piss without losing their place or the laptop. The risk assessment was generally well administered for the first one or two loo visits. Still, by the afternoon, they became less conservative as the booze wore on and the cares in the world evaporated, hoping that the optimistic applications and outreaches sent earlier would be answered with an invitation to interview or discovery call.

Spencer had conceived a backpack device that delivered cold beer through a tube to your mouth and took urine away from your bladder. It was aimed at the millions of festival goers who could now drink and urinate without needing an hour's detour, missing a band or their spot, and avoiding the terror of utilizing a festival toilet. He'd considered calling it "Taking the piss", but it was not thoroughly thought out since who would want to spend all day at a festival fitted with a catheter? Although needing further thought, Spencer considered the idea viable enough to be a backup option should *Shagpad* not reach its undoubted potential. At least with his invention and here at a "Spoons", you could still get pissed at the pub in Central London for under twenty quid before running the gauntlet of heading back to the flat without suffering the fate that befell Surjit after his solitary pint the previous evening. Creationists might deny the theory of evolution but could not restrict the remarkable ability of humans to adapt to their surroundings. Innuits could live in a world of snow and ice, Masai warriors could sustain life in the African desert by drinking oxen blood, and Bedouin nomads could survive a life drifting across the arid sands of the Sahara. Seasoned all-day Wetherspoon drinkers could hold their spot at a pub table for up to half a gallon of ale before requiring a comfort break. They occupied the tables nearest the toilets and the bar, a perfect balance of equilibrium providing maximum efficacy for intake and output. The latter requirement was quickly made obsolete thanks to the downloadable app that brought recurring beverages to a toilet side table with one swipe and a dab of an increasingly disoriented finger on a blurry mobile device.

"We are all greedy, aren't we?" posed Surjit, interrupting the conversational silence held at bay by the chink of Surjit's soup spoon's attempt to remove the pattern at the bottom of the bowl. Then, finally, Mae Li stopped stabbing at a piece of lettuce that refused to be impaled by her blunt fork.

"Innocence and I have had a salad, you have had a bowl of soup; only gannet chops here could be described as greedy,"

"I didn't mean greedy pigs; I meant greed, hunger for success and money", explained Surjit. "I mean, none of us is happy with making just enough. We all want a million or more,"

"A yurrnicong", spluttered Spencer, who had a large bite of his cheeseburger, and two chips were thrown into the chasm before the contents were emulsified by these whirring jaws.

"I think we need a new language for Google to translate, French, German, Spanish, Portuguese, Nepalese, Japanese, and Spencer," remarked Mae li, frowning at the clumsy display of man v food. Spencer took a large swig from his pint glass, the San Miguel washing his palate from mashed beef and starch.

"I said, a unicorn, that's what we all want. I'm not settling for a few million, Shagpad will be worth a billion dollars granted, but that is some serious coin even with AngelTech taking their percentage." He paused to find the time to chew into a beer-battered onion ring before offering the last one to Innocence, who indicated her acceptance with a nod and a smile.

"Happy talk, keep talking, happy talk, talk about things you'd like to do. You gotta have a dream; if you don't have a dream, how you gonna have a dream come true?" sang Surjit, somewhat muted but with a cheeky smile and his eyes darting between the other three who sat bemused by this little outburst of song. Surjit always sat so quiet, very attentive but usually discreet.

"Surj, I didn't know you had it in you. What have they put in the soup? I want some. Captain Sensible, early '80s?" laughed Spencer remembering his dad's awful eighties music playlists.

"South Pacific actually, 1958," corrected Surjit.

"I don't know what you are talking about, but whatever the song or the saying, unless you have a goal, you're never going to score," added Innocence, delicately holding the half-bitten onion ring between her fingers before popping it into her mouth.

"We're just four, regular, average Joes, who hold a dream, one thousand million good luck to us," said Mae Li.

"Not average Joes, unicorn Joes," added Surjit raising his soup bowl as a toast.

"Unicorn Joes? I'll drink to that," said Spencer finishing his drink and pushing his empty plate away.

"Unicorn Joes" toasted Innocence with the melted ice left from her diet coke. Mae Li raised her glass "Unicorn Joes, whatever, babes," she sighed.

"Do we have to go back? I quite fancy whiling away the afternoon in here, downing lagers and discussing philosophy, art and culture, or football if you want to go deep and meaningful," Spencer sank a little into his chair, his hunger for sustenance satisfied.

"I could go back and collect the jackets," replied Surjit, with more than a slight hope the girls might agree.

"Fuck, no" was Mae Li's succinct rejection of the proposal and one that left little to negotiate. "I have work to do, we all have, and if I was to waste the afternoon drinking, it would not be in this place; And you could never converse deep and meaningfully; your idea of philosophical conjecture is whether Arsenal should change their system from a flat back four to a continental sweeper system,"

"What like a Dyson? And it's Chelsea; I don't give a fuck about Arsenal," replied Spencer.

"I rest my case." Mae Li stood up and rolled her eyes at Innocence.

"You know it makes sense. There's no rest for the wicked," added Innocence, smiling.

"Are we wicked?" posed Spencer,

"Not *that* wicked, the wicked meaning weary, from the book of Isaiah, there is no peace, said the Lord, unto the wicked!" She wagged her finger cheekily at Spencer and Surjit.

"Oh…wicked," smiled Surjit, and Spencer laughed as he felt the buzz of another "Chantext" as she referred to her frequent messages. Surjit led the party to the door, encouraged by the laugh he gained from his "wicked" quip. Once outside, they strode across the busy road and the few hundred yards back to the Hive to begin the afternoon shift.

Surjit stood outside the front doors to the gym, wavering. He was wearing black short shorts and trainers, with a white t-shirt, it was the same kit as he had worn at school. Although he'd removed his underpants earlier before pulling on the shorts, Surjit did not like the idea of getting sweaty and having to wear them home. What support would boxer shorts offer under his shorts, and so they were rolled up in his pocket. Then, two tall, fit-looking, muscular guys pushed past him and skipped up the few steps chuckling at a shared joke. Were they laughing at him? He pondered the following steps, the concrete ones that led to the door. He imagined himself a year from now with a forty-inch chest, 15inch biceps, and muscular legs that wouldn't buckle under the weight of a 15kg sack of onions as he did when he helped with deliveries at the shop below where he and his mother lived and worked.

The first session was free. So what was there to lose apart from self-respect and humility? So given that he felt he did not have these to lose, he stepped up and through the doors and into the world of the metropolitan gym; this one happened to belong to a small chain, Sonny Gyms, owned by some guy nicknamed Sonny. He walked up to the reception where an overweight lady sat smiling back at him; not the best advert for Sonny Gyms, thought Surjit, but she was as bulky as he was not, so pots and kettles and glasshouses and stones, and all that.

"Hi, I've come for the introductory session," said Surjit.

"Ok, let's get you to fill one of these out, shall we, and I'll let Micha know you're here." The chubby receptionist cheerily handed Surjit a clipboard. She had the ubiquitous condescending voice like many receptionists did when addressing customers. Surjit sat down and observed the questionnaire. Why couldn't this have been completed online before? Instead, it would probably be manual data fed into a database. What a waste. First question, Sex; "yes, please," he wrote daringly. His name, address, and a few medical questions followed and were easy enough to complete, and then came the most crucial question, bank details from which the direct debit would be collected. He left his blank, this was an introductory session, and he had not decided if he was committed to a monthly outgoing of forty pounds from which he would likely walk for ten minutes on a treadmill twice a month. It took longer to walk to the gym.

"Hi Surjit, I'm Micha. Would you like to come with me?"

"Fuck yes, did she say with or on?" thought Surjit. Micha was stunning, a mixed-race girl from black and white parents with an impressive athletic physique, beautiful bust, and bum. She wore tight black hot pants shorts like a professional dancer, accentuating her toned and tan-coloured legs. Added to this, her smile was wide and stunning, with seemingly perfect teeth; Who knew these days, but Surjit was willing to bet that there was no veneer in 'ere for Micha.

"Thanks, yeah," replied Surjit softly, passing the clipboard across to Leah, the receptionist, who smiled back.

Micha pushed open the door and let Surjit through, and then in three strides, she shot past him to direct him towards the gym on their right-hand side from which, through the glass panels, he could see an array of machines being run, pedalled, pushed and pulled by heavily perspiring people.

"In you come, and I'll get you started," smiled Micha. Surjit wondered if she was married and, if not, by which mind-altering drug he could coerce her to take into accepting his proposal. He looked at her left hand and the third finger. It was long, slender, and ringless; obviously, it was fate.

"We'll start on the mats and do some stretching. It's vital to warm up correctly," explained Micha, and Surjit nodded sagely. Micha stood opposite Surjit and readied herself to show him some warm-up stretches he could follow.

"How are your hammies? Are they tight?" she asked. What on earth did she mean? Best nod in agreement, he thought. She must mean how strong your muscles are, he thought.

"As tight as the next man, but not as tight as I'd like them to be, I want them really tight," and he emphasized the word tight by over pronouncing the t's.

"Oh, ok, well, let's stretch them a little; follow me and put one foot forward, lean forward and gently push your hands down your thigh like this," She turned around and bent forward. The motion was poetry to which the romantics had no allegory, banging on about fucking landscapes, clouds, trees and nature, when clearly, in the 18th century, there was nobody like Micha stretching in little more than what amounted to underwear. Her tight black pants rode up her buttocks, and her arms displayed defined muscles, whilst her braless torso meant that her breasts fell forward under her skimpy vest. Surjit stood and watched in awe, he'd never been this close to a girl in this state of undress, and he would happily leave Leah with his bank details if Micha could run this routine for him every night. But, oh, shit, he thought, please no, down boy, fuck, no, and he covered his front by standing with his hands in front of him, hiding the bulge in his flimsy shorts. So far from it, he was not endowed like a porn star, but even if Micha suffered acute Myopia, she would still notice that Surjit had a bone in his shorts. That would surely mean game over, expelled from the gym, and more than likely added to the registered sex offenders list.

How would he ever get a bride or a job? He thought of Mickey Mouse. He'd once overheard a guy chatting with his mate on a bus that he did this to avoid premature ejaculation. Mickey Mouse, say it and think it, again and again. Mickey Mouse, picture him, an annoying smiling rodent with big ears and a high-pitched, shrilly voice. It was working. There felt some reduction at the front of his shorts. Mickey Mouse is dancing on the spot in his stupid red spotted shorts and waving his hands in those voluminous white gloves. What was it with Mickey Mouse anyway? Surjit did not get it. He'd never found him amusing or child friendly. One hundred-year-old caricature bore no resemblance to any living creature that Surjit could think of with a ceaseless self-satisfied grin and a creepy whiplash skinny tale, whose round ears were forever viewed from a side perspective. Easier to draw, and just how iconic would old Mickey be had he retained his original name, "Mortimer"? But back to more pressing concerns, no pun intended, Surjit thought, but why the fuck had he gone commando? The effect of a hard-on was twice as prominent. Still, he envisaged a short, boring interlude with a fatless young guy banging on about the importance of wiping down the machines, not an up-close and personal experience with probably the sexiest woman on the planet he could ever have fantasized about.

"Surjit, do you want to follow me, do as I do, are you ok?" she smiled, and he fell in love again, if that was possible.

"Er, yeah, just a moment." Surjit held his hand in front of his groin and leaned forward, poking himself in his flat belly with his dick, being watched by magnificent Micha. Thankfully the excitement subsided in direct correspondence to the strain on the back of his legs.

"Ok, let's do some shoulder stretches, arms up high, and rotate those shoulders", urged Micha swinging her arms around, her tits rising and falling with each revolution of her arcing limbs. Oh, fuck not again, he thought as he felt a comeback from the little man down there. Walt Disney's anthropomorphic mouse came back into mind, his big bulbous yellow boots tapping a dance to the thudding beat of the gym's music. This strangely did the trick, and he could replicate Micha's movement for a few loops before she smiled and told him to relax.

"Ok, on to your back Surjit" she barked, and he could not help but imagine that order in a different setting; what man could not have?. A fit woman in nothing more than underwear was, well, a fit woman in underwear, and an aroused cock was hard-wired into a man's libido, no pun intended. If it weren't, there'd be no people to worry about including and diversifying. Surjit lay flat on his back and awaited the next instruction, which surely could never be "lay still why I straddle your body and insert your erect penis into my vagina," or words to that effect. However, what Micha uttered was,

"I want you to raise your right leg and bring your knee back to your chest, place your hands under your thigh and pull back to stretch that hamstring," she said. What was it with hamstrings and stretching? Surjit wanted to build strong arm muscles and a deep masculine chest that was convex instead of concave, not have legs with stretchy muscles at the back. Surjit lay and did as she was told. She stood at his feet and encouraged him as he raised his leg and brought his knee back to his chest. Surjit, Micha, and the shorts that he wore underestimated the agility and skill in Surjit's leg as it flexed back to his chin, with little in the way of muscle mass and strong tendons to oppose it. This, as an action, was not a problem; however, his right and wrinkled testicle, being offered little support by the man-made fibrous lining of his shorts, had no option but to pop out for air and lay exposed sat on his protruding buttock. Surjit grimaced as he pulled the leg tighter to his chin, trying to impress Micha with his effort, but she had turned away in suppressed giggles at this poor unfortunate guy's wardrobe malfunction that stared up at her. During Micha's two years of induction sessions, there were some misdemeanours, including the odd pulled muscle or trapped finger in the weights machine, but this was the first exposed bollock, and she told

Surjit to relax before turning around to face him again. It was too late; Surjit felt the cold breeze of Sonny Gym's air conditioning unit, under which he lay exposing one of his gonads to Miss World, and instinctively knew that something had gone wrong. It was too late to abort the mission, and as he lifted his head to peer down towards his prone legs, the offending testicle still lay proudly outside his flared shorts. Surjit arched his back and readjusted his shorts whilst Micha held her hand to her face, as people do when they can't face an unseemly incident, and she coughed to disguise their embarrassment. Surjit stood up and walked away, then turned to face her to explain. No explanation would be appropriate without further shame for them both. So he turned back again and kept walking, out of the doors that lead back to the reception and out of the doors that led on to the main A3 and from here, he turned left, towards the Elephant and Castle, and walked briskly back home, the cool evening air whistling up his shorts. This baggy old-school gym attire was soon deposited in the bin.

Innocence rechecked the advertisement, lose weight fast, revolutionary process, free trial offer, see what everybody has been talking about. I lost over fifty pounds in three months, claimed one testimonial. These ads popped up in her Facebook feed and other social media sites. The cookies on her laptop knew where she searched and her hopes and fears. It was like room 101 occupied her Macbook. It hung out in the deep cached files that monitored her every tap and click and, worse still, told the whole world about her. She was Innocence, twenty-three years old from Pretoria, South Africa, a graduate of the London School of Oriental and African Studies, loved food, casual gaming, animal rescues, and children in need, worried about her weight, and didn't like her figure. Innocence had a full figure, rounded hips, and a large bust. Her thighs were muscular, and her shoulders square and strong. She was as beautiful as she was that March 1993; her mother, Victoria, screamed one last time to push her out into the world, but Innocence would never accept that.

"What are you looking at, Innocence?" asked her sister, Agnes, as they sat in the small kitchenette of their flat.

"Nothing in particular," lied Innocence, whose eyes gave her thoughts away.

"Don't be paying for more magic diet powders and potions, sister, the only pounds you will lose are off of your bank balance, and that needs more weight putting on,"

"Don't I know it? That's why my game development has to work,"

"Let us both hope for that but even so, be happy that you are fit and healthy,"

"I'm not fit,"

"Perhaps you can't run the London marathon, but you can walk daily to and from your office. Who wouldn't be happy with that?"

"Er, me!" Innocence raised her arms in frustration.

"It is unfair or ironic that most women want to be what they are not. Skin tones are changed with tanning aids, hair colours changed with dyes, tits are made bigger and smaller, lips filled, belly and thigh fat sucked away, bottoms plumped up and cellulite pumped out, bingo wings trimmed, and flabby necks stretched, but ultimately no cosmetic could change your DNA, not yet. That's the secret you want to discover, not some casual game blockbuster, sister."

"Don't I know, but unfortunately, I don't have a degree in advanced molecular biology," replied Innocence.

"People are what they are. They must understand to live and love what they have and what they are. So few younger women do, and some older women never do, chasing youth as fast and elusive as their shadows. It can never be caught. How much are the beauty and cosmetic market worth in dollars?" asked Agnes.

"I'll google it, hold on, half a trillion dollars and set to double that amount by the mid-2020s. Wow, I could do with a piece of that action," exclaimed Innocence. "Get this, over 90% of cosmetic surgical procedures performed on women?" she continued.

"Are we vainer? Are we more prone to self-criticism? Are we the victims of a male-dominated and oriented narrative for what we should look like? Maybe, but I don't think so; surely we are smarter than that?" argued Agnes.

"I'm my own harshest critic", admitted Innocence.

"Is it because you want a man because you think they won't like you as you are for what you are? If so, are they worth your love, sister?" reasoned Agnes.

"No, of course, not, but it's not about that, it's about me, it's what I want, I want a smaller bum and tits," snapped Innocence.

"There you go, you don't want what just about every other woman, and man for that matter, do want, so please be happy with that!" Agnes shouted back.

Innocence stood up. She could not argue with her sister because she was always right, big sisters and mothers always were, but Agnes was brilliant. She looked upon the world with simplicity and logic that the world seldom wanted to be understood by people. Only nature truly understood the world, survive, procreate, and die. If there is time for enjoyment, then treasure that, but that was not what life was about. People did not understand this, so many had the time to obsess about themselves, and time acted like compound interest, feeding off itself. Innocence clicked the advert, saved the website to her "other" bookmarks to consider later, and switched off her computer.

Mae Li lay back on the couch in her bright living area. First, she hmphed listening to her father speak to her in Mandarin Chinese. Then, finally, she replied in English, if only to vex him a little further.

"Father, one more week; the investment meeting is this Friday. I have told you many times. But, unfortunately, you don't seem to listen." Mae Li's father complained she was speaking in English.

"I am speaking in English, which you very well understand. Just because you don't speak it so well doesn't mean you don't understand. Besides, the practice and application of it will be beneficial for you." Mae Li's father explained if she gave up this crazy idea of a Linkedin competitive platform, he would not need to improve his English because she would handle that communication.

"Why can't you back me, invest in me, your only daughter? You're happy to pay me to represent your interests here in Europe, but why not pay me to explore this opportunity? It would save me the time and equity of going through Angeltech?" Mae Li's father disagreed. He already had a good and proven business plan that required investment and her attention. It was about backing a winner.

"It is a great idea, father, and it is a winner, but let's agree to defer this conversation until the weekend. How is mother?" Mae Li was told that her mother was well and dutiful, she would not deny her husband's wishes, and he could not understand where Mae Li acquired this rebellious streak.

"It's in my DNA, father, and I got it from you. First, you pushed back on your father's wishes to become a chemist and study business and commerce at university. You then invested and grew the components business when your father told you it was too competitive and doomed to fail. Now look at you, wealthy, able to contribute to the party and country, and you have a smart and loving daughter as well." She laughed, but her giggles were not shared by her father, who wished her well and closed the call by saying he would talk to her at the weekend when she had come to her senses.

"Good night, father, go to bed. It's the middle of the night for you. I love you, father; it would be nice if you said that back to me," Mae Li leaned over to her laptop and clicked the red button that closed the web call. She then fell back onto the couch and looked up at the ceiling before closing her eyes. She had felt alone these past months. She had few friends. The travails of creating a tech start-up had worn her out, and she harboured doubts that she would not share with her father, but it had been good today to share these with the other guys, the Unicorn Joes as Surjit had coined them. They had worked during the afternoon, sat together as associates, and, dare she say it, emerged as friends. Despite the annoying and puerile Spencer, they felt better than sitting together with strangers. Innocence with her self-doubts about her figure, but with such sweet, naïve bravery. Surjit and his funny traits, insatiable knowledge that lay hidden beneath a demeanour utterly lacking in confidence. And, Spencer, the most politically incorrect twenty-something, more of a dinosaur than a dragon, was he hiding something, a weakness hidden by such enthusiasm and effortless charm? Mae Li was sure he was, and she would find it, and she felt happier going to bed with that endeavour in mind. She walked to her room, removed her pyjama trousers and t-shirt then fished into her bedside drawer. She lay in the centre of the bed, her olive-toned naked body completely unblemished. She closed her eyes. She pictured a young man smiling at her, then kissing her mouth from her wet lips, down her torso, stopping to bite each nipple on her sunken breasts, then tickling her as he ran his tongue down into her pubic region. It flickered like a snake, In and out, up and down, with metronomic rhythm, tickling her clitoris and sensing the warm, damp feel of her vagina. In and out, "eat me inside out, terrible lizard", she thought. Her right hand gripped and pulled hard at the imaginary long raven hair that tumbled across her pelvis. The faint hum of a buzzing implement could be heard beneath the sheets as she dreamt the bobbing head to a climax before she cried out his name.

"Spencer," cried Julian, the red-haired keyboardist, who called the band to a stop with a swish of his arms. "You missed your cue. So what's up, Spen? That's the third time tonight? We have to nail this fucker before Saturday, and this is our only rehearsal before them. It's the first dance, no winging this one,"

"Sorry, Jules, I'm back in the room; let's take it from the top," replied Spencer shaking his head as if clearing an imaginary fog. Phil, the drummer, sat behind a 7 piece drum set and an expansive cymbal collection, most of which he ignored as he patted away at the hi-hat and snare interlocked with a right foot encased in a bumper boot, toe-tapping at the pedal connected to the bass drum. He clicked his drumsticks four times above his head and mouthed the words "one, two, three, four". The guitarist played a few introductory notes before Spencer sang the first line to "Thinking out loud" by Ed Sheeran. Paul, the bassist, nodded his head forward to the beat like a funky pigeon. Who knew? It had probably inspired the same name's online card and gift business. Jules smiled as the song pulled together, and Spencer arrived effortlessly at the chorus; Jules winked at Rick, the guitarist, who smiled back and nodded to Paul before Spencer switched the lyrics,

"So, honey, take me into your loving arms, kiss my cock and finger my arse, place your head on my beating heart; I'm thinking out loud, I've followed through on a big wet fart." Julian was not amused and shot a disapproving look at Spencer before shouting over the instruments,

"For fuck sake, cut it out, Spen." Spencer rolled his eyes, nodded submissively, and finished the song as Ed had intended.

"Great, don't forget the lyrics; Dave and Lisa will not want to toast and kiss their short and unhappy marriage to your alternate version, Spenny, mate. Ok, right, another request for us to get started on "I bet you look good on the dancefloor," how original. So, we'll play this as the penultimate number, they'll go fucking nuts," knowing they could play anything fast and upbeat at that time, and the place would still go nuts. This was a white, un-woke, working-class wedding from Watford. The cake, along with most of the guests half cut by five o'clock, everybody off their tits by the time a brown evening buffet unwrapped at eight to soak up some of the booze, and full steam ahead to half past eleven and the closing track of the band's final set. Still, it paid a grand in hand, tidy money for an evening belting out cover hits to a collective of Mum and Dad dancing.

Julian turned and nodded to Phil, who obliged with his customary four stick clicks, which set off the overdriven guitar sound, whirred up along with a frenetic roll from Phil on his snare, and the song was underway.

WEDNESDAY

Spencer Churchill was in desperate trouble. Another punch hit his jawline, and he recoiled in shock before a roundhouse kick thwacked into his kidneys. How much more punishment could the poor young man take before being floored and out for the count.? Two sharp jabs butted his head backwards, his nose bled, his nostrils discharging the blood like a dragon's fire. Then, a quick chop to the neck and a follow-through knee upwards to the groin split his balls, his attacker was showing no mercy, and still, the onslaught ensued.

"Great work, Mae Li, keep the pressure up, work it, work it, thirty seconds to go, come on, you can do it", shouted the instructor watching her pummel the training bag with a deft variety of punches, kicks, elbows, and head butts. He'd noticed that she was a good trainer, but for some reason, she was going for it this morning; it was as if she imagined somebody she knew was in place. Whack, thwack, whack- whack, thump, and another combination of left jabs with right crosses finished the job. Mae Li stepped back and bent over, letting out a whoop of delight as the instructor's whistle blew, meaning a change of apparatus. She loved mixed martial arts classes. Combining different methods to inflict pain whilst maintaining a high ratio of physical exertion got her in the mood for seizing the day. Carpe Diem could fuck off, beat the crap out of them, was more to boot. But, did she want to hurt Spencer Churchill, the laid-back likeable lothario from Watford or Barnet or wherever it was, somewhere north of London, his raven long hair and mischievous eyes being so unflustered by Mae Li's sternest steely stare? No, but then she wanted to jolt him out of his manner of ease and entitlement around women and for picking up with that tart last night and leaving Mae Li at the table.

Mae Li picked up the skipping ropes and started fast-paced hoops over her head and under her quick feet, changing the style with crossovers and double steps as adept as a professional boxer. She would love to box or fight competitively, not with other women, but with men she could humble and master, but that was not allowed. How boring. Come on, Spencer, make an ill-timed move on me, something inappropriate, and I'll put you on your back. Maybe an arm lock that pincered the elbow so sharp it made him yelp out loud, or a firm forearm across his throat pulled back by an interlocking arm from which unconsciousness ensued in seconds, or just a good old flat palmed strike on the nose, one that made the eyes water. She imagined these outcomes as the rope whip swished faster, beads of sweat forming on her brow. She wore short tight coloured Lycra leggings that matched a tight cropped top, but not so close that it did not stop her firm tits from heaving up and down, struggling to either escape or remain inside the garment. It was challenging to decide which, but whatever their intention, it was something that Dan, the short, stocky guy on the opposite side of the gym, hadn't overlooked. Mae Li had noticed his furtive glances during the session, and it was time to acknowledge his interest in her own way.

"Let's work the pads together", she shouted across as the whistle blew again. She picked up the pads and ventured forwards toward her admirer. He was sweaty with ruddy, puffed cheeks glowing from a combination of the exercise and blood pressure of 200 over 120. He blew hard, jutting his lower jaw like a bulldog, not an inaccurate depiction, and the sweat from his fringe shot up like sparks from a firework. He nodded confidently and swaggered across towards her, rolling his shoulders, different body shape but still Spencer Churchill; you're going to regret this, she thought.

"Ok, I'll go first. You have a rest. I'll show you how it's done, and remember, punch from the shoulders and use your body weight to drive forward." Dan gasped, his body and arms demonstrating the art and skill in slow motion; it was a masterclass, he thought.

"Sounds good. I hope I can keep up with you," smiled Mae Li. She almost sounded submissive.

"I'm Dan, and sure, you can. But, if you need to slow down, just let me know, love," he replied. "Love?" Dan's fate was sealed. He was soon to become desperate, Dan.

"Come on, come on, left, left, left, right, left", shouted Mae Li, offering alternative pads for him to hit, and with each blow, she moved the pillows slightly and quickly. Unfortunately, Dan's punches were missing their mark. He blew in humiliation. The shame of his wild swings missing vexed him further.

"Hold 'em still, love. You're flinching from the power", he exhaled.

"Sorry, I didn't realize you were a beginner; let me slow it down and keep them steady", she sympathized. Dan took giant breaths and tugged at his gaping shorts with his gloved hands. They were losing the fight with gravity as much as Dan was with Mae Li's reactions. Finally, his teeth gritted, punches landed, a final grunt sent snot out of his nostrils, and the round was over.

"My turn, here you go", cried Mae Li, offering the padded mittens used for punch training. Dan bent forward, swapped his gloves for the pads, and wiped his nose across the sleeve of his sweaty t-shirt emblazoned with the word muscle.

"Come on, girl, don't hold back now," he patronized, and Mae Li felt she should warn him that she had no intention of holding back or being that accurate, for one of her punches was going to miss the pads and land on Dan's square and under biting flabby bulldog jaw. Her jabs smacked the cushions with the power and precision of an experienced welterweight, and Dan felt his wrists hurting with each blow. She bounced from foot to foot, a classic style of left-hand leading and right-hand following, and waited for Dan's arms to tire. He dropped his left arm seconds to go, and she countered with a right cross that smacked home hard into his temple. Dan dropped like a stone down a well and slumped to the gym mat. He was out like a candle and lay there poleaxed, like a pig that had been stunned for slaughter. Mae Li shrieked out in a combined mock of surprise and shock,

"I'm so sorry, it was an accident. Is he going to be, ok?" she feigned. The class was curtailed, and Dan was placed into a recovery pose by the instructor; then, once his eyes had opened, he could mumble that he was ok and finally stood up on shaky legs. The short, stout legs wobbled Dan off to the changing rooms, with support under each arm from a male companion. His fight was over with a blow to his head from which he might feel groggy for a few hours, but a blow to his ego from which he would never recover. Dan would swap Wednesday morning fighting fit for Badminton on Wednesday night and competition with men and women to whom power was clearing a shuttlecock over five feet net, hit with a racket that weighed less than a quarter pounder with cheese.

Spencer Churchill was unaware that he had been morphed into an inanimate canvas bag and beaten up by Mae Li that morning. At the same time as Dan was floored by a peach of a right cross by a maddened Mae Li, Spencer was lying in Chantelle's bed, relaxed by a hot mug of tea by the bedside and the pleasuring of his manhood by her left hand as she knelt on the bed applying her make up with the other. Chantelle was a pretty girl, slim with medium-length blonde hair dyed to cover her natural mouse. She wore a long navy skirt and jacket with a white blouse, her silver pocket badge displaying her name.

"Are you ready yet, Spenny? I've got to go to work, darling," she enquired with the deadpan enthusiasm she might use checking in a patient at work. She finished applying the lipstick and smacked her lips together, satisfied with the application.

"It might need some oral encouragement, please", he suggested.

"Spencer, I've just finished putting on my lippy?" she protested.

"Well, something else then, pop a tit out or something,"

"I've got to undo my blouse and my bra's tight. Why have you got to have a wank every morning, wasn't last night enough?" she complained.

"It's not my fault. All men get a hard-on first thing, morning glory and all that," he retorted.

"My wrist aches, Spenny,"

"Swap hands then; you can now that you have finished your makeup," he suggested.

"Ok, there you go, hurry up,"

"I can't work under pressure; where's the fire? No wonder romance is dying out,"

"What's romantic about giving you a hand job, it's Wednesday morning, gone 8 o'clock, and I've got to be at work for nine, and you know what the ring road around Watford town centre is like,"

"Fuck it forget it, don't worry about it. How can I come to a climax when you're sat there pulling at my pork half-heartedly talking about the Watford fucking ring road. I'll pull myself off, chuck us a pair of your knickers." Chantelle went to her top drawer and pulled it open to take the first pair off the top. "No, not clean ones, dirty ones from the basket," he pleaded.

"Spencer", she whined, "I'm off to work; get them yourself. You are a dirty bastard," and she slammed the door shut behind her.

"Yeah. I know, a big wanker, aren't we all?" he uttered to himself. He looked up at the tea and decided to drink it while it was still nearly hot and call off the contest. He needed to urinate, and it was never easy to ejaculate on a full bladder. He thought about heading into the Hive but remembered they had agreed to meet up for a rehearsal after lunch. Surjit was booking one of the meeting rooms. Surjit, Mae Li, Innocence, and Spencer, the Unicorn Joes, had agreed it was a good idea to pitch to each other and for them to play the parts of potential investors, the devil's advocate as Surjit had phrased it. A cup of tea, a morning bifta, and then head in to meet the others later via his flat, it was Wednesday, and it was probably time to change his socks and underwear. No woman would ever want his dirty underwear for sexual pleasure. It was another matter that separated men and women; what kind of sick, perverted woman could wish for that? Having visited the bathroom, he slurped back the tea, shuffled on his jeans, and dipped a filching hand into her washing basket on his way out.

It was a fifteen-minute walk to Croxley Green station or five minutes on the bus from outside Chantelle's parent's house. There was a young lady who stood under the canopy. She wore tight black leggings over her front, revealing a prominent camel toe and a bulging belly hung over a wide gate. To complete the look, Lindsay had chosen a short, black v-necked t-shirt that showed off tattooed arms whilst her sullen face was exposed by her hair scraped back and up into a bun, the Geordie facelift. Spencer stopped in his tracks and walked up to her,

"When is it due?"

"I'm not pregnant; I'm just a bit bloated, you ignorant twat", she replied.

"Not you. The bus," replied Spencer.

"Oh, I don't know when it gets here?" she retorted.

"I'll wait, if only for the conversation,"

"You what?"

"Exactly." Spencer checked his phone; Surjit had messaged the WhatsApp group, Acorn room 2 p.m.

Surjit sat in his kitchen at the table and drank orange juice while fingering his phone. He could navigate between apps and pages with the thumb from one hand. It was said that Homo Sapiens' evolutionary success lay behind the opposable thumb and as an essential part of gripping primitive tools for cutting and carving. This same capability and skill were just as critical in the 21st century; Multi-tasking with a mobile device was at this point on Wednesday morning drinking orange juice for Surjit, eating a candy bar for Innocence, using chopsticks for Mae Li, and in Spencer's case, masturbating. The practice of coordinating mobile phone management at breakfast irritated Surjit's mother, who could at least unknowingly be thankful her son was not Spencer at this moment.

"Can't you put that thing down for one minute and eat your breakfast like normal people" she complained as she wiped dishes from the sink.

"Normal people check their mobile phones at breakfast," replied Surjit.

"No, they don't; you don't see me doing it," she reasoned. A logical inference from her comment would not serve Surjit well, so it was better to think it than say it. That held for almost any thought and potential sentence uttered to his mother. He placed the device on the wooden surface and finished the paratha using his hands. His mother observed him from the corner of her eye. The ability to see beyond 180 degrees of vision was a skill uniquely held by herbivores, mothers, and wives, a fact not acknowledged by anthropologists or opticians.

"What time are you going to your office? You're here much later than usual?" she asked.

"I told you last night, I'm working from home this morning, and then I'm going up this afternoon to meet some friends who are also tech innovators." Surjit waited for the inevitable reply.

"Friends? You don't have any friends. Who are these friends?" she inquired. He could not begin to explain the term Unicorn Joes or that this was what he'd called the WhatsApp group to which he had invited his new friends.

"Just people I met presenting their plans to the same technology investment funding group as me this Friday morning." Surjit's mother stopped busying herself by the sink and strode to make eye contact with her son.

"Then they cannot be your friends. You compete with them. There are no friends in business, just competitors."

"They can be mum because I am not in competition with them, they have different plans and ideas than me, we are trying to help each other. That's what friends do, help each other,"

"Only family helps each other, never trust friends, they will only ever let you down, eventually. Besides, if you are all attempting to secure finance from the same investors, they must be competitors," she reasoned.

"They are, and then they aren't", replied Surjit recalibrating his hands whilst balancing imaginary weights.

"What do you mean they are, and they aren't. You're not making any sense. Are you addling your brain by smoking funny substances or drinking alcohol? Have these friends got you into these habits?"

"No, mum, it means the investors are looking for various projects to invest in, not just one. They specified that they are looking for various propositions to *diversify* their investments. This initial stage funding will support ten start-ups for a year to a stage where a Series A fund is feasible. Ok, mum? Variety and diversity, the spice of life."

"I'll spice your life. Get a proper job with a career path and an employer who will pay you regularly every month, pay you if you are sick, take holidays, and pay towards your retirement. You are a young man with prospects, but how can you find a wife and raise a family without realizing your potential? Mark, my words, go for your investor meeting Friday, but what can it harm to send some applications starting this morning if you are *working from home*. Who gets paid to work from their home? I don't, and I work in it whenever I am here."

Surjit considered this a rhetorical question and so didn't answer it. It was better to leave, out from his mother's mum's

360 degrees of vision, all of its foresight and hindsight. So he packed his bag, kissed his mother, and thanked her for breakfast.

"Where are you going?" she hollered as he opened the front door to their flat.

"Change of plan, going to see a man about a job", he lied. He was off to work from the Hive and then meet his friends at the Acorn Room, booked for them to rehearse from 2 p.m.

Innocence sat again with her sister at the small table in their flat in Dalston. Agnes was pouring coffee and glancing at the digital display of the cooker, which read 08.02.

"Better head off soon, Innocence, mustn't forget my phone, my badge, my purse, my bag, my laptop, my jacket, and what else, I think that's it. Are you walking down to work later?"

"Yes, not until after lunchtime. I'll have lunch here first, see you later, back usual time, after six, I guess. I'll text if not."

"Ok. Sound like nice people, your new friends?" remarked Agnes with a hint of it becoming more of a question; Innocence had mentioned Mae Li, Spencer and Surjit the previous evening.

"Oh, they are nice, just a little *odd*, that's all", and her face switched from a smile to a surprised look as she mouthed the word "odd". Spencer the seducer, Mae Li the enforcer, Surjit, the geek, and Innocence, what was she? The sensible one? Unlikely from what her sister knew of her. She provided balance, patience for Spencer, calm for Mae Li, understanding for Surjit, and drive with a sense of purpose that she shared with them all.

"I know I told you last night, people are what they are," surmised Agnes over judiciously, "although just be careful, because sometimes they are not," and with that paradoxical bent of wisdom, the elder sister left the flat for work

Innocence sat at the table. Another round of toast? Maybe just a tiny scrape of spreadable and the longer route to the office to burn it off? She stood up and peered into the bread bin; two slices left of Hovis granary, one of which was the crust that could be discarded. The other slice needed to be eaten. It was becoming stale, so a couple of minutes later, the toaster popped out the remaining piece, which transformed into toast. Innocence scratched a smear of low-fat spread across its dark brown surface, followed by a more generous veneer of Nutella. She adjusted her diary fifteen minutes earlier to start the walk to work to burn off the Nutella. Her phone pinged, and she was alerted to a message from the newly formed WhatsApp group "Unicorn Joes".

Acorn room booked from 2, see you there, Surj.

It was time to practice her presentation and ignore the biscuit jar before the rehearsals later that afternoon.

The Acorn room at the Hive was a boardroom-styled setting, containing eight chairs, four on either side of a table at the centre of a small office, available for booking by a half-day at £40 for the half-day or £60 for it whole. A large monitor LCD screen affixed to the wall at one end and a flip chart upon which Spencer had already drawn a giant cock and balls in red permanent marker, affirming his maturity level and the subject of his mind's primary focus. From its fifth-floor windows, occupants with the sense to sit on the opposite side of the room could look across to the Old Street side of Tech city with its low-rise buildings before the city emerged with its iconic silhouette, fast-changing to add new skyscrapers.

Surjit quickly linked their laptops to enable connectivity with the now illuminated screen and shared his device with the others. He then clicked the PowerPoint icon and brought up his presentation, one of the hundreds of millions that had bored and trivialized desperate attention across the corporate world.

"Spanner – simple and easy mobile performance management for the consumer at your fingertips – An opportunity to invest in a growing global market by Surjit Ghosh".

"Never mind that old bollocks, show us your wank bank", demanded Spencer.

"Come on, guys, we agreed, 20 minutes pitch, 10 minutes of questions, and then a quick summary, and we do the next one, let's focus", appealed Surjit to Spencer; his hands were shaking slightly.

"Yes, come on, shut up, Spencer, let's do this properly", added Innocence. Spencer nodded in submission and held his hands up to deflect Mae Li's tuts. The room quickly fell silent, and Surjit was able to begin.

"Introducing Spanner, a company and product that revolutionizes consumer management and control of the most important device that affects our daily lives across the globe, the smartphone. Download Spanner and your oyster is the world, erm the world is your oyster card meaning that, erm no, it nothing to do with an oyster card, forget that analogy, the world is in your pocket, which indeed it is given that a smartphone can fit in your pocket. But for much less than pocket money, you too can optimize your phone settings, meaning improved playtime and performance using hundreds of daily apps such as WhatsApp, Instagram, and Facebook. Load times are 13% faster, which means 0.17 seconds quicker with Spanner. Think about how that would transform your life?" Surjit hesitated, then nervously thrust his hands forward to point to the audience before retrieving them and placing them awkwardly by his side, his fists clenched in fright.

Spencer and Mae Li looked across at each other, and both pulled a frowned face. They did not share telepathy, but both were on the same thought train; where was this waffle going? What business or consumer value was loading a popular app pointing something of a second faster than before? Did that improve customer experience in the real world? Small margins mean a big difference in a financial environment, but for the average gambling, punter loading his betting app for a quick Acca, then no, nothing, nada. Innocence smiled encouragingly at Surjit, who was sweating, and whose voice had risen by a couple of keys, not quite an octave but given time, it might get there, and at least Surjit could be a shoo-in for Maurice Gibb in a Bee Gees tribute band.

"Whoa, camel", cried Spencer cutting off more statistics tripping out of Surjit's tongue.

"I'm waffling, aren't I? It's all gone blank; everything I prepared, I might as well be talking about anything," Surjit slumped back down into his chair.

"That's all fine; this is why we're doing this, ironing out a few kinks," supported Innocence.

"A few kinks, I don't need an iron, I need a fucking steamroller; there are more creases in this spiel than an elephant's arsehole," Surjit swore, and he never cussed, and it made Spencer laugh.

"Don't try to remember detailed prose verbatim. It'll never happen; it's better to stick to bullet points. Say what you are going to say, then illustrate it," added Mae Li. "Style will come with practice, but stick to the facts and tell a simple story for now. So what the fuck is loading my Facebook page 0.17 seconds quicker going to do for my life?" asked Mae Li.

"Are we in the questions phase?" asked Surjit.

"Yes, hell, let's start with questions, answer that question", replied Mae Li.

"Here's the deal, most people look at Facebook twenty times per day on their phone, add up all the other popular apps, and it is at least a hundred. So, a hundred times 0.2 seconds is 20 seconds and times that by a week is equal to a minute and a half. So, if you times that by a year, you've got an hour of your life back," Surjit folded his arms; his case was rested.

Spencer responded, "If only we could get this time back, except it doesn't work like that, Surj. You can't virtualize time like you do space, as in storage or capacity needed for application or database files. Each time saved in its entity is too small to mean anything, even accumulated. We can only do that with meaningful elapsed time. If I get to the train right on time every day, not 10 minutes early, all those ten minutes add up to an extra day a year. Except you don't get another day, do you? What you get is stressed the fuck out trying to arrive at the train at just the right time without missing the fucker, and the result is you end up dying five to ten years earlier than you would have done because everybody is pranged out and fucked up, dying to save a little bit of time. How do you want to live your life? Saving the day a year to die five years early, or chilling the fuck out and extending another five years of your life."

"Perhaps ask, who uses a mobile device for business where microseconds count, and that's your market, and that is the sell to the investors," chimed in Innocence, sweet and to the point. It was the Eureka moment Surjit was looking for, and he slapped the lid of his laptop shut.

"Thanks, guys, you're right. I need weeks more for research, and I've got one day left to do it. I wish I'd met you last week," he laughed nervously, his voice returning to normal range, and he meant it in more than one way. He picked up his laptop and retired to the table's far end, dragging his feet as he shuffled along.

"Prepare to be amazed and buckle up because I'm going to knock you out of your chairs," declared Spencer striding to the front of the table by the monitor.

"I guess you'll be going next then. I'm fastened in, hit me," remarked Mae Li folding her arms.

"Good morning, my name is Spencer Churchill, and I am offering you a license to print money. My business is as old as the stars and yet offers a new and innovative twist to the age-old problem, so you want to get your leg over, you have found somebody who is cheap, clean, and discreet to do it with, but you need somewhere cheap, clean, and discreet to do it in. Introducing Shagpad.com," Spencer showed off his new logo design and then moved to a new slide with a few summary bullet points. "Think Air bnb booked by the hour for the discerning fornicator who doesn't get off on dogging and finds attempting the missionary position in the back of a ford focus as comfortable and sexy as somebody putting sand in your KY jelly. Shagpad is a cloud-based platform supporting a mobile and internet app, connecting people with spare rooms and beds with people who need them on a short-term basis. The smart location feature will suggest suitable premises within a five-mile radius of you. You can specify a postcode based on preferences such as price, user rating, etc. 15% in commission from each booking. With prices likely at £10 per hour, that's one and a half quid. When Shagpad goes global, there will be a million bookings per day, meaning a turnover of over £350m per year, with the vast majority of that profit given this is a service-based business. Based on a thirty times multiplier, equivalent to Airbnb, Shagpad is a ten billion pound company, and you can be in on the ground for 0.01% of that, £1 million. So you are in for 10%, an earn-out of one billion pounds and a one hundred thousand per cent return. Now I'll take any questions you have before we sign." Spencer sat back down.

The others sat back open-mouthed. There were two slides, one a logo for Shagpad with the letters g and p replaced with the male and female symbols, and the second said, "Questions?"

"Erm, how about details?" asked Mae Li.

"What details?" replied Spencer, frowning.

"Any details?" responded Mae Li. "It's pure conjecture."

"Yeah, it is magic, isn't it,"

"No, not conjuring, conjecture, meaning supposition without cause, thoughts, dreams, none of this is derived from a logical conclusion," she explained. "Blah blah, bedroom for rent, blah blah, ten billion pounds," she mimicked Spencer's slower, gnarly voice.

"It could do with a little beefing up," added Surjit.

"Look who's talking, made a tool of himself with Spanner," smirked Spencer flinging an arm out dismissively.

"Guys, guys." Innocence interjected. "You're both right; the point was to be objective with each other and to try to help. Think of it from the investors' point of view. What do they need to invest, what does their money go towards, and how does that generate a return?"

"Point taken, I'll add a couple of slides. The devil is in the detail," accentuated Spencer when saying the word detail, looking at Mae Li.

"And the devil is in the advocate," quipped Surjit. "Who's up next?"

"Go ahead, Innocence, show us how it's done," affirmed Mae Li.

Innocence introduced her casual game, consisting of cats and dogs chasing candies for points. Next, she showed some demo gameplay and narrated statistics showing the link between the content, the target audience, and a reasonable rate of return given a target investment of one hundred thousand pounds. Next, she held some additional reasoned arguments as to why it might succeed, how much money she needed to launch it, and the sales distribution model from which games platform providers would deduct a margin but provide a ready market for a potential player. Finally, she showed some projected earnings given from recent comparative data. She concluded that this presented an opportunity to invest in a diverse small games company, predominantly female and black, and the growth potential of future games along the same lines.

"I'll now take any questions you might have", she beamed with pride, "starting with you, Spencer." Spencer shook himself awake; his eyes open, they had been all the time, but his mind had wandered off somewhere soon after the introduction,

"Hi, my name is Innocence Ndlovu, and I'd like to," was all he could remember before his mind meandered. First, how he would take Chantelle that evening, then if he should call Holly, to if it were possible or feasible that Holly and Chantelle might agree to share him and each other for the night? Or just for the evening would be fine, but then as the prospect, however distant, took hold, he felt his raging boner under the table demanding to be fed. Masturbating during Innocence's presentation would be bad manners, not to mention entirely inappropriate and against the code of behaviour rules of the Hive. Spencer switched his focus to the subject of football and contemplated Chelsea's home game versus Bayern Munich in the EUFA Champions League that evening. If only he could have a threesome *and* the match, it could give a new meaning to changing ends at halftime. Unfortunately, his stiffy had not subsided, so it was back to the game. Bayern was cagey and would sit deep waiting to counter, Chelsea had Hazard, and he could skip and jink in between any defence.

"What do you think, Spencer?" Innocence repeated.

"Two-nil to Chelsea and avoid conceding the away goal", he replied. Innocence stood incredulous. What did that mean? Was it some clever business language terminology that she had been unaware of, after all, she had studied Anthropology?

"Oh…Kay…" she hesitated. Finally, Mae Li rescued the situation. "I thought it was excellent, babe. How long do you envisage the prototype mock-up and the full production version is available, and what level of funding is required for that meantime, of no revenue?"

"Great question, six months with two developers funded and three months if we can fund four, then we can revert to two as we maintain updates to the game. That would mean 12 person-months and seventy thousand dollars for a game of this simple complexity. The work would be delivered offshore, with lower rates and high skills. Does that answer your question?" Mae Li smiled and nodded. "Surjit, any questions from you not related to football?"

"Yes, where do you get this developed, and what are these rates?" he asked enthusiastically.

"I can get $20 per hour, a thousand bucks per week, from South Africa. I have a good source, and it's reasonably priced with good quality. Anything else?"

"No, that's interesting; thanks, good job, and good luck, Miss Ndlovu" he smiled with his thumbs pricked up.

"And I guess that leaves me", sighed Mae Li stepping forward.

"The best until last", added Innocence, "we'll see," muttered Spencer.

"Hi, I'm Mae Li, and I'm CEO of treble 8 technologies; it is my pleasure to introduce to you a disruptive social media platform that will bring transparency and honesty to commerce and the people responsible for this, the world over. Dear Investors, I introduce Voracity, the confidential and discreet platform for professionals to offer honest appraisals about co-workers, colleagues, and former associates. Think Glassdoor but for employees, not companies." Mae Li stepped quickly and elegantly through her slide deck with screenshots demonstrating that this anonymous service would revolutionize human resource intelligence. Contacts displaying poetic license, sometimes bordering on fantasy, on Linkedin would be replaced by independent reviews and ratings from people who could verify performance, behaviour, traits, and skillsets. Voracity was to be hosted in China to avoid potential litigation. The corporate entity was established through a network of offshore tax havens, mostly under British jurisdiction, as most are. Subscribers could show support for authentications by a series of justice sword-like emojis replacing the traditional arrow up or down "likes" and "loves" with hearts. Comments and observations could be substantiated or denied with this emoji scoring system or additional comments. Connectivity with the corresponding Linkedin contact enabled it to be compared with Voracity. At last, a single pane of glass into who you are hiring, partnering with, or working with. The numbers were impressive. A fast-growing business with the potential to meet a valuation on the same growth path as Linkedin meant a company worth billions of dollars in under 5 years. Mae Li asked £1m to get it to the first round of funding from private equity investors within a twelve-month plan when shares would dilute, but the severe investment rounds and growth would follow.

"Any questions?" she asked.

"Yeah," said Spencer, "Fancy a pint?" he suggested.

"Serious questions?" added Mae Li.

"How are you going to maintain the integrity of the platform brand when anybody can write anything about anybody else?" probed Surjit.

"You think the bullshit on Linkedin has any value or integrity?" she replied.

"No, but it's bullshit that is at least someway true and verifiable. I mean, who works where and what they do?" Sujrit screwed up his nose a little.

"Even if their posts are re-posts of company announcements with sycophantic likes by their contacts. Who has more than fifty contacts that you seriously connect with? There are people with thousands of connections, especially recruitment firms. Those fuckers suck, not even a personal message, just machine gun requests to connect with thousands of people, hoping one might be recruiting and reply with a request. I mean does that shit work?" posed Mae Li assuming experience beyond her fledgling business experience.

"Good luck Mae Li, you'll smash it, you all will, only mine will fail," spoke Innocence.

"No, your plan looked fantastic to me," said Spencer, "Me too," added Surjit.

"Thank you, guys," she said, sighing, "I'm anxious because I know this can work."

"All the more reason to have a drink. Come on, let's go to the pub," pleaded Spencer.

"We booked this room for four hours, and we've been here less than half that time," scolded Mae Li.

"That's illogical thinking if I hire a car for a day, but I stop and get out when I've finished my journey. I don't drive around until midday the following day because that's when the rental expires. " he shot back.

"I ought to re-work my presentation, but Spencer's right. I also need to relax and start fresh tomorrow. So I might as well wing it anyway. Then, I'll be less anxious," chuckled Surjit, and with some newly found confidence, he added, "Come on mate, I'll buy you a beer," and stood up, collecting his bag, looking at Mae Li and Innocence, ready to go, "Coming?"

"I'll finish up here," replied Mae Li, and Innocence confirmed that she would stay with Mae Li too.

"Ok, I'll update the group chat where we are if you change your minds later?"

Surjit and Spencer left the room, their preparations none the better for the rehearsal, whilst the girl's content looked in pretty good shape, just final adjustments and, of course, how they presented on the day. Time would tell, and time was ticking on towards Friday morning, just over a day to go, T-1.

Spencer led Surjit to the Griffin, a short ten-minute walk between Leonard Street and Ravey Street and at the heart of

Shoreditch. It served craft ales from a burnt umber tiled exterior and a laid-back, homely interior with a long bar. It was Spencer's style of pub, full of character and a hostelry that could tell thousands upon thousands of tales from customers that had boozed and splurged their hard-earned cash from the markets, shops, and factories that thronged the busy lanes of Shoreditch and Hoxton during the 19th and 20th centuries. In 2016, it was one of a few small survivors from an environment that had undergone dramatic change during the past fifty years. The "Griff", as some locals referred to it, offered independently brewed beers despite the exterior signage denoting the long-defunct local breweries of Charrington's of Bethnal Green, and Whitbread. The latter turned out 4,000 barrels of beer each week during the 19th century from the vast, sprawling brick-built Brewery with its tall chimneys in Chiswell Street that ran East to West between Moorgate and Barbican.

Spencer and Surjit ambled through its double side doors and strode to the bar. It was half-past three in the afternoon; drinkers sat hunched around the wall-lined tables, sipping and supping at pints of varying shades of autumnal-coloured beers, one or two with wine glasses. Spencer surveyed the clips on the beer pumps, some new that he hadn't yet experienced.

"What would you like?" asked the red-haired girl with a black apron tied around her petite waist.

"To be balls deep in your mouth" was not an appropriate answer, thought Spencer, and so he followed the social etiquette when ordering drinks and enquired as to the taste and strength of the Camden range, which he knew well, but it offered a short time to converse with this young lady.

"I don't know. I don't drink the produce. I only serve it. I can offer you a sample if you like?"

"No, I'll stick to the beer, thanks. I'll admit to being into some kinky stuff, but not urophilia. Perhaps you could offer a small beer taster?" he smiled. The red-haired behind the bar giggled spontaneously.

She gripped the pump and pulled a smidgen of "Camden pale ale" into a shorts glass. Spencer could not resist the thought that entered his head. Perhaps he needed therapy, every utterance or action by a woman he fancied offered a sexual connotation or innuendo.

"Thanks, that's quite hoppy, smooth, and not too bitter", knowing full well what Camden pale ale tasted like. "Tell me, might I try the Ink Stout? I might be in the mood for something darker, more chocolatey, and bitter?"

"Sure, here you go," She pulled the pump gently with her pale knuckles flexed around Ink Stout's handle, and Spencer imagined his shaft where the pump stood erect. It was true he did need help.

"Deftly, done, have you worked here long?" he smiled, acknowledging the delicate splash of stout that immersed the small glass.

"Just started a week ago", she replied,

"Oh, that is intense, strong, but a little more than I was looking for on Wednesday mid-afternoon. So I'll stick with the Pale Ale. Please pour one for my friend and have one for yourself, a drink that is, not the Pale Ale. You mentioned you don't drink the stuff." He smiled, eyes as dark and as intent as a wolf's glowering at a lamb.

"Thanks, I'll have a small glass of wine, but I'm not allowed on duty; I'll have it later," she replied, pulling at the pump, her small right arm bicep flexing under the white short-sleeved shirt that she wore under the apron. Surjit stood back, watching, listening, and learning. He did not want the beer but did not want to interrupt the dialogue. He could buy an orange juice later; Spencer could manage two pints easily.

"I could join you if I knew what time you finished?" Spencer hunched his shoulders submissively; it was a cheeky but innocuous ask.

"Not until much, much later, but I appreciate the offer", she politely declined, peeped up at him between swapping glasses and smiled nervously.

"I get the message. No need for more beers. I'll be crying into this one enough," Spencer smiled and paid the twelve pounds with his contactless payment card. Thanks were exchanged, and the boys turned on their feet, found an empty table to deposit the beers, and sat pulling their chairs beneath them.

"I don't want this beer," admitted Surjit.

"Get it down, you, for fuck sake, we had a fucking nightmare rehearsal. So let's chill the fuck out with a beer or two and work things out here. In the pub, admittedly, more ideas were created and forgotten than any office meeting room full of fucking pens and flipcharts." Spencer took a deep swig of the beer and replaced it on the table with a clunk, the foam settling on his top lip like a milky moustache.

"I'm not sure I want this. I don't drink," appealed Surjit.

"Get it the fuck down you," growled Spencer. Surjit took a sip and closed his eyes. It was more substantial than the shandy from Monday, with a slightly bitter and sour taste. He took a stronger swig and swallowed, the smooth ale followed his trachea into his belly, and within five minutes, the alcohol would soon permeate his bloodstream.

"The conversation you just had with the girl behind the bar", whispered Surjit.

"Yeah, what about it?"

"Do you often do that, you know, ask the girl out?"

"Not always, no."

"Not always when?"

"Well, not if I don't fancy her or not if I am already with somebody and she can overhear me, not usually if somebody else can overhear us, but you didn't count, so no, not always."

"Oh, what do you mean, you don't count? I mean, I don't count", asked Surjit.

"It meant you were standing off the bar, kind of listening but not listening, so it didn't make her uncomfortable. She has not been working here long, not in a bar long, judging by the time she took pouring two pints, and has not become immune to the bullshit advances and hits she will get on a daily occurrence. I deduced all that from the short charade of not knowing the beers, so I was gentle, charming, not too pushy, complimentary, and a nice guy, all of which I am. And because of that, when I come in tomorrow and ask her out again, she might just say yes, because she knows me, trusts me a little more and probably fancies me too, given that her pupils dilated, her cheeks reddened a little, and she breathed gently. Her hands around the pump did not tighten in a fight or flight response to my bold inquiry as to whether she might like my company with her small glass of wine," Spencer took a pause and another swig.

"You're a fucking legend, so much to learn, I could never think and remember of all that", sighed Surjit.

"You don't have to, you fucking arsehole," laughed Spencer to Surjit's bewilderment, "I just made that all up. It was just a little banter, that's all. You're a nice guy Surjit. You can be hilarious, don't try too hard, engage in a conversation, then be direct, ask her out? Why wait days and weeks? They usually know within minutes if they like you or not. Either shit or get off the pot, there's a queue outside the door; it's a numbers game; the more you ask, the more rejections, but the more some might say yes, or in the case of Nicola Roberts over there, it wasn't a fuck off, it's in the folder marked pending, so I'll try again, understood?"

"How did you know her name is Nicolas Roberts? But, Crikey, you are good," admired Surjit; how had Spencer known her name already? He was sure he had not asked.

"I didn't; she's the ginger one in Girls Aloud, you twat, fuck me," hissed Spencer.

"Girls, who?" Surjit was more confused than before. He took a stronger gulp from the pint, the effect was kicking in on his weak tolerance, and he felt a surge of calm fall from his shoulders and through his arms. He was talking about women in the pub with a mate in London. He smiled and relaxed a little.

"What did you get up to last night?" asked Spencer changing the subject; Surjit was elated that Spencer seemed genuinely interested in Surjit's life.

"Oh, I went for a gym try-out, but it turned out I dropped a bollock there," quipped Surjit, who proceeded to tell Spencer the tragic story, who then laughed out loud and punched Surjit playfully. Surjit chuckled back, and laughed at himself, was it the beer, or was it Spencer or both, but he felt that he didn't give a shit about things so much, but in a good way. So he picked up his phone and tapped a short message to the group.

Mae Li and Innocence were sat in the Acorn room at the Hive, each focussed on their screens, although in truth, each was thinking different thoughts from fine-tuning their presentations. In Mae Li's pocket and on the table in front of Innocence, their phone's announced a new message. Innocence was the first to pick up,

"They are in the Griffin pub, in Leopold Street," she said slowly, then looked at Mae Li.

"Good for them; they need a drink," replied Mae Li after a few seconds' delay.

"What did you think of the guy's presentations?" asked Innocence.

"Shocking, they've got no chance," replied Mae Li, "and you?"

"Needs more work. I'm not sure about, ahem, Shagpad. It's a good idea but is that the sort of thing Angeltech will invest in?"

"I don't know, but one thing is for sure, I can't see Spencer appearing on Dragon's Den anytime soon. So can you imagine (mimics Spencer's deep tones) Hi Deborah, my name is Spencer Churchill, and I want you, in the Shagpad babe, I'm looking for a sugar mummy? I'm willing to offer you a big portion in return for a loan that's all alone, with me babe and my big swinging dick." And Mae Li stood and swung her hips back and forth. Innocence giggled; the likeness was good. Had Mae Li practised?

"What about Surjit?" goaded Innocence. Mae Li stood with her hands clasped between her legs, feet together, and shoulders hunched a little, chin down. Then, eyes peering up a little and spoken with a quiet south London accent, she mumbled quietly, "Spanner, the must-have tool for all women, with many attachments meaning satisfaction guaranteed every time. Easily handled for manual tasks or comes with batteries for Spencer mode, for when you need a helping hand for those hard, to-reach places," stop it cackled Innocence, "You're being very naughty and funny. Oh, sod it, shall we join them at the pub?"

"How about we stop off somewhere else, I have my bike, so I'm not drinking, or perhaps come back to my place?" suggested Mae Li.

"Sure, that can work; I'll walk and catch you up if you give me the address. It's near the University, isn't it?"

"Yes, babe, but no way you are walking. I've got a spare helmet in the luggage compartment on the bike. I'll give you a ride; it'll only take five minutes," and Mae Li stood and packed her bag. She put on her leather jacket, picked up her helmet, and walked towards the door as Innocence followed her out of the room and the building. Innocence pushed the motorcycle helmet over her afro, fastened the straps, and then slung her bag over her shoulder before attempting to straddle the passenger seat of the big bike.

"I'm not sure I can get my leg over", appealed Innocence,

"Come on, you sound like Spencer. Tuck, your skirt between your legs, swing your right leg up and over, like this." Mae Li stood adjacent to the bike to show her. "That's it; hold my waist and lean with the bike when we corner," instructed Mae Li before lowering her visor. Unfortunately, Mae Li failed to notice that Innocence's skirt had hooked on the back of the luggage box. It covered her backside adequately, but the big bike was stationary. As Mae Li and Innocence took off, the voluminous skirt billowed like a parachute, baring Innocence's Rubenesque derriere to the East London traffic. As Mae Li swung the machine between the startled trafficVan drivers peeped, and uber cars tooted horns if only to confirm sexism was alive and well in 21st-century contemporary London. The sight was amplified by Innocence leaning forward, her back arched, and legs gripped tight around the seat as she sought additional purchase over and above the belly-to-back bearhug she embraced Mae Li with. After five minutes, her modesty was restored as the bike's roar fell to a purr synchronized with Innocence's skirt falling flat. The episode was unnoticed by either of the passengers, "See what I have to put up with every day, fucking men drivers who don't like a woman over and undertaking them," snapped Mae Li.

"I see what you mean; we could not have had more attention if I'd have shown my backside to them," agreed Innocence, removing her helmet and shuffling off the bike. Her dismount was more accessible than the attempt to climb aboard, and she acknowledged her feet touching the ground with a little cry of satisfaction. She followed Mae Li through the doors and up to a first-floor landing where Mae Li's large apartment stood opposite another doorway.

"Come on in and make yourself comfortable," pointed Mae Li to the door leading to the lounge area and removed her jacket. She disappeared into her bedroom that stood off the large hallway. "Won't be a moment, babe, just getting out of the leathers," She was back in the open planned lounge with two large windows that overlooked a tree-lined street within moments.

"This is lovely; how many bedrooms?" asked Innocence,

"There's two, but I live alone. I'm a solitary animal," smiled Mae Li.

"Like a leopard", acknowledged Innocence. "Leopards only bear another one for mating."

"I know how they feel," agreed Mae Li.

"Not like lions; sisters stay together for life and kick out the young men at two. They put up with dominant males who fight to the death for them and are never around, except sometimes for dinner or sex. So it's the sisters and daughters who stick together and make up the pride," she said quietly, remembering her native and beautiful Africa.

"Please sit down, so what can I get you to drink?" asked Mae Li.

"Could I have something non-alcoholic? Just water is fine,"

"Tell you what, I'll make mocktails; any fruit you don't like?"

"No, I love it all. Please go ahead with whatever's easiest,"

Mae Li crushed fresh mint leaves and sugar, cut limes, squeezed them freshly into glasses and added crushed ice from the freezer before topping them with soda water.

"Voila, a virgin mojito for Innocence, quite befitting," she announced, passing one of the glasses to Innocence.

"Innocence by name, Innocent by nature?" posed the young African.

"I don't know. I'd say so, you tell me," replied Mae Li.

"You're right. I'm not promiscuous. I could never dance on a stage in front of men or women. I don't have the body for it anyway," Innocence sipped from the tall glass "ooh, this is very tasty."

"Thanks, and yes you do, and yes you could, if you so wished. You have fabulous figure Innocence, pretty face, full-bosomed, muscular arms, and legs," warmed Mae Li.

"And a big bottom, you did not mention my big bum?" Innocence wagged a finger at Mae Li, smiling and toying with the ice.

"Women would kill for your arse, babe; it's fantastic, not skinny like mine,"

"Maybe we could swap then. I'd love to wear tight skinny jeans. I mean, they are always tight, but not so skinny," sighed Innocence.

"Be proud of what you have because it is what most men desire, a woman with a full bust and hips. So you've got it, babes, cheers?" said Mae Li.

"So do you think Spencer and Surjit will be talking like this?" asked Innocence.

"What examining their full bust and hips?" laughed Mae Li. "Spencer has a full ego, and I bet he has a tiny cock,"

"Mae Li! Are you going to find out?" shrieked Innocence, cradling crushed ice between her lips and coming close to spitting it out.

"Am I fuck, arrogant cock" she replied.

"He's not arrogant; he's just super confident, super cool. I wish I had some of that,"

"I'm going to boost you up, babe, get you to see how beautiful and talented you are. You've got a lot going for you, and I hope you get an investment offer on Friday morning," said Mae Li playing with her hair.

"Me too, and you too," nodded Innocence, and her phone buzzed, "It is Unicorn Joes, they're still in the pub, they're asking are we coming? That would be a not tonight boys, early to bed, early to rise, makes a woman health, wealthy and wise," tapped her long brown fingers with clear immaculate nails.

"They're not coming," stated Surjit reading the group message.

"Good, they'd cramp our style anyway. I've still got my eye on Nicola over there," replied Spencer turning and smiling at the bargirl, then pouting his lips and wiping tears like Pussycat reacting to being turned down for a lift by Cliff Booth in Once Upon a Time in Hollywood. Nicola Roberts laughed and shook her head pitifully but in a playful way. Spencer Churchill was in.

"What will I do if you start chatting with her?" posed Surjit.

"Look, mate, she's working. I'm laying the groundwork for tomorrow or whenever she is off next, I just need to get another round in. Anyway, look over to your right. A young lady sat on her own, keeps looking over…at you," teased Spencer.

"No way, she's probably looking at you," replied Surjit, eyeing the mousy brown bobbed girl, looking furtively across the room.

"She can't be, mate. I'm sitting here, which is out of her eye line. That would be you, dude, exuding power and charm, the proud owner of Spanner Inc., and soon to be the next UK unicorn. If you are worth several million, you will not be able to beat the women off you with a shitty stick, shallow as fuck women, mark my words. You should say hello and tell her to have an investment meeting tomorrow, but you would love to take her for lunch if she is available afterwards," suggested Spencer.

"It's that easy? What do I say again?" asked Surjit.

"Words to the effect, tell me to fuck off but do you fancy lunch tomorrow," quipped Spencer, not fully paying attention; his mind was elsewhere. He'd never shagged a girl with ginger pubes; he wondered how red Nicola's might be? Buoyed by the pint of ale and enthused by Spencer's flattery and fair heart attitude, Surjit took Spencer by surprise, stood up and drew himself to his full height, and strolled in the direction of the mousy bobbed girl. He leaned over, and they exchanged words briefly. Finally, Surjit turned and walked back to the table, a notable quickening in his step.

"Drink up; we're out of here", he hissed.

"Hold fire, what's up? What happened?" asked Spencer with just a creep of concern in his voice.

"Humiliating, I shouldn't have listened to you", hushed Surjit under his breath.

"Whoa, what did you say?"

"I did what you said. I went up to her and said, tell me to fuck off, but do you fancy lunch tomorrow?"

"Eh? What the, er, what did she say?"

"Fuck off", replied Surjit flatly.

"Jeez, Surj, I didn't mean it literally. I was paraphrasing, warm her up first for fuck sake, a little light banter,"

"Well, next time, keep your paraphrasing to yourself, not that there will be the next time. I'm heading off," Surjit walked towards the door before remembering his last painful post-pint experience. "Where are the loos, please," he asked Nicolas Roberts.

"Just over there on the right", she replied, smiling and pointing in the direction of the mousey bob.

"Fuck", swore Surjit again.

THURSDAY

"Breakfast? Coffee and croissants at the Hive for 9? Our table awaits," wrote Surjit to the Unicorn Joes What's App group, and he added a photo of their table, an empty booth at the ground floor cafe. He had arrived early again and commandeered "their" table on the fifth floor. The four seats were snagged by four high visibility vests he'd brought in place of the assorted clobber that adorned the seats the day before. The lurid yellow vests, borrowed from some random stock in the store below where his mother worked, were much easier to transport and had the look of officialdom. Nobody would sit down with these deposited around the four seats belonging to "their" table. Spencer had suggested that he would arrive earlier that morning, but that was a statement of intent made yesterday afternoon in the pub, a lot of time and probably the purpose had passed since then. The girls did not appear at the Griffin, at least not before Surjit left, after one more pint later, a shandy this time, and nursed so that he felt confident that he could make it back to the Elephant and Castle without any unfortunate interludes. Spencer had offered more valuable tips on how Surjit might successfully pursue a relationship with a female of similar age. They agreed that Surjit should join an online dating app. Surjit thought this through and made sense; it cut the crap, the small warm-up talk with strangers in bars, the uncertainty of the answer to a simple question to a girl he had met and liked, might you go out with me sometime? He imagined the dialogue,

"Let me be frank, no, not a bloke called Frank; I'm Surjit. So I'll start again. Let me be candid. I'm searching for some warm, funny, and intimate conversations and mutual feelings through shared social experiences and collective happiness. And I'm desperate for sex."

They selected "Secs in the City", which matched predominantly heterosexual female administrative London-based professionals with higher-earning, metrosexual men. The format was simple and if things didn't go well during the initial call, then no date, never mind, plenty more fish in the sea, pebbles on a beach, and all the consolatory waffle aimed at softening the blown-out blow. On the flip side, if a positive mutual conclusion was reached, the app's calendar arranged a convenient time, place, and activity for a follow-up date. Spencer signed him up that previous afternoon in the pub, where all things reckless made sense, despite Surjit's protests that he would rather wait until after the weekend. It was a seminal week. The dissent was countered; nothing had to happen this week, it was all to be run at his own pace, and before Surjit had left the pub, he was registered with a profile and a picture, selected by Spencer, uploaded to his account. A free trial month's membership started. It was time for the app to alert Surjit that a potentially promising partner was waiting for a first-time call.

Innocence bounced into and onto the office floor, her smile beaming as she acknowledged Surjit's frantic waves.

"Good morning Surjit."

"Hi, how are you? Was it a nice walk-in?"

"Lovely, thank you, the sun is shining; this time tomorrow, we'll be standing at the precipice of fame and fortune,"

"I'll take the fortune part. I'm not interested in becoming famous. I could not take the attention. So, hey diddly dee, a quiet life for me," sang Surjit, which made Innocence giggle. She thought Surjit quite sweet and funny.

"Are the other two Joe's coming in?" enquired Innocence.

"Oh, I don't know. The message was viewed but without a reply. You never know with Spencer," he chuckled.

"How was your afternoon in the pub? Did you get any work done?"

"Well, Spencer was working on something," that much was true.

"I think that so long as they like your idea, the detail does not matter so much. All that can be worked out as part of the follow-up appointment" nodded Innocence.

"I hope so. I still haven't resolved the legal issue regarding invalidating warranties," Surjit admitted sorrowfully.

"Don't worry about that. Why not OEM the technology to the manufacturers?" suggested Innocence casually, opening her MacBook.

"OEM? Oh, you mean sub-license the technology to them. Yes, OEM it. Why not indeed. Why didn't I think of that? Innocence, you've just made my morning, my day, my week, who knows, maybe my life." Surjit was elated and sprang open his presentation to add this critical opportunity. His brow frowned, and his tongue licked across his lips in concentration like a child colouring a storybook. Innocence noted that part of him and smiled again.

"Morning wankers," Spencer slammed his bag down on the desk with a thump and pulled the chair out noisily to sit down,"

"Hi, Spence," remarked Surjit looking up from his screen. The shortening of his name felt good; it indicated he was a mate.

"Good morning Spencer, a good morning would suffice; please do not call me a wanker," requested Innocence.

"Fair enough, but you do, don't you?" he shot back.

"Do what?" she replied.

"Wank. Girls wank as much as boys. Don't tell me they don't," frowned Spencer. Surjit looked like he would not add to the argument and rolled his eyes.

"It's not something I am going to debate right now", declared Innocence.

"No, but it is a mass debating point. Get it?" Spencer hung on the words looking at Innocence. She declined to answer.

"Mass debating, masturbating", he added.

"Oh, Spencer, get on with your work", she protested, shaking her head, realizing the pun and being none the happier for it.

"Hi guys, what's going on?" chirped Mae li. She was in a surprisingly upbeat mood.

"We were just talking about wanking. Did you have one this morning?" enquired Spencer. Mae Li paused and took a short but sharp take of breath.

"No need. I had a man inside me for most of the night. He fucked my brains out. But, mind you, a real man with arms like a gorilla and a cock like a baby's arm. Not a man with arms like a baby and cock like a gorilla," she uttered, looking Spencer up and down.

"Have gorillas got small willies? Innocence, have gorillas got small dicks?" asked Spencer.

"How the hell should I know how big a gorilla's ding-dong is? Do you think I have slept with one?" she snapped.

"No, but because you're from Africa, and that's where they live, so I assumed maybe you knew how large King Kong's ding-dong was," replied Spencer folding his arms.

"Africa is over one hundred times the size of England, gorillas live in the Congo, I am from South Africa, I've never even seen a gorilla, so I don't know how big his" she shook her head in exasperation, "his thing is."

"Relative to his mass, the gorilla has an exceedingly small penis and testicles compared to the male human. The average length of an erect penis in a gorilla is one and a quarter inches. It measures one and a half in an orangutan, three inches in a chimpanzee, and five inches in a man. Testicle size and the conspicuousness of the penis vary correspondingly," remarked Surjit.

"Thank you very much, David Attenborough. How the fuck did you know all that, and how would somebody know how big a gorilla's boner is?" asked Spencer.

"Googled it while you were arguing, but I can't say I know who discovered the length of gorilla's hard-on," replied Surjit.

"Well, I'd be disappointed with five inches, but I guess you can dream, Spencer," Mae Li pulled a sarcastic smile before returning to her usual mean, bitch face staring at him.

Surjit smiled, Spencer had been at the table for less than a minute, and an argument had already broken out about female masturbation and gorilla genitalia, not that the two were related in any way, but it was outstanding.

"Now that we're all here and have our spots, shall we have a coffee and croissant at the bar?" suggested Surjit.

"No, fuck off, and not now", were the sharp, simultaneous replies from Spencer, Mae Li, and Innocence. Surjit sank back in his chair earlier that week. Although such a volley of responses would have destroyed him on Monday, it was Thursday morning, and he chuckled to himself; a week was a long time in business. His pocket buzzed from an inbound message alert. Surjit retrieved his phone, and the notification made his heart skip. The dating app notifies him that somebody wants to meet up later, and a virtual speed meets as the process required. He opened the app and pondered the photo and biography, shielding his phone from Mae Li's line of sight, who sat next to him. Suddenly the phone was pulled from his grasp, plucked with speed by the long reach of Spencer Churchill. In this respect, he did have arms like an ape.

"Who is the lucky lady then?" cackled Spencer.

"Spencer, give me back my phone", shrieked Surjit under rasped hushed tones. He made a desperate lunge to snatch it back, but Spencer's reaction was too quick, and it was pulled further into his chest from where he peered down at the message.

"Jojo, thirty-four, an administrator in the city, suggests a speed meet at lunchtime with a view to a date tonight. Although not a bad-looking bird, I reckon thirty-four might be a fib, but then you're not exactly a millionaire either, are you, Surj?

"What are you doing, Surjit?" asked Innocence.

"Nothing, Spencer is taking the piss, as usual", lied Surjit unconvincingly, "fuck, you've accepted already, 12.30 p.m., today!"

"Calm down, Surj; you'll have a nosebleed, anyway; it'll be good practice," replied Spencer.

"Good practice, for what?"

"Bullshitting in front of the investors tomorrow and closing a deal", exclaimed Spencer.

"She's never 34; I'd say 43. Maybe she got the digits the wrong way round," remarked Innocence, peering over Surjit's shoulder.

"Let's hope she doesn't get Surjit's digit the wrong way round," smiled Spencer, "or maybe he'd like that."

"Chuck it here, babe, let me see, please?" instructed Mae Li, and Surjit did as she asked and slid his phone diagonally over to her, the angst in his eyes showing.

"She'll have you for breakfast, young man. She is, in social terms, what they call a cougar," Mae Li informed him. Surjit swallowed hard and figured the easiest way out would be not to show up. He did not want to be prey for a woman defined as a feline predator? But, perhaps he should ask, he did so hesitantly, "What's a cougar, apart from the obvious answer?"

"A woman in her forties seeking a sexual relationship with a younger man," replied Innocence.

"I'm cancelling. I'm not interested. It's not good timing," stammered Surjit.

"It is perfect timing. It'll keep your mind off the meeting tomorrow. You're going out for a date. Maybe you're both up for a fish supper. You're not asking her to marry you," declared Spencer. Surjit sighed, and his breathing felt a little deeper than usual. Mae Li slid his phone back to him, taking another look at Jojo, the cougar. The picture showed her laughing; her teeth were straight, but if it were a top plate, they would be? Her eyes were staring straight at Surjit; he avoided a direct return contact and looked away.

"Why don't we all go out together just to start? Then, we could say you're my employees?" suggested Surjit.

"Don't be daft. We are not coming out with you and your date, Surjit. Besides, Mae Li and I are going to a fitness class tonight together," said Innocence, flexing her biceps.

"I'm out with Chantelle, got a pleasant evening planned, taking her to the Harvester, Croxley Green. Sticky ribs, sticky fingers, and sticky toffee pudding," added Spencer rubbing his hands.

"You lucky girl, Chantelle", muttered Mae Li. Spencer wasn't listening. He led forward to Surjit, who was sitting opposite him,

"Looks like you are on your own, squire. In any case, maybe you don't connect that well in the pre-meet call at lunchtime."

"I can make sure of that. I've just got to be myself!" Surjit frowned.

"Just play it cool, talk about her, ask her questions," said Mae Li,

"What questions?" asked Surjit,

"What football team does she support, and does she agree with the offside rule as it is currently interpreted?" joked Spencer.

"Ask her about her job, the family where she lives, what she likes to do, the five f's, films, food, fun, and…." Innocence did not have time to finish her sentence,

"Fellatio," added Spencer. Mae Li laughed and then suppressed it.

"Sorry, perhaps it's fearter?" suggested Spencer.

"It is family and friends", completed Innocence. "Theatre begins T and H, not f wally brain. What do you like to eat, and what are your favourite foods? Preferred style of restaurant? Films? What was the last film she liked? What genre of film is her ideal? What does she like to do for fun? Ask about her favourite activities or sports, whether she has a small or large family, who are they and where, who are her best friends, what are they like, and why she likes them?"

"Food, Films, Fun, family and Friends and another F, favourites, you said that four or five times, but thanks, I'll remember them," replied Surjit, having typed them judiciously into his notepad app.

"I still think asking if she likes fellatio and fucking is more important," resigned Spencer.

"Maybe he will find out," replied Innocence. Surjit felt his stomach tighten. There was a surge of adrenaline at the thought, no pun intended, and he needed the loo. He excused himself, saying he needed a coffee and headed to the landing where the toilets were situated. He found the first cubicle empty, pulled some toilet tissue from the holder, and simultaneously checked sufficient capacity to complete the task. He'd learned this since enduring the penguin waddle around to another cubicle, his trousers around his ankles restricting foot movement. He flushed the bowl whilst holding loo paper and settled onto the pot, loosening his trousers and pants that fell to his ankles. Food, films, fun, family, and friends. Remember favourites too. He repeated the words, and since he was in a private and quiet place, Surjit practised his patter.

"Hi, I'm Surjit. You can call me Surj. If we were to meet at a restaurant tonight, what type would you prefer it to be? Then if we went on to a film, what would your preference for genre be? What do you like to do in your spare time?" That was a good start before Surjit was horrified to hear a waspy, effeminate male voice reply,

"In the order, you asked me, I'd say Italian, some sort of drama and photography. Why, how about you, and are you asking me out?" asked the voice.

"Fuck no, sorry, I was just thinking aloud", stuttered Surjit, pulling up his trousers.

"Oh, I see, just a prick teaser, or have you bottled it. You're a closet, aren't you? Just fucking come out, Surjit, or should I call you Surj? You followed me in here?" said the voice. Surjit scrambled at the door and flew out of the bathroom, no turning back for fear of making eye contact with the voice that now knew his name. He walked smartly to the stairwell and skipped the steps to the next lower level, his eyes bulging in embarrassment, his heart pounding, and his stomach needed the toilet bowl more than it previously felt, which was a seven or eight on a scale of one to ten. He was now in the nine's, and he prayed the cubicles would be accessible where he would complete his business in silence, or at least without asking a stranger out for a gay date. Fortunately, the booths were unoccupied, and so were Surjit's bowels within moments. He returned to his desk and avoided eye contact with the other three; he felt they would know something had happened because he could not pull a poker face.

"Where's your coffee?" asked Spencer.

"What? Oh, I drank it. It's what you do with coffee," replied Surjit. Spencer looked up at him and smiled curiously before adding,

"The lady doth protest too much," teased Spencer.

"What, lady? There was no lady. I just grabbed an espresso, chucked it back, and here I am, flipping heck, can't get a coffee without the third degree," smarted Surjit.

"Calm down, Surj. Are you on your beeriod?" posed Spencer.

"Beeriod?" quizzed Mae Li, looking up.

"Yeah, beeriod, same as a woman behaves on her period only for a man coming off the effects of beer the night before, you know, ratty and uptight," explained Spencer.

"Is there any limit to this man's linguistic talents?" asked Mae Li rhetorically.

"I didn't have many beers last night, just the two that you practically forced down me in the afternoon," declared Surjit.

"There is no beeriod, period. Surjit is just anxious about tomorrow, we all are, and we all show it in different ways, have some empathy," suggested Innocence.

"I'm not anxious about tomorrow. I couldn't give a toss. If Angeltech can't see the gilt-edged opportunity I'm offering them, I'll find the money some other way." Spencer exclaimed.

"You can't rob a bank. So there are barely any branches left open and contactless means there's no actual money left in them in any case," suggested Surjit.

"I can't see you as a bank robber," smiled Innocence.

"Oh, and why not? It's the quiet ones you have to watch out for," he replied.

"You haven't got the bottle, babe," remarked Mae Li.

"How do you know I haven't got the bottle for it?" snapped Surjit, trying his best to assert himself.

"Because you messed your pants thinking about having a three-minute video conversation with a woman old enough to be your aunty. So storming the Walworth Road branch of the Nat West, armed with a shooter, isn't going to be high up on your list of capabilities, babe, just stating facts," remarked Mae Li.

"You don't know what I'm capable of," drooled Surjit, and he clasped his hands together, holding a mock gun before swinging round and repeating Honey Bunny's infamous line from Pulp Fiction,

"Any of you fucking pricks move, and I'll execute every motherfucking last one of ya." As he swung around, he knocked the coffee from the clasp of a young, well-built man shuffling past Surjit's seat. The coffee cup dropped to the floor, splattering from under its lid as it bounced off the hard floor and across the guy's shoes, splashing up his aptly coffee-coloured chinos.

"Watch out, oh, you're the fucking prick. What are you doing?" gasped the guy, his feet stepping gingerly over the mess.

"Oh, I'm so sorry. I'll buy you another cup." Surjit stooped down to retrieve the emptied coffee cup, clearly flustered. "I'll get some kitchen roll; I'm so sorry again."

"Yeah, well, as I said, you're the little prick", smarted the guy inhaling deeply. Surjit looked away, shrugging his shoulders, humiliated.

"Don't worry about it. It was a freebie from the Nespresso machine; your shoes will wipe clean," added Spencer in a conciliatory tone.

"Yeah, on his arse," huffed the guy holding up his shoe for closer inspection. His white muscle-fit t-shirt extolled two bicep guns nicely defined, a blue vain bisecting the left one. He had fair hair and wore coffee-splashed chinos. Good upper body, thought Mae Li, but do you train your legs? She regarded the skinny definition of both his quadriceps that made no impact on the slim-fit trousers and thought, no, I didn't feel that you would do that.

"He has apologized twice, I trust that is acceptable, and if you want an arse to clean your shoes, you can try mine," smiled Mae Li, and her smile turned to her mean look bitch face.

"I don't beat chicks," he sighed and prepared to move on.

"Oh, I bet you do, but you'll never beat this one," replied Mae Li. The guy paused for thought and then walked away.

Moments later, Surjit had mopped up the spillage and returned to the kitchen area to deposit the damp towels. He returned to his seat and glanced up at the other three gigglings. Surjit thought of something witty to say in response.

"Oh, fuck off," and he said it, and then he looked across at Mae Li, who looked back at him and smiled warmly.

"Thanks," he added quietly.

"No problem, babe," she replied without looking up.

Surjit darted his eyes towards the bottom right-hand corner of his screen. It was T- 3 hours and 15 minutes regarding his appointment with Jojo, the cougar from Clapham. He felt the same twang of adrenalin as before, but the commotion with the coffee cup and cubicle meant that he was going to sit this one out; best stay in one place and keep your head down for a while, he thought.

The morning meandered on, Spencer was scolded by Mae Li for humming the tune "The Eye of the Tiger", and Innocence dipped another Galaxy ripple into a warm, milky tea. Eventually, the time came for Surjit to make his call as his increasingly deeper breaths foretold his friends.

"Are you going to call Jojo then?" asked Innocence.

"For crying out loud, it's my business. Are you going for another chocolate bar and tea?" he snapped back.

"Go and grab a conference room; there's always some spare. You'll be alright for a few minutes. No one will kick you out in that time, fella. I'll stand outside if you like", suggested Spencer.

"No, you won't, earwigging my conversation and laughing no doubt," retorted Surjit, "why do I want to be doing this?"

"Then don't, hit the cancel option, put yourself out of your misery but on the other hand, a quick chat and you might have some fun tonight, nothing ventured, babe," supposed Mae Li.

"It's only a quick conversation, right? Food, films, fun, family and friends," he rehearsed.

"Not forgetting fellatio and fornication," added Spencer laughing.

Surjit rose from his chair and checked his phone; it was ten minutes to show time; he was cutting it fine, but then as a busy CEO, being a minute late would make sense. He checked his blind spot for large males carrying hot coffee, and when the coast appeared clear, he trundled off to the stairs and up to the next-floor meeting rooms. He slipped into the first one that was unused and closed the door behind him, checking at first that the others had not snuck up behind him. They hadn't, although Spencer had suggested it. Surjit was nervous, and his hands trembled as he placed the phone onto the table, upright and at an angle that he could both speak and be seen by the camera. He checked the display, reversed the camera to see himself, and tried various cool poses. Firstly, with his arms folded like Lord sugar on the Apprentice, then with his hands spread under his chin like a novelist looking thoughtful on the back cover of their book. Finally, he settled on his hands clasped together, looking forward like the Chancellor of the Exchequer giving the television party political broadcast after the budget. He then flipped to the app, started the meeting, and waited. There were three minutes to drift slowly, but enough time to rehearse the five F's. Food, films, fun, family, and friends. Food, movies, fun, family, and friends. Damn it, he'd write it onto the back of his hand, and he retrieved his black biro from his pocket to scribble the words. He licked the nib several times to encourage the ink to form on the light brown skin of the back of his left hand. His senses were awakened like a predated animal when the screen suddenly changed, and a woman's face stared and then smiled back at him.

"Surjit?" she confirmed. It was like his name was being called out at the doctors.

"Coming, I mean, yes, I am here," his throat went dry. Fuck, why didn't he bring a drink? He swallowed, desperately trying to draw any saliva from his tongue with which to swallow. It had abruptly become like sandpaper, coarse grade.

"Hi, I'm Jojo," she replied, nodding.

"Hi, I'm Surjit," and there was a pause. It was perfectly natural, but it seemed like the thirty-second clock on Countdown, each annoying metronomic beat drumming into his flummoxed brain to Surjit. He looked at his left hand, and the words unscrambled his panic.

"Do you like food?"

"Yeah"

"Films? Do you like films, ever seen a film?"

"Yeah"

"Do you like having fun?"

"Yeah"

"How's your Mum and Dad?"

"They're fine, thanks,"

"Have you got any friends?"

"Yeah, thanks, I've got mates,"

"Good," said Surjit nodding back. There was another pause whilst the countdown clock counted down its 180 degrees. Jojo broke the suspense.

"Fancy a fuck tonight?"

"Err, yeah, alright", squeaked Surjit, his throat still hoarse.

"My place or yours?"

"Yours"

"OK, I'll send my address. I like your tats," Jojo added. What did she say? Tits? He was not transgender, was there a mistake? Had Spencer fucked things up? He looked perplexed.

"The tattoos on your hand. Do they go up to your arm?"

"Yeah, they do, both arms and my chest," Fuck, what had he said? She was bound to notice that there wasn't any ink on his body apart from the five words beginning with the letter F etched into his hand like a schoolboy cheating at school.

"How tall are you?"

"Five ten", he lied and added four inches. Fuck he had done it again. What was he to do, stand on his tiptoes until they were horizontal?

"A bit short, but that's ok; what do you weigh?" Fuck, what was this a medical? Better not lie this time.

"58 kilos, but I keep it light. That's my boxing weight, super featherweight, like Lloyd Mayweather,"

"Do you mean Floyd?" she suggested.

"Yeah, him as well,"

"Cor, a boxer. I love tall, fit men with tattoos who can fight; see you later, Surjit," she smiled.

"Yeah, see you later", replied Surjit. He was not tall, not fit, had no tattoos, and he certainly could not fight. The call went well, apart from misrepresenting himself and setting an expectation that would be impossible to meet. Surjit closed the app, picked up his phone, and stood up, feeling sweat run down his hind legs, at least he hoped it was.

"How did it go?" asked Spencer. Surjit sat down at his place opposite him.

"Alright, I suppose. So where are the girls?" Surjit sniffed disinterestedly.

"Gone for a bite, gone for a shite, who cares, "alright, I suppose" what's that supposed to mean?" interrogated Spencer leaning forward.

"It means, supposedly alright, she is sending me her details, and I'm meeting her tonight. Are you happy?" shrugged Surjit.

"I'm happy, I'm fucking laughing and giggling, I've already got a shag booked solid tonight, no doubt about it, one Harvester, one bottle of Lambrini, and Robert is my uncle as the saying goes, or in this case, Spencer's on a promise. Are you happy? That's more to the point cos you don't look it? What did she say?" quizzed Spencer.

"It's not what *she* said?"

"What did you say then? Fuck me, cough it up, son, it'll soon be Christmas, and I haven't done my shopping,"

"Well, she asked me if I had tattoos, and I said yes," admitted Surjit sheepishly.

"You could have hidden on your arse or somewhere; that doesn't matter, mate," Spencer folded his arms.

"I said they were all up my arms and across my chest," Surjit looked up at Spencer.

"Why the fuck did you say for? That's not so easy to conceal unless you keep your fucking coat on," Spencer gasped.

"I don't know. I just did. It's because Jojo saw the biro on my hand; she thought the scribbles were tattoos, I said yes because it made me sound cool, and then I went too far, that's all,"

"Up your arms and across your chest too far, you might as well have said you've got your balls inked" Spencer looked across, and Surjit looked down at the floor, "Tell me you fucking well didn't,"

"No, of course, I didn't." Surjit paused and breathed deeply, "But I told her I was five foot ten inches tall," He looked at his friend, who gawped back at him.

"Fuck my old boots. You're a real Bobby bullshit when you're let loose. You make me look believable. I don't know how you will pull that off, and by the way, you will pull it off tonight. On your own as usual," hissed Spencer.

"Will you help me?" pleaded Surjit.

"Yeah, I'll go and get my tattoo gun, and when I've finished, I'll hang you over the balcony and pull hard at your legs." Spencer sat back.

"Oh, and I told her I was a boxer as well. I had to. She asked how much I weighed, and it was the first thing I could think of to explain my nine stone, three."

"Fuck me, a boxer, you couldn't smash a packet of marshmallows. At least that look is easily rectified. I'll break your nose with the tattoo gun."

"A packet of marshmallows is not that easy to smash because of their soft and flexible consistency and form. You might have said crisps, and you'd have been right."

"Never mind the pedantry; what are you going to do?" asked Spencer. He thought some more, and then his eyes lit up, "I've got it; my flatmate has got some temporary arm transfers, silly stuff, you know to soak in water and apply to your body. He puts them on for festivals, looks trendy and hipster, and then washes them off the following week. So you can come back to my flat, and we can set you up.

"What about my height?"

"Lifts, shoe inserts that lift your height, you'll need to wear trainers, or you'll flop out of your slip-on," remarked Spencer observing the moccasin-style slip-on shoe he was wearing today.

"Where will we get those? Let me search," Surjit tapped furiously at his phone. "There's a shoe repairer's with accessories not far from here, Kings Cross, says it stocks Heelix, elevators in 1-, 2- and 3-inches inserts,"

"Get the two-inch inserts, and wear a pair of Nikes Airmax, that'll get you thereabouts five-ten. We can get those from Sports direct in Ludgate Hill and cab up to Kings Cross after. Come on, let's go,"

"Hold on, what about the girls?" paused Surjit.

"Message them. They've taken their bags anyway. We'll be back here in a couple of hours. So leave the bibs on the seats. It's pretty quiet today. It's Thursday. That means long lunches and some of them on the piss early," jibed Spencer throwing his bag over his shoulder.

"What about…ahem, after, won't she notice my real height when I'm putting them back on?"

"Keep the room dark, mate and who cares? You've done the business; just walk tall," laughed Spencer ironically.

Mae Li and Innocence sat in the downstairs lobby of the hive following Surjit and Spencer's suggestion to meet them there to wish each other good luck before heading off for the evening. They would all meet next time following the Angel-Tech interviews, as prearranged. It was close to five o'clock as the revolving doors swung anti-clockwise, and in strutted Spencer, tall, long-legged, ray-ban shades adorning his hair which was swept back and shoulder length. His black leather jacket was well worn, and his jeans faded and frayed.

He looked up and saw the girls, and his head tilted slightly in acknowledgement. They formed smiles that turned into surprised gawps as the doors ejected a mini version of Spencer in his wake. The young man with a white t-shirt and a dark armful of tattoos up to the hand that swung a leather jacket over his shoulder, and his dark shades betrayed his line of focus as he approached them. For a moment, they thought it was Surjit, but this guy was taller, his hair slicked back, and his demeanour more confident than their bashful associate.

"Is that? No, it can't be. So who is that with Spencer?" asked Innocence.

"I don't believe it, babe, fuck me," replied Mae Li.

"Introducing Mr Surjit Gohst, millionaire owner of Spanner Technologies and amateur regional featherweight boxing champion," announced Spencer, his hand leading to the slender frame of Surjit, who stopped short of the girls to readjust the jacket.

"You could knock me down with a feather, Surjit. So what happened to you?" enquired Innocence.

"Got me a makeover from Spencer. What do you think?" he asked.

"Are they making Grease 3? It's Danny fucking Zuko," gawped Mae Li open-mouthed.

"Where did you get those tattoos? They're all over your arms?" gasped Innocence.

"Henna transfers. Cool, aren't they?" cooed Surjit.

"You seem, how can I put it, taller?" remarked Mae Li.

"Yeah, got lifts in my shoes, makes me 5 foot 10, I love it, I can see eye to eye with people", declared Surjit.

"Steady tiger, but I know what you mean," uttered Spencer, who stood six foot two inches.

"What's with the new look?" asked Innocence.

"He told his shag tonight he was a tall, lean, millionaire boxer," said Spencer deadpan.

"With tattoos", added Surjit.

"With tattoos", finished Spencer.

"Any why would you do that?" asked Mae Li. Spencer shook his head and wagged a dismissive finger back at her, "Just don't go there."

"But it's…not you, Surjit," shrugged Innocence.

"Exactly", he replied.

"Oh! Kay," replied Innocence quizzically.

"She's going to be disappointed when you take off your shoes and find that she's got four inches less than she thought she had, babe", cracked Mae Li straight-faced.

"I'm sure he can find another four inches from somewhere else; besides, he can always keep his shoes on. Then, you know, wrestle her down onto the couch in a bout of unstoppable passion, rip her clothes off, drop your trousers and keks and seize the moment," eulogized Spencer, his eyes glinting with menace.

"That won't work. I wouldn't be able to get my trousers off if my shoes were still on," replied Surjit shaking his head. He pulled his shades from his face and rubbed his eyes as the light from the lobby poured into them. Spencer shook his head, and Mae Li looked away, grinning.

"The course of true love never did run smooth," observed Innocence, staring distantly beyond the lobby. The conversation was uninhibited to a point they would never have believed when they met on Monday morning by chance. Mae Li noticed her social check on the tactical advice offered to Surjit to fornicate with a stranger without the length of his legs being of any note and changed the tune.

"So are the business plans for Shagpad and Spanner ready to go for tomorrow morning, given tonight's social interludes with Chantelle and Jojo?"

"Yeah, I'm happy they don't want too much detail. They'll either dig the idea or not. I don't care; Shagpad is too big to fail. Only a fool could fail," he smiled. Yeah, only a fool, thought Mae Li, who looked at Surjit and raised her eyebrows as if to indicate, "your turn."

"Me? Oh, I'm happy. I'm more nervous about tonight if I'm honest," he swallowed deeply.

"No need to be honest; you couldn't hide that anyway", laughed Mae Li. Innocence screwed her face a little in sympathy and reached out to put her arm on Surjit's shoulder before remarking,

"I hope she goes gentle with you because you'll need a good night's sleep and all your strength for tomorrow, Rocky," and she giggled sweetly.

"You make tomorrow sound like a prize fight," he countered.

"It is; there is a prize, and we have to fight for it; desire counts as much as detail, guys," instructed Mae Li."

"Are you both ready, too?" asked Surjit. He looked at Innocence first, who responded.

"As I ever will be, it's all about pitching it now and getting that seed funding," she breathed in deeply and looked at Mae Li.

"I'm good to go, and whatever happens, there are other early-stage funding options, so it's not shit or bust, is it?" she conjectured. They all agreed and nodded.

"Well, good luck. I might see you tomorrow at the offices. But, if not, see you tomorrow at the pub at 12.30 as we agreed. We'll all need a drink by then," remarked Innocence.

"I think I need one now," admitted Surjit,

"Well, if you fancy one, they are open", suggested Spencer.

"No" was the chorus of returns.

"Ok, well adios amigos, keep your guard up and chin low Rocky, remember what I said, a quick drink, then suggest you go back to hers for a fish supper," said Spencer reminding his protégé of his advice garnered during the makeover. He turned to Surjit, mimicking a boxer, and then he drew Surjit into him for a man hug. Surjit looked overwhelmed and terrified simultaneously; the moment had come, and he was heading out for a date in Clapham.

"Yeah, bye boys, we're off for some fitness fun at my gym, a health supper, and an early night in bed," said Mae Li.

"What together?" smiled Spencer focussing on the bed part of the admission.

"Fuck off, babe," was the reply. At least the term babe could be loosely interpreted as an endearment, which was progress given it was already Thursday and Spencer. The group left the building, and the girls headed to a waiting taxi whilst the boys walked the short distance to Old Street Station before heading in their respective north and south directions.

Spencer Churchill arrived at Croxley Green tube station, bounced out to the roadside, and turned left into Watford Road. He strode along quickly to consume the three-quarters of a mile to the Harvester, where he would meet Chantelle for an early dinner and then back to her place for afters. She had driven from the dental surgery and was waiting in the car listening to Ed Sheeran playing "Shape of You" on Capital Radio. She was singing along, her head bobbing to the rhythm, thinking how much Spencer did not like Ed Sheeran since he had to learn one of his songs this week. Spencer did not know Ed Sheeran personally; if he had, he would probably think Ed was a good bloke and talk about blokey things like football and girls. But no, Spencer did not appreciate Ed Sheeran and his gimmicky sampling and tiny guitar, lack of live drums and bass. Spencer considered Ed Sheeran a clever karaoke stint, catchy tunes but not an act Spencer could go and stand in a stadium like Chantelle had cheered and adulated what was essentially a 21st-century one-man band? If Ed Sheeran played the Croxley Harvester, then sure he might listen whilst eating his chicken and chips with a salad on the side, but anything more than that, no way, and as for the millennium dome or Wembley stadium, then people must be mad. Spencer had long since learned that generally, people were. Another track, Party in the U.S.A, bopped its way through Chantelle's blue Vauxhall Corsa with Chantelle on lead vocals trying to out-sing Miley Cyrus. Sadly, she failed to come close, but it was of no consequence to anybody else because her windows were wound up and the sound muffled. Spencer strode into the car park and walked up to her car from behind, she had parked straight into a bay, slightly skewwhiff, but it would do. He approached the driver-side door and pulled hard on the door handle,

"Police, do not move; put your hands on the wheel," he shouted. Chantelle screamed and looked up,

"Spenny, for fuck sake, you frightened me,"

"Come on, darling, let's go inside. I'm Hank Marvin; phwoar, have you been farting in here? It's as ripe as a sumo wrestler's nappy?" he joked, stepping back sharply.

"Piss off Spenny, no, I haven't only you do that, and you hold my head under the sheets when you do, choking me, you bastard," she laughed.

"Your head better be under the sheets tonight, and I'll test your gag reflex," he cooed crudely and planted a kiss on her cheeks that she enjoyed all the same.

"Spenny, what are you like? So behave. We're at a decent restaurant, mind your manners," she told him.

"It's the Harvester Croxley Green, not the Ivy. I think I can handle it. Oh shit, I forgot my bow tie," he teased. They walked towards the double-doored entrance, and Chantelle reached for Spencer's hand as they crossed the car park. They broke hands as Spencer opened the right door, and Chantelle stepped forward to enter before Spencer cut across her and entered first with the door swinging shut; Chantelle skipped inside. They were seated, presented with menus and drinks orders taken within minutes, a spritzer for Chantelle, and a pint of San Miguel for Spencer.

"What do you fancy, Spenny? I don't know what to have?" posed Chantelle perusing the large Perspex form.

"There's chicken, steak, burgers, all done different ways, ribs, loads of ribs, fish, there's fish if you fancy fish darling, Salmon, Cod, and chips. Do you fancy fish, darling? No, you're not a fishy guy, are you, more of a meat man, burger, steak, or chicken. The salad comes free, so we can get that ourselves. How about chargrilled skewers? There's peri-peri chicken, surf and turf, halloumi, no you won't want that darling, that's funny cheese, isn't it? There's a choice of chips, and some meals come with chips or a baked potato. What do you think, Spenny?"

"Do you know what I think? I think I can read the menu, Chantelle," spoke Spencer calmly.

"Don't be like that. I'm making conversation, darling," reasoned Chantelle.

"But you are not, are you? You are reading the menu to me like I'm a fucking five-year-old. Making conversation requires uttering some words that have come from your original thoughts, not words inspired off the Harvester menu."

"Have you had a bad day, darling? You're uptight about tomorrow, aren't you?"

"I've had a good day, and I'm not phased about tomorrow either," he replied, sighing.

"Aren't you going to ask me about my day?" she asked.

"How was your day?" he asked,

"Same as usual, booking clients for fillings, hygiene, check-ups, and extractions," she replied.

"Not unsurprising, is it? Given you are a dental receptionist, you're not going to get an unexpected call to fly to Boston to deliver a speech to the World Orthodontist Conference," he replied with his gaze still fixed on the menu.

"I sometimes have to go to our Hertford branch as cover," she corrected him.

"Sorry, I forgot about that; no idea how that escaped me," His sarcasm was interrupted by the waiter bringing their drinks.

"One spritzer and one San Miguel, and have you decided yet, would you like lite bits to start with?" asked the server, a pimpled student in a black apron and green shirt.

"We're still choosing," replied Chantelle.

"12-ounce rib-eye, medium cooked, no sauce, Mac n cheese, and a rack of ribs with the Jim Bean glaze," replied Spencer handing back the menu.

"I haven't decided yet? What am I going to have?" Chantelle looked bewildered.

"My beautiful fiancée will have the 1983 Harvester Combo, a wonderful year for the combo, I gather, thank you," replied Spencer.

"Very good, thank you", replied the student marking the orders on his hand-held device before retrieving both menus and turning away.

"I do love it when you order for me, Spenny. You are all dominant and masterful" she smiled before her face fell, "What's the 1983 Harvester Combo?"

"You tell me you're the current Harvester menu mastermind champion,"

"I don't remember that one, though; what is it?"

"Half a rotisserie chicken and a half rack of BBQ glazed ribs. With sage & onion seasoned chips, buttered corn, and speciality chicken gravy," replied Spencer sounding bored.

"I can't eat all of that", she protested and jabbed a finger at Spencer.

"But I can, so you'll be fine", he added before quaffing at his pint.

"You'll get fat eating that lot,"

"No, I won't because even though both dinners amount to around 3,000 calories, my required daily intake is two and half thousand without exercise. I've walked four miles today and eaten fuck all, which is a deficit of 500 calories, meaning I'm exactly at equilibrium. Unless I eat dessert, I'll be in calorific surplus by a thousand, so I'll have to burn it off by having sex which at two hundred calories an hour at a steady pace means I'll be shagging you all night." He laughed.

"And what about that pint, that's another half an hour?" she teased.

Mae Li pulled tight the laces to her Nike trainers, stood upright, and flexed her muscles. She was lithe, solidly built, 5 feet 8 inches in height, relatively tall for a Chinese girl. Next to her, Innocence was pulling up her black leggings and loosening her tee-shirt. She was shorter than Mae Li by a few inches and solidly set with a large bust and fuller hip. She rocked her shoulders like you do when getting comfortable in sports clothing. Her frizzy-styled hair had been combed straight back into a tight bun, and a yellow scrunchy held it fast, which matched the colour of her top, which had a black cat silhouette on the front.

"Ready, babe?" enquired Mae Li.

"As I'll ever be, let's do this," replied Innocence, and she turned on her heels to follow Mae Li from the stylish changing rooms and out to one of the fitness rooms where other ladies waited attired in tight leggings, vests, and assorted tee-shirts. The class instructor stood at the front adjusting her phone from which the Latino-themed music would be blasted through the room's speaker monitors.

"Ease yourself in, babe and enjoy. Zumba is my fun workout, so cool." Smiled Mae Li.

"I will try. I hope it is easy to pick up. I'm going to the back and out of the way," stated Innocence.

"Ok, but she kind of moves you around the class anyway, so don't worry, just enjoy", replied Mae Li.

The instructor checked her phone; it was 18.00. Chrissie hit the play button to her selected playlist. Ten tracks of metronomic Latin twisted music thumped out to a tempo of 70 beats per minute, a rate which might be described as a beginner to intermediate. Depending on the intensity and fitness of the participant, either glowing skin or deep breaths would emit, alternatively, hot sweats and gasps for air extracted like being trapped in a furnace. Luckily, this room, like all the club, was air-conditioned.

"Ok, people, step it up nice and high now," shouted Chrissie bringing her feet from side to side and lifting her knees to the beat. The class followed in synchronicity, feet stepped, thighs raised, and hands clapped in unison, excepting one pair that clapped off the rhythm. Chrissie smiled at Innocence and accentuated the clapping timing to help her synch into the class. Three more loops expired, and nope, the off-beat clap was still there, and Innocence smiled joyfully. Chrissie decided to move on to the next step. Perhaps that would reset the coordinates of the black girl in the bright yellow tee-shirt.

"In and out now, follow me. One to the right, two to the left spin around and one to the right," cried Chrissie completing the manoeuvre and arriving at the same point, marching on the spot. All the girls followed in unison, one skip to the right, two hops back to the left, and one more skip, and they were in the same spot, apart from Innocence. She had cut across her classmates and now clapped offbeat one place forward and further than before. The class readjusted skilfully, shuffling into place before awaiting the next instruction.

"Same again, everybody, watch my steps" she shot Innocence a prolonged glance and accentuated the commands. "One to the right, two to the left, spin around, and one to the right. Ok, now your turn and a three, two, one and," Chrissie paused as Innocence was already on the second spin, to her right, not two to the left, and her flailing arms swung within range of a classmate who ducked to avoid a backhand slap to the side of the face.

"Wahey," screamed Innocence with enthusiasm. Chrissie continued the class between the sideways glances and steps to avoid the random moves thrown by Innocence. Mae Li could not fail to notice and was surprised that Innocence popped up in front of her by mid-session, given that she had begun several classmates away. It all added to the fun, the not knowing where the young girl in the black and yellow gear might buzz by, like an errant bumble bee, the sound of her buzz replaced by irregular claps and hoots of delight.

The class warmed down, and after hamstrings, calves, quadriceps, and glutes were gently stretched, Chrissie cheered and clapped for a final time to indicate the "fun" was over.

"Woohoo, I am not fit. Walking to and from work does not do enough for me. I need to come to this class every week," shrilled Innocence.

"You do? I mean, yes, you do. There is bound to be a class nearer where you live," suggested Mae Li wondering if she could maintain focus or respect if the random dance generator arrived at class in tow every week like today.

"Yeah, probably, but I like this one. It's nice to go with a friend," she reached out and touched Mae Li's arm before drawing her in for a cuddle. Mae Li felt strange and did not react. She was an only child and had few friends, the giving and receiving of affection was seldom felt in either direction, but this felt OK.

Surjit stood outside the aptly and ubiquitously named Railway Tavern on the corner of Voltaire Road and Clapham High Street that led to the train station of the same name. The traffic rumbled slowly and noisily to his back as he surveyed its dark indigo blue exterior framed by large windows of a three-story corner boozer with its name marked proudly beneath the flat roof of the building to which it stood. He peered in the front window of its High Street aspect, wondering if he could spot Jojo's ash blond shoulder-length hair. Although he was apprehensive, and his stomach felt tight from the nerves following a large intake of breath, he pushed the double doors that bisected the corner walls and headed straight for the bar. He held on to the bar with his left hand and spun around slowly, carefully surveying the room for any sign of his date. The tables were occupied. Six o'clock was a busy period for the tavern, as commuters stopped off from the station and the nearby Clapham North tube station for a quick drink or, for some, an all-evening bender, given that it was Thursday.

"What can I get you?" asked the young girl with a nose piercing and green hair.

"Just an orange juice and lemonade please?" asked Surjit. "Just an orange juice and lemonade?" Why did that sound like an apology? Because it was not alcohol, or it was not a full-price drink?"

"£3.40, please," stated the pierced girl with the green hair. It was a full-priced drink, so there was no need for an apology there, thought Surjit. He produced his debit card, tapped the reader, and turned to face the walkway from the doors to the pub. What were his first lines going to be? Family, friends, food, fun, and films, or not in that order. But then he'd done all that earlier that day. What else was there to talk about? People sat around him, deep in conversation. What were they talking about? Was anybody listening, or was pub conversation just a monotonous cathartic rant to accompany drinking?

Surjit thought he'd eavesdrop on the young couple stood to his side who had just ordered drinks. Instead, a guy with shoulder-length curly hair and a canvas man-bag stood with his back to Surjit and conversed with a young girl of Asian appearance, with red lipstick and a round face.

"It's like, I do want to go to the gig with her, like, but then I don't want to go, do you know what I mean?" he said.

"Yeah, like, I know what you mean," she replied.

"I mean, like, I like, but do I like them that much, like, do you know what I mean like?"

"Yeah, I do, like, you like something, but then, like, do you really like something?"

"Yeah, like, yeah, I like it, but then do I really, really like it," he repeated.

This was too much. What had Surjit learned? The banalest retarded utterance of an informal adverb, like, which meant nothing to Surjit. None whatsoever, and yet the two people conversing seemed to understand the meaning of the language. What was it with the repetitive deployment of the word "like"? So many young people used it, yet it meant nothing more than a pause, utterly useless and an annoying phrase, often used with its actual meaning as in the conversation he'd just heard and only adding to its frequency. Why could natural language not be replaced by computer languages, code, sentences, and sequences that meant what they were designed for, no innuendo or hidden meaning in C++ or Java? Say what you mean and mean what you say in the most efficient manner possible. Debug if needed and be sure it all adds to a logical and executable task. No arguments, no miscommunication, no body language experts, no movies, no poetry, no lyrics, no thesaurus's, just meaning, intent and output wrapped up in code, blissful.

"Hi, Surjit?" said the female voice. Surjit swung round, and there stood Jojo. She was his height, that was his height in the lifted shoes that he wore, and he looked down at her feet. She wore flat shoes with bare feet and a short denim skirt that drew into a tight waist. His eyes scanned back to her face, back to her feet, definitely no heel on those slippers, and then back to her face quickly. She was smiling confidently but then slanted her gaze quizzically.

"Something wrong with my feet?" she laughed.

"No, no, just admiring your shoes. They are nice, er what do you call them, well, shoes,"

"They're espadrilles, light and comfy. Besides, I'm five-nine, which is tall for a woman, I didn't want to tower over you, but you're slightly taller, so no worries there," she nodded.

"Definitely, yeah, like. No worries there," Surjit paused between the words, slurped his drink, and swallowed deeply.

"Are you going to offer me one of those? A double Vodka and Orange, nice shout," she agreed.

"Oh, yes, of course, where are my manners, a double vodka and orange, please," called Surjit to the green-haired bar girl, who acknowledged the order by spinning with a slim jim glass towards the Absolut optic and following up with a double jab before pouring orange juice over ice.

"Find this place, OK?" she asked.

"Couldn't miss it. I live south of the river, over in Elephant and Castle," he replied.

"£6.50, thanks," interrupted the bargirl.

"What, oh, yes," the price surprised Surjit, ten pounds for two drinks, and that's with his being soft one, and that resentment was not meant in any other way. Another tap of his debit card batted away the recently accrued debt, and Jojo led him by the hand to a recently vacated table and sat down. Surjit felt engaged with her, not in any matrimonial way, but as a woman had not held him by his palm since his mother had to lead him to his first day at Crampton Primary School. That was twenty years ago. Jojo was probably a similar age as his mother would have been; perhaps it was an affectation that thirty-something women did. He'd soon find out that if it was, then in some cases, like Jojo, they also did much more.

"So, you're a boxer?" she inquired.

"Er, yeah", replied Surjit, attempting to look tough by furrowing his brow and speaking as low as possible. Her face was quite close to his, she had shoulder-length blonde hair, not natural, but it suited her brown eyes and a wide mouth that smiled and made her eye lines pretty. She was in her late thirties but fit. Her arms were brown that showed prominently from her blousy white t-shirt. She wore a gold necklace, and he noticed only one ring on her fingers, a single gold band on the third finger of her right hand.

"I like a man who knows his way around the ring. How many fights have you had?"

"Quite a few, just amateur, friendlies, to be honest. I haven't fought recently, what with the business and all." Surjit was trying to change the subject from something he knew almost nothing about to something he could lie about more convincingly.

"You don't look like you've boxed. Your nose and ears look like they've never felt a glove,"

"Only the back of my mum's hand", he laughed nervously, "I was too quick to get caught. I can run quite fast if somebody's trying to ram his fist into me" he nodded innocently.

"I bet you can", she cackled "you're quite funny, Surjit", she added.

"I am? I mean, yeah, I am. Think a good sense of humour is a must in a man; women have always laughed at me," he affirmed and sipped at his drink.

"I like your tats; they look quite fresh," she remarked, looking at the bold ink on his hands and forearms.

"Yeah, got them done this afternoon," he replied.

"You what? Don't they still hurt?" she looked surprised.

"Nah, they were done pretty quickly. Coldwater and a sponge are all I needed," he admitted.

"God, your dead hard you are, Surjit, at least I hope so," she was warming to this baby-faced assassin.

"What are they Polynesian?" she asked. Surjit paused from sipping his drink,

"Synthetic, so probably poly something", he replied, and she spat out her drink, laughing out loud, "oh Surjit, you are such a laugh; I'm going to like you. "Do you want to know something intimate? My knickers are quite wet," she leaned forward as she told him, and he listened intently and thought if she was being so open, then he should empathize too, so he leaned forward towards her and whispered,

"Easily done. I pissed my pants at London Bridge Station earlier this week; the loos are over there if you need to attend to yourself," and she roared with laughter which Surjit found flummoxing.

"So, Mr hard man, funny man, what do you think we should do next?" she asked and crunched on a small piece of ice as she said next. Surjit wondered if this was the time to suggest a retreat to her nearby flat but remembered something Spencer had mentioned during an earlier pep talk. Spencer said Surjit should advise returning for an early fish supper to ensure she was up for fun early in the conversation.

"Shall we go and get fish and chips?" suggested Surjit.

"Why are you hungry?" she seemed surprised.

"I do fancy a sausage in batter." Surjit had not eaten, and maybe this would offer some energy.

"Now you're talking, Rocky. Come on, let's finish these and go back to my place. You bring the sausage, and I'll provide the batter." She stood up, pulled at his hand, and led him out of the door and directly back to her flat whilst Surjit wondered if they would perhaps order the food by delivery or whether she would cook.

Innocence and Mae Li sat at the gym bar, a table by the second-floor window that looked out to the street below, each slurping a smoothie through a straw, their kit bags at their feet. The glow of the Zumba class was beginning to wear off, and they idled away chit-chat, mainly to be polite and to run down the clock with the prospect of the morning meetings at the forefront of their minds and nerves.

Two male members sat opposite, one tall and lean with olive skin and dark features, the other a far eastern male, cleanly shaven and of average appearance in terms of size. Both wore tracksuits, their bags by their feet, and tennis rackets zipped up in their protective cases placed neatly on top. They were both whispering and glanced across at the girls on more than one occasion. Their attention was not returned, although Mae Li was alert that Innocence and she had created interest. Mae Li had garnered two types of male interest; One that was harmless, a man could not help looking at a woman and considering her as a sexual experience, conquest, or whatever the correct term was. It was hard-wired into them. They were fuckers, and women were to be fucked, which worked both ways. This sort of attention was not always gratefully received, and worse, it was not to be considered fuckable in the first place. Still, fortunately regardless of a woman's level of appearance, age and consciousness, there was at least somewhere, a man who would be up for screwing her.

The second type of male interest was direct, incoming, and inevitable. Once committed, few men would abort an attempt to communicate; only the method would vary. Some men tried a humourous reproach and some with flattery. Others started a conversation on the back foot, an apology hoping for sympathy; how desperate? Finally, a few would try a physical action demonstrating strength, bravery, or kindness to gain more favourable odds. Mae Li sensed a close encounter of the second kind, she had good intuition for such things, and it would not let her down on this occasion.

"Hi ladies, I'm Nicolas, and my friend here is Lim, and we were wondering if by any chance you played tennis?" interrupted the Mediterranean featured guy. However, this approach could be shut down quickly. Nicolas had opened with a closed question. Simply saying "no, we don't" would leave Nicolas floundering for a comeback.

"I do, and Mae Li told me she does in the summer, so yes, we do", replied Innocence eagerly and openly. Mae LI shot her an unnoticed glance and waited for Nicolas to volley home.

"Would it be forward of us to ask if you would care for a mixed-doubles this weekend? We can book the courts here, that is if you are available? Would you be?" added Lim. Perfect, two closed questions, yes, it would be forward to ask, and no, they would not be available, thought Mae Li.

"Sounds like fun. I'm up for it; when were you thinking?" smiled Innocence. Mae Li breathed in deeply and exhaled slowly.

"How about Saturday afternoon, the weather will be fine, and a court is available at 3 p.m. Then, we could meet here for smoothies at half-past two?" suggested Nicolas.

"OK", chirped Innocence, "I'll need to buy a racquet, or do they hire them?"

"Don't worry about that. We've more than once each. We'll bring enough for us all to play doubles," added Lim.

"Should we play with your balls too?" asked Innocence, smiling. Lim looked hesitantly across at Nicolas, who responded croakily, "Er, yes, we'll bring those too. They're all fairly new, plenty of bounce left in them," he looked down at Mae Li, who remained poker-faced and tight-lipped.

"Ok, sounds like fun, doesn't it?" said Innocence, looking towards Mae Li.

"If you say so," Mae Li quipped, emphasising "you".

"Ok, it was nice to meet you, Mae Li and?" Nicolas paused and looked at Innocence, who replied with her name, "and Innocence, we'll see you back here Saturday, we'll book the court and bring everything, bye." So said Nicolas, and they left swiftly; Lim looked over his shoulder and smiled as they pushed through the double doors.

"Fuck me, you play hard to get, babe?" sounded Mae Li, folding her arms.

"It's a game of tennis, not a date. Besides that, I've not played since school, and I would love a game,"

"Hello, Earth to Innocence; of course, it's a date; we're meeting two guys for a social interaction that will lead to drinks and then a dinner suggestion," exclaimed Mae Li.

"And then what?" asked Innocence.

"Then what do you think, back to theirs for coffee and a game of scrabble?"

"It's just a game of tennis. We don't have to go for dinner. I'm not interested in a date, I'd just like a game of tennis, and they asked."

"Then ask me. We can have a game of tennis,"

"But doubles is more fun, especially mixed," beamed the young African.

"Then we can ask Spencer and Surjit," snapped Mae Li. She stopped and looked at Innocence, who returned her glare, the corners of their mouths twitched, and they laughed out loud.

"Let's see how we feel Saturday. We can always blow them out," replied Innocence.

"I thought you didn't want this to lead to any action," gibed Mae Li. Innocence stared back for a moment and then tittered, "Mae Li, you could shame the devil, come on, let's go before we get asked and agree to mixed martial arts with a couple of hunky guys," and she stood up.

"Now I could go for that," sighed Mae Li, gathering her bag and leaving the table.

Surjit followed Jojo into her flat in Gauden Road, just off Clapham High Street. The ground floor, basement apartment of a four-floored terraced house split into four flats with a communal hallway. They'd completed their drinks quickly and walked the five minutes it took to reach this point, and with each step, Surjit's apprehension heightened. Perhaps he should have had a vodka steady the nerves. What was he doing? Spencer had talked him into this encounter the day before, one of the most important meetings of his life. He was walking into a flat with a fit City secretary, wearing lifted heels, meaning Surjit, not her, covered in henna transfers pretending to be a millionaire white-collar boxer.

"I'll put some music on. What do you like?" asked Jojo, removing her jacket.

"I'm easy, anything that you fancy," replied Surjit trying to keep his voice composed.

"You are quite the gentleman, Surj. Do you like Lana Del Ray," she posed.

"I don't know; I've never been to Spain," he said, shaking his head slowly.

"What are you like?" she laughed, clicking her phone and starting the music through the Bluetooth speakers cradled on the cabinet. She ran her hands through her hair, and the blonde locks fell effortlessly across her shoulders, and Surjit could not but help notice her bust, which was full and sculpting its image from within the fabric. The music was slow and rhythmic. Jojo turned her hips slowly to the beat and smiled back at him, "come and dance with me?" she tempted. Surjit was not an experienced dancer. He'd tried it once at a party whilst in university and had not felt it was something that came naturally to him after ten minutes of rudimentarily rocking from one foot to the other, as indeed most men did, without any style. Now was not the right time to repeat the performance, so he stood motionless, biting his lip. He folded his arms defensively, unsure what to do with them and the rest of his body, for that matter. Jojo shimmied slowly towards him, twisting and smiling sexily as she drew nearer.

"Making me do the work, are you tough guy" she whispered, kissing his ear lobe. The delicate touch made Surjit shudder, and he felt the hairs on his arms and chest stand out. This was scary but very pleasant. What should he do in response? He decided to play the tough guy and stand still. She could take the lead, and he would follow, so there he stood, like a statue, as Jojo flounced around him, nibbling his ears and running her nails across his neck. She felt him tense up as she did it, which only encouraged it more. Surjit's eyes shot from side to side and up to down, following her every move, looking as terrified as a small mammal eyed by a hungry predator.

"Relax, hard man, let's take this into the bedroom," she cooed, emphasising "hard" as she cupped his groin. Surjit could not help but think this was almost surreal. Jojo, an attractive and fit woman, was asking Surjit, a mid-twenties penniless virgin, into her boudoir with the intention of a sexual encounter. And this match was engineered within minutes or hours by a small mobile phone application that made redundant and obsolete hundreds of years of social etiquette that ranged from days to months or even years. But Spencer was on to something. Not everybody could be discrete within their homes; not everybody was like Jojo. She clasped his hand and led him into the room off the small lounge. Jojo stood by the bedside and embraced his body with her arms thrown around his neck and shoulders. They kissed, and Surjit sensed the sweetness of the orange juice still on her lips and smelt the coarser essence of the alcohol. Her eyes burned into his, and instantly, his anxiety left him, he was a man, and a man had to do what a man had to do. But, something strange was happening to him. She took his jacket off, slung it to the floor, and ran her hands up his arms, feeling the biceps or at least trying to find them. She then started to undo his belt; when the task was complete, she unbuttoned his jeans, unzipped his flies, and then dropped to her knees to unlace his shoes. Surjit was excited and relieved to feel himself become harder at the sight and experience of this suggestive woman undressing him.

"You need to take your shoes off, or I won't be able to drop your trousers and pants," she commanded, looking up at him from her knelt position. She stood up, facing him as he scuffed the heel of his training shoe, trying to find the leverage to complete the task. She kissed him delicately across his mouth and felt his feet unhinge from his shoes. She stood opposite him within inches of his mouth, with her warm breath and bosom pressed against his chest. She lifted his shirt and pulled it over his head, then repeated the action on her own, her big breasts hanging down; Surjit could see them within his perimeter vision; wow, this was simply wonderful. They gazed into each other's eyes like boxers at a stare-down, and then it happened. Surjit leaned forward for another kiss and flipped both the trainers off, and suddenly he found himself pecking into her neck, and she stared down at the top of his head. In the moment of impending passion, he had forgotten about the shoes and six inches were instantly cut from his height as she screamed out loud.

"What the fuck? Where did you go?" She stepped back and stared at the shorter man in front of her.

"I'm still here, just not as much as me as you thought before," squeaked Surjit, as much surprised by his dramatic downfall.

"And look at my hands; they're black. Are those tattoos rubbing off?" Jojo looked at the dark inky palms of her hands that had run up and down Surjit's perspiring arms and then across at the blurry images that went from his forearms to his shoulders. Then, finally, she stood back and folded her arms, lifting her tits as she did but not in any enamouring way, more in defiance.

"Is anything about you real, Surjit, you're not 5 foot 10, and your tattoos aren't real, is the rest of it true?" she inquired.

"I've never boxed, and I'm not a millionaire, but my name is Surjit," he exclaimed.

"I don't give a fuck about that part. You can call yourself what you like. My name is not Jojo, Alison, but I am a City PA, and this is my flat, or rather it's rented," she admitted.

"Does that matter? What I earn and what I am, physically?" he appealed.

"Do you want the truth?"

"Yes"

"Of course, it matters, but only the wealth bit. You don't think Bernie Eccleston's wife thinks he does it for her, do you or Trump's wife, or any other short, fat, wrinkly, or ugly old fucker that's got grade A cunt on their arm, do you? A wife can always find a fit fella for a fuck, but a fit fucker who's earning, that's as rare as hen's teeth, and at the end of the day, a dick is a dick; any dick can be blown, and it's fucking disgusting, but a dick that can buy luxury, that's worth it."

"I'll be worth millions one day. I've got a seed investment meeting tomorrow morning," objected Surjit.

"Well, until you are, you can keep your seed to yourself," replied Alison, aka Jojo "pop your Cuban heels back on, and go and have a sausage in batter, then have a shower and wash that muck off your arms," she sighed, then nodded towards the door. Surjit grabbed his t-shirt from the bed, the bed where he'd almost lost his virginity to a woman who was only in it for his money. Why had Surjit mentioned he hadn't any? Jojo or Alison might have still been on for it? He was too honest. Spencer had remarked upon that trait in the pub. Message to self, how about a credit scoring app for a sugar daddy or bounty hunters, a real-time low down on potential victim's finances with a shag rating commensurate to wealth? Nightmare, thought Surjit, he was beginning to think and speak like Spencer, and he'd only known him for four days. Surjit suddenly felt a massive surge of relief, no more lies and pretence, be yourself, be successful, and never mention or show your affluence. The woman who loved him for who he was would have it all. Maybe it was romantic and noble for 2016, but Jojo, Alison, or whoever she was, had taught him a lesson. He reached down for his shoes and was ready to ditch the lifts, but then he thought, what the hell, why not? Strut back to the Elephant, and walk tall like Spencer had told him, but don't forget to remove them before you get in and keep your arms covered up. Mum will have a fit. The door clunked behind him, and Surjit walked out of Gauden Road and turned North onto the A3. It was a lovely evening for the straight two and a half miles and an hour clopping along in his high shoes that it would take to get home and to his mum's cooking.

"I'm just popping to the loo," excused Chantelle, stepping up from her seat and leaving the table and the barely touched 1983 combo. Spencer looked up and nodded, he could not sputter with a mouthful of sticky ribs, but he would have tried had there been any need to. Spencer had an enormous capacity to devour food at a single sitting for a slim guy. He had the eating habits of a predator, gorging when food was available and then going for more prolonged periods whilst typically a kilo of some sort of dead animal, fried potatoes, and cheese worked through his digestive tract. The emerging fad was called this intermittent fasting. Still, realistically, it meant the same number of calories consumed in short intervals, without the additional calories consumed by grazers who picked and dipped at food all day without really noticing it. Spencer was not surprised that the fattest animals in the world were vegetarians, elephants, hippos, and cattle. All ate poor quality grasses and vegetation. When did they last eat three-quarter pounders with cheese and fries on the side? OK, fries were vegetables, but the point could not be mistaken. You would not see a lion with a belly overhang, a tiger with love handles, or a leopard with a triple chin. Did a wolf or a fox have a muffin top or cankles? Fuck no, they did not, and it was why Spencer followed a mainly protein-rich diet made up of meat, fish, and dairy. Vegans could fuck right off, the self-righteous, pasty-looking hypocrites wearing leather shoes and utilizing fuck knows what of the animal by-products. Throughout their self-obsessed, virtuous day, they moralise to the world or anyone who could give a toss about cow farts' effects on the planet. Spencer was much influenced by his Dad Winston and his uncle Gary when it came to such matters rather than contemporary studies published in the New Scientist and regurgitated by the Guardian. Chantelle returned some minutes later, and her dinner had been reduced considerably.

"Alright, babe, you were a while, just had a shit?" mused Spencer.

"No, I haven't. I'm afraid it is not good news," Chantelle whispered. Spencer stopped chewing a thought for a moment.

"You didn't make it in time, and you've followed through?" he half-smiled.

"No, stop being like that, no, nothing like that. Well, sort of?" she said awkwardly.

"Sort of what?" he asked.

"I've just started,"

"Started what? For fuck sake, please finish it quickly if you've just started. The suspense is killing me, not," he complained.

"I'm on. Ok? I've just come on, which means tonight, is off!" she said through tight teeth and not wishing to be heard.

"Why are we whispering? We're the only two fuckers in here, so you're on, big deal, I just won't go down on you," he sniffed deadpan and began working on the pile lifted from Chantelle's plate to his own.

"Spenny, sorry darling, but it's tough love; I'm bleeding like a stuck pig," and she looked across at Spencer, sucking at the ribs, and then looked away with a shake of her head.

"Ok, babe, no worries," he replied. She breathed in deeply then her eyes squinted.

"What's all this babe nonsense? You never called me babe before; now it's babe this and babe that?"

"Is it? Sorry, I did not notice; it must have been something I heard," he answered.

"Are you having dessert? I'm not. I just want to go home," she pleaded.

"Sure, babe, I mean darling. I'm stuffed, let me pay up, and I'll meet you in the car. Can you drop me at Darren's?" Spencer wiped his chin.

"Aren't you coming home with me?" she looked surprised.

"Well, not if you're not well, you need your space, and besides, Darren's got a table booked for 8 o'clock," he said, retrieving his wallet.

"You've only just stuffed yourself," she remarked.

"A snooker table", he replied, standing up.

"Oh, fuck off, Spencer," shouted Chantelle and got up and stormed off out of the restaurant.

"Got the painters in, a bit hormonal", sniffed Spencer to the spotty waiter, who scanned his card and said nothing. Spencer followed Chantelle out of the door minutes later and stood staring at the empty car park space. He examined the vicinity hoping that she might have moved the car out for efficiency, but that hope was not expected or held for long. He picked out his phone and tapped a quick message,

SPEN*"Daz, come get me at the Harvester. Cheers, mate."*

FRIDAY

The reception area was not untypical of any London tech city office. It was of a minimalist design, with hard, black leather seats and a large, thin smoked glass coffee table adjacent on which a modern piece of art sat oddly in the middle. A water cooler was stationed in the corner. Monographic photos of the London skyline adorned the walls on either side of a wiry gold logo displaying the name Angeltech with a strapline in smaller font underneath, "where electric dreams become a reality", how cheesy thought Spencer.

The young receptionist appeared to busy herself at the desk, peering into a Facebook screen and looking at Spencer. She had seen large numbers of budding entrepreneurs bouncing through the frosted glass doors of Angeltech in the six months she had started. First, as a temporary and then as a full-time receptionist, when the opportunity to sit, smile, introduce visitors and pour coffee permanently between the hours of 8 and 5 each day was too good an offer for any aspirational writer to turn down. So, in between mundane tasks, Sarah wrote and edited her first novel, the story of a temp at an advertising agency who would sleep, lie, and charm her way to the position of Creative Director, the female antipathy of Don Draper of Mad Men only set in the 2010s. In essence, she convinced herself that for £24,000 per year, plus benefits, she was paid to write, which was better than servings drinks or food for less money and not having the time to deliver her first masterpiece, at least that was the plan. She had seen many aspiring money makers, some shy, most nervous, others brimming with confidence, but none had come through the doors so utterly wankered as this young man. He slurred his name by way of an introduction, yawned like a lion and then appeared to totter on the spot as he blinked heavily whilst being asked to take a seat. He was dishevelled, smelt of alcohol, and was likely to pass out as he sat on the hard black leather seat on the opposite side of the room. He felt shit; if he felt it, he knew what it felt like to look it, his eyes withdrawn and sullen, the dark shadows under them accentuating a good or bad but indeed long night out.

"Excuse me?" uttered the debut novelist.

"Er, yeah?" fogged Spencer slowly.

"Would you like some water?" She stood up and walked towards the water dispenser carrying a tumbler glass in her left hand.

"Yeah, that would be cool. Have you got any uppers or Charlie?" he grunted.

"Er, no, I don't, but I'll make you a strong coffee and add some cold water so you can drink it quickly", she sighed, looking at the young man whose head was buried between large hands.

"Thanks", he managed. It was ten minutes to eight o'clock, and Spencer had staggered from the Fox and Hounds on Smithfield, where he had finished the bender with his mate Darren only 30 minutes before his appointment. His presentation had been emailed the day prior, so arriving without his Mac book was not the disaster it might have been.

"Here you go, Mr Churchill," and the coffee was passed to his trembling hands. He cupped his hands and hunched into the cup to slurp back lukewarm liquid; to take the cup up to his mouth risked a considerable spillage. He finished the coffee and asked for another whilst excusing himself to head to the bathroom outside the frosted doors on the landing. Once inside the sterile bleached environment of the male designated bathroom, he leaned over the sink and splashed cold water up and into his astonished flesh, desperately trying to encourage life where there stood near death. He looked into the mirror and saw the raven black hair unkempt across his face and scalp, his eyes looking like urine pierced holes in crisp white snow; that was the familiar adage that people referred to hungover people. Spencer was more than hungover. He was coming down from an epic night of booze and drugs that his liver and kidneys struggled to handle. They were collapsing under the surge in demand for toxin purification. It was like the Alamo, Rourke's Drift, and Stalingrad into one overwhelming onslaught of shit. He felt ill; he needed to be sick. He staggered into the cubicle, projectile vomited across the closed seat of the white toilet and threw out an arm to stop himself from collapsing onto the floor. His stomach convulsed further, and he wretched with an almighty roar that could be heard in the adjacent reception area. The bathroom that had contained the sound of running water, flushing lavatories, and almighty farts could not suppress the sound of Spencer's Thursday night and Friday morning. It erupted through his gaping mouth like an evil genie escaping the lamp after a thousand years corked up in a filthy abyss.

"Is Mr Chruchill alright? He's apparently, very nervous," remarked Andy Wyatt, one of the investment committee who comes into reception to greet Spencer Churchill.

"I'm not sure, Andy; I'll send him in when he comes back, give him a few minutes to compose himself", replied Sarah, the receptionist novelist. Andy agreed and returned to the room where two other directors sat peering at the submission synopsis,

"Shagpad – a quick buck from a quick fuck, sounds…. interesting," muttered Stevie Moon; he thought he'd seen everything. He was about to.

Spencer blew through trembling lips, emitting gunk that had stuck to his tongue and from the back of his mouth. His legs shook, and he felt moisture across his groin and back passage. Please God, not the triple crown, he shuddered. Throwing up, coming, and shitting yourself at the same time. He'd experienced Feculent vomiting or "shomiting" but never the triple. He lowered his back jeans and pants; damn, he'd only changed these Wednesday and peered into the gusset. Nope, thank God almighty, just sweat, but still uncomfortable. He waddled like a penguin into the main bathroom and stood beneath the air dryer. He encouraged the downward blast by placing his hands beneath a large silver nozzle, withdrew them quickly and directed the draught towards his open gusset. The machine cut out. The procedure was repeated several times, and for a moment, Spencer was on to another idea, a bathroom dryer designed specifically at waist height for such accidents. He could not have been the only one to suffer this predicament. What about splashback from taps and toilets bowels energetically spurted from and into? Another idea for the pending tray. Just focus on getting back into the reception and meeting with a functioning brain and some basic motor skills to get you there.

He was thirsty, dehydrated, his tongue was as dry as a crusty towel, his throat hoarse, and his salivary glands as dry and crisp as a coconut husk left in a tropical sun for a month. Spencer fumbled at the taps, and they were those annoying water-saving taps that you had to press for a short burst meaning each hand to be washed separately while the other pushed the stiff tops fully down. Short sharp pumps could just about generate a steady flow of water. Who the fuck came up with this shit, he thought? Jabbing with his right hand and left hand scooping up the jet, he drew precious fluid into his orifice that felt as dry as the floor of a budgie's cage. Water dripped from his chin and onto his dark shirt that wore remnants of the guttural outburst that had pebble-dashed the cubicle, a decorative effect that Spencer could not and therefore had not cleaned up. Following numerous scoops and slurps, Spencer let out a simultaneous belch and fart that echoed around the bathroom like a foghorn in the Albert Hall. He held his stance a moment to check that he had not followed through; once reasonably confident his pants were undisturbed, he turned and shuffled the few yards across the landing and back into the reception. Sarah was astounded. Spencer Churchill looked worse than when he had walked out to freshen up, which took some beating. In terms of makeovers, it was a disaster that forbade the interview.

"Would you like to come through Spencer," gestured Sarah, her arm leading him towards the meeting room to the right of the corridor behind her desk.

"Yeah, just a moment. Have you got another one of those coffees?" Spencer rasped.

"Sure, here you go, I made another," and she passed him a black mug displaying the gold-lettered "Angeltech" logo. Spencer took the cup, drank its caffeinated content back in a single continuous chug, and shook his head vigorously after.

"I think that's better," he said and passed the mug back to Saah before strolling towards the door. He walked inside to be presented by three people seated on the opposite side of a large back, boardroom-style table. They introduce themselves as Andy Wyatt, Stevie Moon, and Kathryn Cook, associate directors of the firm and prospective investors.

"Please sit down, Spencer. Would you like a tissue?" asked Andy Wyatt, noticing his shirt's sickly spew.

"Nah, I'm fine, thanks, I'm only allergic to rejection, and there's not going to be any of that in here", smiled Spencer, pleased with his positive and intelligent response.

"Well, let's see about that. Walk us through your presentation and tell us why we should invest money with your proposition. Here you can use this clicker to step through. It's already pre-loaded into the display," added Kathryn passing a small device to him. He fumbled it as he received the wireless Bluetooth AV component, dropping it to the floor. As Spencer bent down to retrieve it, the room swam around him, the floor rippled like a wave, and his legs became unsteady. He held the table firm and drew himself back up, his palms placed flat on the table for balance. Suddenly, the events of the previous twelve hours flashed back to him. Daz picked him up from the Harvester car park, and they shot a few frames of snooker with an equivalent number of pints of lager. This led to them getting the taste, as evident by several strong continental beers in Watford Town Centre. These were quaffed with some vodka-induced shots shared with some girl technicians who were bar crawling, having earlier stopped, just for the one, after work at the nail bar. Having popped some pills and another round of shots, Daz suggested a club, and they took a taxi into North London where they met Spencer's flatmate Adam and his colleagues from working at a north London estate agent chain at a club in Kilburn. Following several more rounds and a binge on Charlie, Spencer had felt euphoric enough to consider finishing the night at Fabric in Farringdon. He thought that at 6 a.m, he could walk to the Hive, grab an hour in an armchair at the Honeycomb, the ground floor café, and then trot across to Angeltech in Old Street to triumphantly smash home the investment required by Shagpad. Those plans were waylaid by the hunger left by the booze, coke, and dancing, and the insatiable prospect of a porter's breakfast consisting of steak, sausages, and eggs, washed down with a couple of points of beer at the Fox and Hounds pub in the next-door Smithfield's market. Daz and Adam had left in an uber for their respective works, an Estate Agency for Adam, and the borough council for Darren, who worked in the council tax office. The effects of the night's indulgences wore rapidly off during the short walk to Old Street. This left the sedimented dregs to stir their way to the surface, as evident by his bloodshot hollowed-out eyes that felt like they had nearly burst from the guttural retching attack in the bathroom.

"Spencer, are you alright? Would you prefer we postpone this meeting for another time," asked Kathryn Cook. There was no immediate reply; Spencer was still recalling with sincere regret the evening and night's display, shocking.

"Spencer?" prompted Stevie Moon.

"Oh, yes, any questions?" replied Spencer confused.

"Well, we haven't started yet, walk us through your presentation and tell us why we should invest our money in your enterprise, er, Shagpad?" repeated Kathryn. Spencer stood up and drew in a large breath to oxygenate his blood without a chemical reaction to the cocktail of drugs he had taken such that his stomach, although undoubtedly recently emptied, should find more contents to bark across the meeting room table. Should these three be sitting with plastic bibs like diners tucking into lobster, the thought amused Spencer for a moment, and Spencer smiled, but the smile curled into the expression of a man pained by the feeling of being utterly sick. But, he thought, never again, never again, never again. Another deep breath and he started.

"Never start a presentation with an apology, but I feel I must. I have gastroenteritis but was so determined to win your trust that although I should have stayed in bed this morning, I hope my determination and commitment to succeed overshadows my dishevelled state. I assure you the illness is not contagious. Still, I must warn you, my hunger and enthusiasm to succeed are." Andy, Kathryn, and Stevie exchanged glances, ten out of ten for bullshit and attempting to rescue a dire situation but get to the meat of the bone.

"Shagpad, is a social media platform that connects people with places, with people who need places for a short but intimate time with somebody else. The problem, hotels, B&Bs, Airbnb, and studios all charge by the day, check in after 2 p.m and check-out before noon the next day. That is up to twenty-two hours for people who need, on average, twenty-two minutes to perform a personal and private activity with another consenting adult. The solution is a digital platform for anybody to rent property, for a limited time basis, at a price that reflects equivocal value for both buyer and seller. Booked online and transacted with a discrete payee identifier, Shagpad means any property owner can make money at any time they choose, for as little or as long they like, at a price of their choosing. Their value is reflected by a scoring system by customers who rate it for cleanliness, convenience, and friendliness. My next slide will show conservative projections," Spencer was interrupted.

"Spencer, we need to stop you there. This is not something we can invest in. Angeltech invests in projects, start-ups, and firms that fit our core values. We were clear on the application criteria that we would not be considering funding for any pornographic or socially unacceptable businesses," remarked Andy.

"What's socially unacceptable about two people having a fuck somewhere in private? Are you a prude?" shot back Spencer.

"There's nothing wrong with that, just that we won't promote it," added Stevie.

"There's nothing to suggest renting rooms by the hour is immoral. People could be meeting up for a game of chess. What they do in the room is their business," replied Spencer.

"With a name like Shagpad?" repealed Kathryn folding her arms.

"Change the name, I don't give a fuck, call it chess club, roomfor2, air b no b, no, that spells airnob, er, call it whatever, offer the service, let the customer decide how they wish to consume that service. You can buy and take Viagra for sunburn if you like?"

"Why would somebody do that?" sniffed Andy,

"Keeps the sheets off your legs", replied Spencer, and Kathryn tried hard to suppress her laugh.

"It is business, and if you don't want a part of a multi-million, no billion dollars opportunity to provide a perfectly legal and respectable service because of outdated attitudes to business and consumer demand, then perhaps you're not the investor I'm looking for. You're discriminating against people of all sexual persuasions and people who desperately want to sweat their assets," Spencer felt invigorated.

"Sweaty assets are all I can envisage, I'm afraid," said Stevie. "Sorry, but it does not fit the corporate culture and code we comply with," he added.

"Then why did you ask me in? What a waste of time" complained Spencer.

"Sorry, Spencer, we no longer vet the applications, we lost some good opportunities by being too presumptuous, and besides, it's the people we invest in as much as the idea," explained Kathryn.

Spencer felt the recoil of his stomach twisting as it kicked back at the acidic assault of the night's excess.

"And why can't you invest in me" he demanded. Then his eyes shot across the room towards a small black cylindrical tin resembling a waste bin. It would have to do, and he lunged towards it as his stomach cramped and shot more biley gunk up through his trachea and out of his gaping mouth. Most of the spurt made it towards and in the general direction of the floor-based unit, but some shot side-ways and Andy became a collateral casualty of the misdemeanour. Spencer howled as the cramps continued and spat out the remaining globules from his disgusting mouth. He sniffed and inhaled deeply, leaning against the wall like a night-time drunk taking a piss.

"Do you want us to answer that?" reacted Andy sharply, wiping his shirt with a serviette.

"Nah, you're alright. Fuck it, I'm off. You can stick your investment up your arse," replied Spencer staggering towards the door and wiping his mouth with his sleeve. He opened the door, and before he left, he farted loudly, it sounded wet and flappy and hung in the air whilst Stevie shot up from his chair to open the window.

"Name that fucking tune," cackled Spencer, and he was gone.

"Hi, good morning," smiled Sarah, looking up at Innocence, whose smile was beaming with nerves.

"Good morning; my name is Innocence. I have an appointment at nine o'clock," she whispered gently.

"Yes, that's fine. You'll be meeting with Stevie, Kathryn, and Andy. They'll be in the boardroom shortly. We are just letting it air a little. Please take a seat, and they'll be with you shortly," gestured Sarah, who resumed her attention to her Instagram account. Innocence sat at the same coffee table as Spencer had, about an hour earlier before he had left in a hurry, minus the contents of his stomach and lower bowels. She breathed deeply and thought about the outline of her pitch. She had not over-rehearsed this upon her sister's advice. Too much to remember meant loading up on more nerves and not thinking clearly. Just remember the outline and prepare to have an enjoyable conversation. Innocence said a little prayer. She asked for God's strength; she would do great things with this venture's success. Kathryn Cook, dark-haired and slim, wearing navy trousers and a plain white blouse underneath a navy jacket, strode into the reception. She introduced herself and invited Innocence to follow her to the boardroom. Innocence felt a surge of excitement in the pit of her stomach, which, unlike the previous applicant, had hosted just fruit, yoghurt, a weak milky tea, and a small Cadbury's dairy milk. Innocence noticed the room was airy but had the faint smell of sickness like she could remember when her younger siblings had been ill as infants.

"Sorry about the smell, we've opened the windows, but unfortunately, a previous applicant's nerves got the better of him. However, there is nothing to worry about. We just want to have a very informal chat about your business plans. Hi, I'm Andy," said Andy creepily.

"And I'm Stevie," said Stevie sat with Andy and Kathryn on the opposite side of the table, and a chair had been set with water, where Innocence was beckoned to sit. She wore a colourful dress, orange and green, with a brown cardigan. She unpacked her laptop but was told the presentation was preloaded, and she was offered the same clicker device that Spencer managed to fumble and set the room off spinning when he had swooped to retrieve it.

"Take your time and walk us through your pitch. Tell us why we should invest in you and your idea?" posed Kathryn.

"Sugar Rush is a casual game that lets players choose between either cats or dogs and take control of their selection to compete in many increasingly difficult tasks. The gameplay is addictive and fun, and it offers a multitude of levels and scenarios. Casual gamers are typically twenty-somethings, and advertisers for that market will be attracted to this platform. The next slide shows that this market across smartphones is expected to grow by 30% per annum as more customers acquire these devices meaning a market doubles in size within three years." Innocence paused; her nerves had diminished, and she asked if there were any questions so far? The three investors shook their heads, smiled and listened to the presentation conclude with some sample gameplay that was smart and well-executed. Her audience seemed attentive and polite, nodding and smiling as she spoke softly and purposefully in between occasional sips of water.

"That concludes the presentation. Now I will be pleased to answer your questions," summarised Innocence; the pitch had reduced thirty minutes to barely a registered blink. But, contrary to pre-meeting nerves, the experience had been enjoyable.

"How many casual games are there?" asked Stevie.

"Thousands for Smartphones," replied Innocence.

"How will yours stand out and be selected for play?" he countered.

"People like cats and dogs. They identify with these animals more than with people. It will help direct traffic to my Sugar Rush," she smiled nervously.

"But according to elementary search, there are hundreds of casual games featuring cats and dogs, little friends, catastrophe, doggie town, dog's life, nine lives, literally hundreds of cute furry critter themed games. So how can Sugar Rush attract the multiple tens of thousands of players needed to secure a thousand dollars per week of advertising revenues?" Stevie specialised in gaming and tech for leisure. He recognized Sugar Rush as a competent, nicely presented game but ten years behind the curve for release. Released in 2012, Candie Crush acquired millions of players and dollars in annual revenues. But, unfortunately, that wave had surfed and crashed on the shore where Sugar Rush would fail to launch.

"People I have shown the game like it and say they would play it," countered Innocence.

"People like who?" asked Andy, leaning back in the chair, his shirt tightening across a plump belly, the buttons straining but holding firm.

"My sister, her boyfriend, his sister, her friend Shelley, other people I have encountered, they all say they like it," replied Innocence.

"So, people who would have a reason not to upset you or no reason to be impartial. How about gaming reviewers, gaming groups, pre-launch groups, or maybe some gaming journos? Have you any feedback from these types?" suggested Kathryn.

"Not yet. I thought I'd get the funding first to fully develop a beta release with more play levels and advanced features." Innocence reached for a glass of water; her hands quivered as she drew the tumbler to her lips that were drying from the questions. She swallowed the cool liquid and waited for the next volley. It didn't come, but the rejection did and swiftly.

"Innocence, thank you for your presentation. Very well thought out and well delivered. Unfortunately, we will not be pursuing this further. Gaming is highly competitive, and only a few make the returns we seek with this investment. I wish you very well with this venture but would advise that you look for a different theme, something new that stands out from the rest. Thank you for considering *AngelTech*. We would be happy to see you again in the future if you develop something more in line with future trends, but until then, thanks again." Stevie Moon sat up straight and tilted his head, pulling a sympathetic frown that Innocence found that, surprisingly, she at once wanted to punch straight out of him.

Months of work with precious little money from part-time employment, short-term gigs, packing, serving, counting, and data entry support the inception, planning, and building of a prototype game that she thought was entertaining and compelling to play. She looked at the three young investors, each not seeming much older than herself. What the fuck did they know? A rage engulfed her emotions as the enormity of the furnace that she had stoked these past months was snuffed out at a pinch by Stevie fucking Moon. Who the fuck are you, you tousled-haired tosspot? Language surfaced in Innocence's mind that she would be ashamed to think, let alone utter. But yet here she was in a professional environment struggling to contain words that she wanted to scream into the face of these three wankers that could not comprehend the potential that Sugar Rush offered. She rose from her chair and contemplated her options, continue handling the objections or admit defeat. Perhaps this was a test of how much she wanted it. A measure of her commitment and desire to fight for her dream, or would the desperate attempt to rescue a lame-duck idea humiliate her further? Or perhaps it was best to just walk out, say nothing except a polite thank and use the experience to drive an insatiable appetite to make Sugar Rush a global success. The subsequent interviews in high net worth reading material referenced the rejection by an investment funding trio she would name at every opportunity. She would follow the mandate of Mario Puzo's Don Corleone; revenge was a dish best served cold, let the heat and emotion cool off, and plan a calculated response; they'd be sorry.

Innocence took the latter option, "Thank you," was offered quietly and gently, and without returning their glances, she stood up and left the room.

"Who's up next?" asked Andy, glancing at his phone and noticing the time had reached 9.30a.m, nothing interesting yet, but the day was young. There were six more opportunities to review before beer o'clock, a decent session on the lash with mates in Shoreditch followed by cocaine, rum-based shots, and ogling fit women at one of the gentleman's dancing bars nearby.

"Says here a chap called Surjit Gosht, from Spanner. He's developed a mobile performance utility," replied Stevie.

"How exciting", sighed Kathryn, rising to pour another cup of coffee from the machine cradled in the corner of the room. She was tired. After work, a Thursday drink had extended beyond the 9'oclock curfew placed on a school night, but she could cruise on a Friday when the opportunity reviews took place. She'd arrived home late, well pissed and Abbey, her flatmate and partner, took advantage of her mood to embark on an hour of sex, several minutes of which she slept through as Abbey's tongue worked its way in and around her lower half. Abbey was not amused to surface from mowing the grass to find her femme unresponsive and deeply asleep. Hmph, bloody women, she'd thought!

They caught up with emails, social media, and other personal-related items before a polite tap on the door, and Sarah popped her head in to announce Surjit had arrived for his appointment. Andy offered to "get him", and within minutes Surjit sat in the same chair occupied by Spencer and Innocence. The same courteous and frank instruction to present his idea for thirty minutes and then be prepared for questions was offered to Surjit as the others. Finally, after his glass of water had been poured, the presentation loaded, and the clicker passed to him, Surjit Gosht was ready to begin.

"Hello, my name is Surjit, and I'm the founder of Spanner, a company specialising in mobile digital optimization technologies. Have you ever been debugging code remotely using an IOS interface, and the task has run down your mobile battery quickly, or wondered why it can take seconds to load some applications when others are instant? How about having experienced sub-optimal performance connecting Bluetooth to a Wi-Fi proxy to circumvent the very lag you were trying to eradicate through pairing two wireless protocols? I know I have,"

Kathryn yawned deeply, the coffee had not dug in yet, and she apologized.

"Spanner is a technology that runs deep-rooted into the operating system of mobile devices and will speed ultra-user performance by over 20% by optimizing machine code written into the kernel of the sub-operating system. I know you are all dying to know how I can achieve this and to show you I'd have to kill you afterwards, and so, by definition, that statement must be true" he laughed nervously. "But seriously, I will explain how I can achieve this and what that means to the mobile device market opportunity."

Andy smiled back "fascinating stuff Surjit, please do go on", and Kathryn gave him a dig on his foot with her heel. Andy kicked back playfully. Surjit continued his pitch. He felt confident and empowered, and his nerves had disappeared. A week that had started by audibly farting in public, desperately urinating, asking women out, meeting for a date, all be it briefly, and going down the pub with a mate had emancipated him. Thank you, Spencer Churchill; you're not all bad. Now, he was cruising through a business pitch with three investors sitting up and making notes.

"Thank you, Surjit, that was interesting, exciting," noted Andy sincerely and surprised. The pitch was good, made sense, and most importantly, made money potentially. "So, 2% of mobile device users would consider better performance tooling, and at a one-off $5 payment or .50 cents per month, given the huge size of the market, even a niche that offers sizeable revenue returns" Andy nodded and screwed his mouth up, he was interested. He looked across at Kathryn, and she took his cue,

"Yes, international markets like East Asia where high-performance gaming is in high growth and could offer lucrative returns if we found a partner to market this," she added. Surjit's eyes widened fuck. They were interested, "exciting", to quote Andy Wyatt. Stevie stepped in,

"Surjit, we're going to make you an offer. Subject to due diligence, which takes about a week, you know to check this is your IP, erm intellectual property, erm I know you know what that meant. We would look to draft a joint venture MOI, erm memorandum of intent, to take a 50% investment in Spanner, reducing to 40% upon certain KPIs, erm that's key performance indicators, being met. Then, over twelve months, we'd invest half a mill, five hundred thousand pounds, to scale this out and get to a series A funding round, where we go for more finance and a proper business plan. How does that sound young man?"

"Apart from a little patronizing from a guy not much older than myself, pretty good, damn good indeed," thought Surjit. "Yeah, that works well," he stammered.

"Excellent. We will send DocuSign heads of the agreement later today. Please sign and return that Surjit. Next week, we'll schedule an appointment to map the plan and sign the full paperwork. Thank you, Surjit, congratulations and great job," said Andy standing and offering his hand across the table to Surjit. Surjit took it and shook it, surprised at how quickly the decision was made.

"Are you OK, Surjit, you seemed a little shocked, but you did exceptionally well; we were impressed", smiled Kathryn.

"Oh, sorry, I'm fine. I'm delighted. I guess I was expecting more hard-hitting questions around the tech," admitted Surjit.

"No, that all made sense. Andy is very well versed in this area of the market, and if he is happy, then we are," offered Stevie.

"Then that's great. I was worried you'd be concerned with the breach of warranty that running third-party code might impact the user," chirped Sujit.

"What was that?" remarked Kathryn looking at Andy, concerned.

"Jeez, completely disregarded that. But, of course, that could be, no check, that is a major hurdle. But, oh dear, I think we jumped the gun here, guys. So hold that offer, I'd better check this out, but of course, it will be running executables, which will invalidate warranties." Pondered Andy out loud.

"Dead in the water?" asked Kathryn.

"Fraid so," said Stevie screwing his face. "Sorry, Surjit, this is a very fair point, and we admire your honesty, had you kept schtum, we'd be five hundred grand into this and committed down the pan. We appreciate your honesty."

"Down the pan," murmured Surjit, which summed up his week.

"What about an OEM deal? We sell the IP to Motorola, Apple, or Samsung," snapped Surjit, remembering Mae Li's advice.

"Great idea," remarked Andy, and Surjit's eyes relit, and his frown turned into a broad smile. Still, Andy continued, "But not quite our bag, not the returns we want, plus it's a bugger to prove once you show them, and they reverse engineer the stuff. We've tried it before, unlucky but a great idea," he consoled. Surjit shuffled towards the door, thanked them for their time and opportunity, and closed the door on them and his dreams behind him. He walked out of the reception, where Sarah was still navigating Facebook and into the fresh April air. He needed a drink, an hour or so to meet the others, and he would have one or several.

Mae Li lifted her left leg that extended to a high-heeled boot and a side karate-style kick towards the reception door of Angeltech but stopped short of smashing it inwards and neatly pushed it open. Sarah looked up from her novel that she had finally started and smiled.

"You must be Mae Li?" asserted Sarah, half questioning by raising the intonation of her voice at the end of the sentence. She sounded like an Australian whose manner of speaking meant they spoke in uncertain terms even in the most earnest of situations. An Australian doctor who told you that you had nothing to worry about could never erase the uncertainty in their tone upon the words "nothing" and "about". Sarah had realized this herself and was pleased since she could cleverly inject this observation into her updated 21st century, woke Mad Men update. Mae Li accepted a seat and waited in the same black and gilt-themed reception that made it look more like the foyer or booths of one of the clubs she danced at during the early part of the week.

Kathryn came out to meet Mae Li and invited her to the same meeting room that had rejected three prospective unicorns. Spencer had been sick, Innocence too bland, and Surjit too honest. Mae Li had received a group update from each of the Joes, one-word "bollocks", wrote Spencer. "I need a sugar rush even if they don't, see you at the pub," remarked Innocence, and "defeat snatched from the jaws of victory, tell you later before I get drunk", had written Surjit. Had Mae Li felt any pressure to emulate the success of the others, and she hadn't, she could do no worse than receive a rejection.

Mae Li observed the panel whilst listening to the introductory remarks and explanation. There was something familiar about Andy Wyatt, the chubby fair-haired guy with round glasses and a permanent smirk. She'd love to wipe that from him, maybe a roundhouse kick to his lower jaw or an elbow into his temple. Kathryn smiled simperingly, far too condescending for Mae Li's liking, and there was something about her that she looked like a dyke. For sure, Kathryn was some butch's bitch. Then there was Stevie Moon. Not Steve, but Stevie, the addition of I to give the name two syllables like footballers did to each other, only Steve looked like he couldn't kick the air out of a balloon. He had a bouffant hairstyle at the front of his prominent forehead, making it seem even longer. Wrong styling Stevie. Why the long face? she thought. Stevie smiled pleasantly and disarmingly, which aggravated Mae Li. She was here for a fight, not a love-in. With the pleasantries completed, Mae Li managed a smile and began her presentation.

"What is the truth? Philosophers have argued and reasoned the nature of the truth since the Ancient Greeks and Chinese pondered this several thousand years ago. And yet, are we any closer to knowing the truth about space, time, the universe, or each other? Ask any business owner, director, or leader what their most important asset is, and they will answer their people, employees, and colleagues nine out of ten. But what do they know about these people, what is the truth regarding these employees, and can they ever be honest about their colleagues? The truth is whatever the commonly observed facts are about a product or a service, or a person. If the perception of service is inadequate, unreliable, and costly, then that is what the market will believe. Is that then the truth? What about people? Where do we find out about the people who make up companies, products, and services? Do we go to Linkedin? Is this the source and the truth about workers and professional people? How can it be when it is written by the same people themselves? Colleagues are only ever invited to write nice things about them. If not, it is edited from their profiles in a heartbeat. Linkedin, therefore, contains some truth that a person works or works at a company. What about the job title and job history? Is that true? It is about as close to reality as a CV, and yet this is where we go to find out about people, professionally speaking. 99% of the content on Linkedin is misleading. It is not the truth. It is a colossal, evolving platform of the most unimaginable bullshit like northeast Australia's great barrier reef. The difference is that it is beautiful and deadly. Yet, Linkedin is alive and growing, an amorphous digital fog of lies and untruths with no verification or validation other than that by the perpetrators themselves. The market value of Linkedin is billions of dollars, $100billion, yet more than 90% of its content is untrue. Therefore, I ask you, of what value is the truth? Nothing, or a trillion?

Kathryn sat up fuck, this was heavy shit. Why could Mae Li not pitch a new eco-product, an algorithm that saved money to consumers, a novel online betting exchange? But no, she was raising philosophical dogma. She was pitching the truth. It was only ten past eleven on a Friday morning, and Kathryn's fingers trembled from the strong coffee and withdrawal of alcohol? Andy's eyes stared back at Mae Li through his thick lenses. They looked glassy and still, unblinking like a serpent as if mesmerized by some spell this witch was casting. Stevie sucked thoughtfully on his pen. At least, that was the impression he wanted to give. The truth was that this observation hit home. He was one of the Linkedin warriors that trumpeted Angeltech's s every step as if it were his own. He fluffed up his importance, achievements, worth, and value as a sharp-eyed angel investor when the truth was that he could no sooner come up with an original, innovative idea himself than he could fly out of the third-floor window. This was what he was ever more likely to experience if Mae Li had her way. She spun the story further for the remaining thirty minutes, creating a dark web professional networking platform that sought to tell the truth about everybody. All she needed was funding to get started and prove that she had what it took. Her father would provide the rest.

"What if somebody tells a lie about you?" asked Andy.

"Profiles will be able to respond to it, and other profiles are invited to comment. In addition, having a platform hosting claims and counterclaims will be entertaining enough for people to want to join in any case," Mae Li argued.

"So, it's not about the truth. It's about the show, a kind of Jerry Springer meets Linkedin?" enquired Kathryn.

"That can only add to its attraction, but the purpose of the show is to arrive at the truth about somebody, and that can only come from witnesses, opinions, and corresponding facts from statements made by people in the know," replied Mae Li.

"We cannot support a venture that utilizes the dark web," stated Stevie.

"Fine, then we run it on the web and host it from China or anywhere Western libel laws are not recognized."

"But that's just it, the platform might not be sued, but the people who comment on it will be. They are still subject to the laws of their respective jurisdictions. So this has the potential to be the biggest viper's nest of litigation in the history of commerce," remarked Andy shaking his head. "It's a fantastic idea but completely unworkable or certainly from an investment perspective we could not be seen to be a part of it," he hmphed.

"Why not?" asked Mae Li. "It's about making money, isn't it?"

"Yes, but it is being seen to do so in the right way", replied Andy. "AngelTech has a reputation to uphold, to be seen to be on the right lines in terms of moral compass," Andy folded his arms.

"Does that include attending lap dance clubs, Andy?" asked Mae Li. Andy blushed and unfolded his arms, and Mae Li continued,

"I thought I recognized you, you regularly attend Lollipops, the club in Shoreditch, but I guess you may do as you please outside of office hours," Mae Li raised her eyebrows and held her arm to her mouth, her forefinger pointing towards her lips. Stevie interjected.

"Erm, let's keep this conversation to the proposal. Andy's point is that any conditional investment approval needs to be made on the basis that there are reasonable grounds to expect no legal challenges or considerable funds required for litigation as part of this process. I think it fair to say that there is enough doubt in Voracity to step back from this opportunity at this moment in time. Although I do wish you success in finding investment, it is certainly an intriguing thought to have an open platform where one's colleagues, customers, and associates are far franker about their experience working with you," nodded Stevie.

"So, you are going to turn this down? An opportunity to make billions, not millions?" countered Mae Li, looking puzzled.

"We have to. It does not fit our core values," remarked Andy.

"You hold no values, you fat frog-faced fucker," snapped Mae Li.

Mae Li stood and withdrew her items to her bag. She maintained eye contact with each of the three before turning sharply on her heels and leaving the room without saying goodbye. Stevie, Kathryn, and Andy sat speechlessly and stared at their respective screens. Stevie was the first to break the silence,

"Early lunch it is then."

The glass-panelled door to the Old Fountain pub swung open, and in stepped Spencer, his demeanour decidedly more alert than the wreck that had poured into Angeltech just four hours earlier. He had taken an Uber back to Barnet and slept the forty-five minutes it had taken the driver to traverse the London traffic headed primarily in the opposite direction. A big shit, followed by a much-needed shower and two fried egg sandwiches with a pint of tea later, and he felt human again. Only the young can recover from an all-night bender. Spencer took advantage of his youthful body's resilience to such abuse. Still, it was already being pounded into older biological age. He'd drank a bottle of Evian, consumed two pre-workout caffeine shakes, taken the Northern Line back into Euston, and walked the mile back to Old Street via Kings Cross and the City Road.

The crisp April morning air invigorated his senses with every step, and by the time he had arrived at the Old Fountain to meet the others, he was already looking forward to a pint. He'd changed his clothes, new pants and fresh socks, deodorant had been sprayed liberally across the three b's, back, bum, and balls, and his manful hair combed back and hung across his shoulders like a sixties poster child. He ordered a Camden Bells lager, something cold and refreshing to maintain the momentum of waking up before the inevitable effects of it, and God knows how many more to follow would take him back into the abyss. Spencer contemplated his life. He was either getting pissed, pissed, or getting over getting and being pissed. There was no state of not being in any of the other three conditions, and something had to change, but just not today. He checked his phone and ignored the three separate new texts from Chantelle that had arrived this morning. At first, she was angry that he had not wanted to spend the evening with her, then angry because he had not replied, then worried. After all, he had not replied. Finally, Spencer replied, talk tomorrow, out with business associates all day. I'll come round tomorrow. Love Spencer. This appeased Chantelle, who responded with a single love heart; she was still upset, so the usual five or six would have to decrease until after the reconciliation. He looked over at the door as it swung open, and Mae Li strode purposefully towards him like a model on the catwalk.

"Just you then?" she posed.

"Don't sound so disappointed," he replied. Mae Li feigned a smile.

"Buy me a drink then,"

"What would you like?"

"Lots,"

"Start with a half lager,"

"Fuck a half. Get me a pint of what you are having,"

"Since you asked so nicely,"

"Here," Mae Li handed Spencer a roll of ten pounds notes bundled up; there must have been three hundred pounds. "The kitty I'm buying, you are procuring," she ordered him.

"I can buy you a pint", he protested.

"No, you can't; you're broke, Spencer, the same as Innocence and Surjit is. So I'm buying the drinks and lunch. I need to launder this dirty money," she smiled and accentuated the word "dirty", which Spencer found a turn on, recalling she pole danced for cash during the week.

"Down boy", he muttered, feeling his cock stiffen in his ripped jeans. Not good to have a hard-on walking up to the bar; uncomfortable but not insurmountable.

As Spencer ordered Mae LI's pint and another for himself to save getting and going up again, Innocence and Surjit entered the pub, and with drinks agreed, they returned to the table where Mae Li sat with four pints of lager. They sat down, looked at each other, and took hesitant sips from the pints except Spencer, who downed his first pint and moved the empty to an unoccupied adjacent table.

"Whose first? Spencer, you were up first. What happened to you?" asked Surjit.

"I think they liked the idea but could not invest on ethical or moral grounds, bullshit, bullshit, blah-blah, ta-ta." Spencer did not elaborate further and sniffed dismissively, shaking his head.

"Was that it?" nudged Mae Li.

"Pretty much, yeah. Oh, and I thew up in the waste-paper bin," Spencer added.

"You did what?" remarked Innocence open-mouthed.

"I had a chunder. But, purely tactical, needed to be done," said Spencer, non-plussed.

"Were you hankered?" asked Surjit.

"Nah, not hankered, wankered. I came in off the back of an all-nighter." The others looked at each other astounded and then erupted into laughter,

"I thought it smelt funny when I walked in, they had the windows open, and there was a strong smell of bleach," cried Innocence.

"That was on account of my feeling so shite, I barked up my breakfast, and some collateral flew the way of that tufty-haired ponce, Stevie TLA Moon. I thought I did well to present at all, I deserved a fucking medal or an Oscar," appealed Spencer.

"All that work and you blow it on a binge," tutted Mae Li.

"Binge, minge, it's never wasted. Besides, it was only a fortnight's work. I got the idea pissed up at Uncle Gary's house, and he gave me the money to research and pitch it," exclaimed Spencer.

"You must have spent longer than that. I've been working months on mine. The submissions were last month in any case," observed Surjit, taking another swig of his lager.

"Yeah, I know, but I only started working on this on Monday when we met at the Hive. I thought this place might help me concentrate and seek inspiration, which it did meeting you guys," Spencer scoffed.

"So, if you have only been working on Shagpad since this week, what do you usually do?" asked Innocence.

"A bit of this and a bit of that, anything really," he replied.

"Give us an example of a bit of this?" asked Mae Li, intrigued.

"For example, I'm a wedding singer," came the reply.

"A wedding singer? What's a wedding singer do?" asked Innocence.

"Doh, answers on a postcard; please, I sing at weddings, in a band. We perform requests. "What are the most requested first songs? Asked Innocence.

"Depends on the brides, but Watford weddings a Gary Barlow or Westlife number, something upmarket, north London, Finchley, Golders Green, then you're talking Al Green's "the way you look tonight" or Elton Johns. "Can you feel the love tonight". Look up wedding classics on youtube or Spotify; we do them all," he continued.

"We?" asked Surjit.

"Yeah, the band, a five-piece, Midnight Sun, drums, bass, guitar, keys, and me on lead vocals. I can sing anything," he laughed.

"That explains the constant tapping and humming," proclaimed Innocence.

"Yup, I usually learn vocals, lyrics, and new songs. We're booked out most Saturdays and sometimes Fridays. Sometimes mid-week, weddings, Bar Mitzvahs – Jacob on drums is Jewish; it helps get those gigs, corporate functions, anything that pays decent money, Christmas parties, birthday parties, we're booked out. We get between a grand and two for a gig, depending. Two sets, forty to fifty songs from over a hundred and fifty we can do and growing, plus, as I said, the requests. Three hundred and fifty quid a week on average, tax-free," he replied.

"That's a bit of this. What's a bit of that?" asked Mae Li.

"Labouring for Uncle Gary, driving vans for his mates, I'm an acting extra,"

"What like in Ricky Gervais?" piped in Surjit, smiling.

"Yeah, exactly, £100 per day for when I've got nothing else. I've done modelling, helped out in kitchens, and gig economy stuff, but that will not pay a mortgage or make Chantelle happy?"

"You'll never make her happy," thought Mae LI.

"Right," said Innocence, nodding, then looking up at Surjit and Mae Li, "It's Ok for you sugar tits, your daddy pays for you, and Surjit, you live with your mum, the rents paid and the food on the table, not for Spencer and me, it isn't." Innocence jabbed her finger into Surjit's belly, who recoiled playfully.

"Who's up next?" asked Spencer,

"Steady on, I'm not anywhere near finishing this," protested Surjit picking up his pint,

"Nah, I meant the Angeltech experience," finished Spencer.

"I was after you, so I'll go next. Let me tell you all about it, all forty-one minutes of it, I didn't even get an hour," admitted Innocence.

"Me neither, but go on," urged Mae Li.

"I followed my script, showed some great materials and sample gameplay. It all went smoothly, and they were attentive and smiling; I thought I must be doing something right here. Then I finished and asked for questions," Innocence quaffed the lager before continuing,

"Then that bloody Stevie Moon, you know, the "floppy-haired cunt" interrupted Spencer, "yes, him, starts asking why my game will stand out when there are so many of them? What's different and I explained, but he is like, yeah but it's an old market, that ship has sailed, and it made me so mad, they all did," Innocence started to cry, tears welled up in her eyes, and she stopped and wiped her cheeks with the sleeve of her brown cardigan.

"Babes, don't cry, they're not worth it, but you are," comforted Mae Li, pulling up closer to Innocence and extending her arm around her.

"It's not them. I care about the months I put into this, and now I'll have to leave London and England. I needed this sponsorship to retain my temporary work permit, which runs out in June, and other people depended on this becoming a success," she sniffed.

"We'll think of something. What's your story, babe," asked Mae Li, looking up at Surjit.

"Oh, mine is epic, I can't top Spencer throwing up, but it comes close," he shrugged.

"How so?" asked Innocence becoming recomposed.

"I got an offer," declared Surjit.

"Hold on, I thought you said, well, that's fucking great news, congratulations, let's celebrate, fucking well done, Bro," cheered Spencer slapping Surjit across his back which made the table jump and some of the beer spilt over the pots.

"Hold the phone, Spencer. It got rescinded within minutes," choked Surjit.

"Why? Hold on, no, noooo! You fucking well didn't do you, tell me you didn't," snapped Mae Li leaning forward.

"Didn't what?" asked Innocence.

"Tell them about the warranty issue. You did, didn't you" replied Mae Li.

"I might have mentioned it", murmured Surjit squirming awkwardly and taking a bigger sip of his drink.

"Fuck my old boots, Bro. When?" startled Spencer.

"On the way out, they said about sending documents to sign and stuff, and I didn't want to go down that route without mentioning it in case it got me into trouble,"

"How much were they offering?" asked Spencer.

"A half", replied Surjit.

"Only half what you wanted?" asked Innocence.

"No half a million." Surjit picked up his drink and swallowed the remaining contents. The others sat in silence, gawping at their naïve and lovely friend.

"Well, stuff my old boots," remarked Spencer. Mae Li spoke next,

"It would have probably been picked up before any funds were transferred, the offer was conditional, and due diligence would identify this as inappropriate risk."

"Yeah, exactly what I thought, anyway; what happened to you?" continued Surjit trying to reassure himself he did the right thing. He appreciated Mae Li's comments even though she did not entirely mean them, but she felt protective of her new friends.

"Pretty much the same scenario as Spencer," Mae Li started.

"You threw up in the boardroom too?" remarked Innocence.

"No, not that. Has all that sugar rush to your brain? No, they felt my proposal unsuitable as a profile for their investment portfolio, legal implications, and so forth. That guy Andy Wyatt, you know the podgy little twat with the round-rimmed glasses,"

"Yeah, he's probably been around a few rims himself", piped in Spencer; Surjit coughed back into his pint as he was mid-slurp.

"Yeah, him, I've seen him at the club where I dance, pervy little fucker always taking a private dance and salivating into his drinks, I'm going to give him a private dance then knock him out if I see him, I'll say he touched me up, the security will back me," Mae Li scowled.

"Guys, let's not dwell on this too much. It's all negative. Let's think about something positive," smiled Innocence.

"Like what?" posed Surjit. The four of them sat in silence and looked at each other. Spencer contemplated how he would get away from singing at functions, driving Uncle Gary's van, and completing orders for his mate's internet gym equipment business. Surjit wondered if his mother was right and if he should update his CV and apply for a job as a software engineer. Innocence contemplated finding sponsorship to remain in the UK within the next two months before either staying illegally with little likelihood of well-paid work or accepting that she would have to return to South Africa with similar prospects. Mae Li considered what her next call to her father might be like if she admitted the project she held secret but had been working on had failed and that she should represent his business interests here to remain in the UK. They each held their thoughts a little longer and felt the pang of regret that the morning's prospects had not fulfilled their potential. The silence was broken,

"Let's get hammered. What are we drinking, same again? I'll get them," announced Spencer standing and unrolling two ten pounds notes from the bundle Mae Li had given him," he shot her a nervous glance. Mae LI looked back at him, and her steely look morphed into a smile, and she said,

"Sure, thanks to Spencer, and Spencer," he stopped in his tracks and turned back to look at her, "keep them coming, babes," he laughed handsomely and started to sing, "Can't take my eyes off of you" and better known as "I love you baby" by Frankie Valli and the Four seasons.

SATURDAY

Surjit snored himself awake, a big pig-sized snort that vibrated his eardrums to such an extent that they scrambled his brain into consciousness. It took a few moments for his eyes to focus, and then panic as the vista of a strange room drew into focus. He was not home and had not woken in any bed other than his own since leaving University nearly three years earlier. Where was he, and for that matter, who was he? Surjit Gosht was an entrepreneurial software developer who lived with his mother above a convenience store in Brook Drive, near the Elephant and Castle. Back to the first question, where was he? The room was dark, the curtains drawn, and clothes were strewn on the floor. He could feel warmth in the bed, a soft and gentle air tickling across the back of his neck. His feet stretched to touch the leg of another human being, and he moved his leg and foot with care and explored the limb of the person in bed with him. It was warm, firm and soft.

Surjit could not remember anything until this point. Think hard, he thought. He remembered the interview at Angeltech, the mortifying moment that the investment was snatched from his grasp cruelly and quickly as it had been offered minutes earlier. He remembered walking back to the Hive and sitting in the café area nursing a cup of coffee with Innocence, who had stopped for tea. Following this, they met Spencer and Mae Li in the Old Fountain. Everything after that blacked out. Alcohol was not good, his head hurt, and his mouth felt sore, dry, and sickly. The body next to him moved slightly.

Could it be that Surjit managed to score and head home with a woman in the purgatorial chasm of drunkenness? The dull, thudding ache in between his temples would be a price worth paying if the woman next to him was both attractive and remained at least indifferent that Surjit shared her bed. "Think hard, Surjit," he thought, "where did you meet her? Where did you go after the pub behind the Hive? What time did you stay out until? What time was it now, and was it still Friday or Saturday? Surjit's blood began to pump faster around his brain as the adrenaline demanded. It was not lost on him that following its journey from his cerebral cortex before returning to his heart, his blood went via his cock, which was starting to wake up too. This situation could become interesting. He was lying in bed wearing just his pants, tartan boxer shorts that belied his Indian heritage. A lovely pattern and flimsy enough to not support his cock, growing in stature like a snail's antennae emitting from its head following a stint inside its shell. Perhaps the analogy was not flattering to Surjit in terms of size but assuming it was scaled correctly, then that was accurate enough to reflect that Surjit had a morning glory hard-on that was pushing through the fly of his tartan boxers. The tepid breath stopped caressing his neck and a throat cleared from behind him. Who could it be he was about it find out? Surjit hoped she'd at least sound sexy and waited in exalted anticipation.

"Morning, darling, put the fucking kettle on. We've had a Weston," croaked the familiar North London overtones of Spencer fucking Churchill. Surjit's eyes widened, his mouth opened and his head spun around like the possessed girl in The Exorcist, and his cock retreated into his foreskin and pants like a sea urchin that had just been prodded by a snorkeller's spear gun.

"Mother of God, what are you doing here with me?" cried Surjit.

"You cheeky fucker, it's my bed. You insisted on coming back with me last night, and after you had polished off my Jägermeister, you crashed here. I'm not kipping on the couch or the floor, Surj, so I got in with you. I'm on my usual side. Now get that fucking kettle on. I've got a mouth as dry as a nun's snatch," rasped Spencer. Surjit groaned and apologized. What a week? He stepped out from the bed, checking there were no wardrobe malfunctions, Spencer was a man of the world, but Surjit still did not want to add to the embarrassment of waking in his bed. Instead, he used his feet to feel and fish for his trousers and shirt. Then, quickly dressed, Surjit headed for the bathroom to unleash more than a pint of urine that seemed to take forever to finish. Having gushed to a tinkle, then stopped, he started several times more. After a night of heavy drinking, it felt like his bladder was stretched like an uncooked pizza base. He made his way to the kitchen from where he filled the kettle, found the teabags, and minutes later poured two cups of tea topped with milk that, given it was Spencer's flat, was unusually in date. Spencer ambled in, yawning and scratching his scrotum before fumbling with the same hand in the bread bin and retrieving three slides of bread. It was all that was left.

"Toast?" he yawned again.

"Er, no thanks, I'm alright with a cup of tea, then I'll get off. My Mum will be wondering where I am?"

"No, she won't. You called her from here last night," replied Spencer.

"Shit, I called her? You're lying. What did I say? How did I sound?" shrieked Surjit.

"Shitfaced, and you told her you were moving out and in with me," remarked Spencer.

"I didn't, did I?" Surjit was anguished.

"Well paraphrased, yep, but don't worry, I think she hung up on you before you said too much," Spencer popped the bread into the toaster and dunked the leftover slice into his tea. Needs must. He was starving; they had not eaten since sandwiches at the Old Fountain over twenty hours ago. Surjit reached for his phone, three missed calls from his mother last night, and it was now twenty past eleven this morning. His head hurt, and the tea was a relief, added to which Spencer passed him two paracetamol and told him to knock them back. There were other messages too, Unicorn Joes, from Innocence and Mae Li, asking "guys, where are you?", sent at 9.30 p.m and repeated at 10.03 p.m the previous evening.

"What happened last night, where did we go, and what did we do?" asked Surjit.

"It's sketchy, but we had a fair few in the pub with some sandwiches. That was a good call, Innocence. We chopped pints and shots all afternoon, left at sixish, and were well pissed. We went over to a bar near Spitalfields that Mae Li knows. You got asked to leave when you started dancing on the table and refused to get down, and that was an instruction to get down from the table, not groovy get down. You were already groovy getting down, which is why you were asked to get down, if you get my drift? So after a couple of heavies pulled you off the table, we were thrown out. I think that's when we said we'd grab a kebab and meet the girls back outside at half nine, I'd guess, and go somewhere else, but we got waylaid, ended up in another bar because we met a couple of chicks outside, and we bought drinks and chatted with them. By the end, you could not stand up, Surj, so I called an Uber, grabbed you, and headed back here. That's when you got a third wind and had a nibble at the Jägermeister, but don't worry, there were only a few shots left, and thank God for that.

"It is scary. I don't remember any of it. I could have said and done anything, I could have woken up in a cell and be told I'd committed murder, and I would not be able to refute any of it,"

"Fuck I've got a message from a person called Linzi, *"Hi, Surj, this is my number. Call me soon, Linzi,"* read Surjit, astounded.

"You must remember Linzi?" posed Spencer.

"I wouldn't know her if she walked in here and pissed in my tea," appealed Surjit. Spencer laughed with a mouthful of dry toast. Surjit was beginning to sound like himself.

"Linzi, short, blonde, nice tits and a good giggle, works in development at Google. Mates with Sarah, who we met at Angeltech, you know the receptionist, do you remember her?" prompted Spencer.

"I remember her at Angeltech, but nothing after that. Honestly, everything is blank after the first few rounds and the sandwiches. After that, I blacked out, fuck me, I blacked out," groaned Surjit, and then he looked astonished, "Let's do what, what did I suggest to her?" He looked across at Spencer, who smiled, shook his head and recounted what happened as far as he could.

Spencer and Surjit were stumbling down Commercial Street when Spencer spotted two girls walking towards the Ten Bells pub on Commercial Street and the corner of Fournier Street. One of them looked familiar. She had a short wedged bob hairdo, a blue flowery blouse, and a white mini skirt. The girl from the reception at Angeltech had made Spencer some strong coffee and tried to help him get it together that morning.

"Hi there, remember me?" he shouted across, the girls stopped in their tracks, and Sarah recognizing Spencer, waved excitedly.

"He's the guy I told you about, fucking ace. Hi, Mr Churchill, Spencer, isn't it?" she shouted as he and Surjit approached.

"Yeah, and I'm Surjit," confirmed Surjit. "I'm not Sir Jeet, I'm not a knight of the realm, so I'm not Sir Jeet. I'm Surjit, just a mortal," he explained earnestly; nobody was confused, only Surjit.

"Hi, are you feeling any better? You were shitfaced this morning," smiled Sarah, looking at her friends nodding.

"Well, nothing's changed much since then; come on, I owe you a drink, you tried to help me out this morning, which I appreciate, so it's the least I can do. Come on, let's go in here," appealed Spencer, and the girls and Surjit followed him into the busy pub. They approached the old wooden bar in the centre of a bar bedecked by brown leather seating adjoining the walls and the large tiled mural depicting olden Spitalfields scenes. They ordered half lagers, which Spencer and Surjit were happy to match, given they'd already drunk through their capacity for beer.

"You caused quite a stir. Nobody's ever been sick in the boardroom before," laughed Sarah, who introduced her friend Linzi, a shorter girl with a large bust and cleavage on show.

"You never get a second chance to make a first impression, cheers!" cracked Spencer raising his glass, "I'm sorry you have to work with such wankers, assuming they're not friends," retorted Spencer.

"No apology needed. I'm only a receptionist, I started temping, and it led to a full-time offer, and it works for me because it's pretty quiet, and I can focus on what I like to do," shouted Sarah; the pub was noisy. Background music with a generic dance beat throbbed in the air.

"And what's that, help entrepreneurs in distress?" enquired Spencer.

"Ha-ha, yes, that as well. I like to write, nobody pays me for it, well not yet, but I get a lot of time to write, so in effect, it's like being paid twenty-eight grand a year to write, which if somebody offered me fifteen grand for a book, I'd take it, any day, so that's my story if you know what I mean? What's your story Spencer?" she asked, taking a sip of the lager. Linzi turned to Surjit to open a parallel conversation,

"Are you OK? Let's sit here," said Linzi, who pointed to a spare two seats. Surjit seemed a little unsteady on his feet. She would take one for the team since her best mate Sarah seemed interested in Spencer. She'd let their conversation develop long enough and alone for Spencer and Sarah to swap numbers, and then they'd regroup and head their separate ways. Linzi could chat with Surjit long enough for her half a lager to be downed and for them to excuse themselves after Sarah had finished hunting.

"Thanks, I don't usually drink, er; I do drink, of course, just rarely alcohol. It would be impossible not to drink, although some animals can get all their water requirements from water-rich foods, like the Kangaroo rat. It gets its water through the seeds it eats. Tortoises in the Sonaran desert survive by drinking their urine. Still, it begs the question of which came first? The urine they drank or the urine they peed, never mind. There's the thorny devil, that's thorny, not horny, Spencer's a horny devil you know, you're not interested in the thorny devil are you, if you are google it, but not humans we need to drink daily, 3 days without water. You would be close to death, which is probably the same as ten hours with a lot of alcohol the way I'm feeling." Surjit smiled, pulled an ironic grin, and focussed on Linzi. He noticed she was small in stature, with blonde-coloured hair and an ample bust accentuated by a low-cut t-shirt that exposed a cleavage upon which a gold heart was suspended from a gold-plated chain. She laughed at his clumsy but intelligent response.

"Ten hours? Did you start drinking at midday? Good darts Surjit, why the early start?" posed Linzi.

"We all pitched, sorry that's Spencer, Mae Li, and Innocence, that's friends, who we left at another bar. I got asked to leave because I was dancing on the tables, which was not good given that I couldn't dance and the tables were full of glassware. So we all pitched our respective ideas for investment this morning at the company where Sarah works as a receptionist. We all met earlier this week, and we agreed to meet after to celebrate or commiserate." Surjit was surprisingly lucid; despite ducking several rounds, he'd consumed several pints of session lager and several shots after a lifetime of abstinence.

"And are you celebrating or commiserating?" asked Linzi, intrigued by his answer.

"Regrettably, and certainly in the morning because I am completely pissed, not in celebration but defeat. My idea for an optimization utility for mobile devices was not considered as investable, rather boring, compared to a time travel device or a potion that immediately sobers you up. Still, the upside is I'm intoxicated enough to have the confidence to hold a conversation with somebody as lovely as you. Without excess alcohol, which until I met that man, I swore I'd never touch, I would be tongue-tied and unable to engage in eye contact or conversation. That's the sad truth," Surjit smiled uninhibitedly and looked directly at Linzi, who held his gaze.

"I'm sorry to hear that, not the boozy bit, I mean the investor part. I'm sure you will find another," consoled Linzi.

"No, I don't think so. The same problem undermines the concept regardless of the investor, and I won't bore you anymore with that. I'll bore you with something else. What about you, what do you do?" asked Surjit, changing tact.

"I'm a software engineer," replied Linzi. "I'm working on a cloud project. Just general business app integration stuff, nothing too heavy or low-level like yours."

"Oh cool, freelance or for a company, and for how long?"

"I work for a small business integrator. It has been two years now, the work is quite varied, and I can be wherever I like most of the time but get paid for being in London," nodded Linzi.

"Getting paid, that part I like the sound of," stuttered Surjit.

"You can get paid work easily, Surjit, a man with considerable talents," she nodded.

"Not as considerable as yours," Surjit meant politely but dropped his inebriated gaze towards her fully endowed chest as he said it. He quickly averted his attention elsewhere and then drew it back to Linzi, hoping she overlooked the indiscretion.

"Give me your phone; I'll give you my number; we can connect on Linkedin,"

"Definitely interested in contacting you. How about tomorrow?" suggested Surjit fumbling for his phone. Linzi laughed,

"I mean for networking, maybe to help get a job," said Linzi, adding her details to Surjit's phone.

"Have you pulled Surj? You're a fast mover," laughed Spencer, noticing the activity and wrapping his arm around Surj's shoulder.

"Just networking," replied Surjit smiling and then asked Linzi. "If not tomorrow, maybe we could network Sunday? It's going to be fine. We could go down to Brighton; After all these years, I've never been."

"I'll think about it," said Linzi, looking at Sarah.

"Thanks, I will too," replied Surjit. As he spoke, his eyes closed slowly.

"Hey, Surj, let's go home, bud. You can come back to my place," barked Spencer, grabbing Surjit's arm and pulling him up.

Any recollection or thought in Spencer's kitchen hurt Surj's throbbing head. Alcohol was terrible, and the liberty of his inhibitions came at a painful cost the following day. How long was he to feel like this? What was the cure? Going home and burying himself in his bed for the rest of the weekend seemed like a good idea. But, his mum would not allow that. Work in the store downstairs beckoned stacking booze; it would make him sick.

"You were too fucked up to leave in a Cab on your own, so I brought you here," Spencer knocked back the tea and reached for the kettle; another cup was required. Surjit screwed his eyes together, struggling to his feet and said,

"Thanks, Spence; I gotta go home and die. It was nice getting to know you this week. You changed my life. I'm not sure in a good way, but you changed it, Spencer Churchill."

"Fuck off. You need to go home, have a big greasy breakfast, a bigger greasier shit, a hot shower and an even hotter mug of tea, and you'll be right as rain, my son. See you around, stay in touch and be lucky."

Ten miles further South from Barnet, Innocence woke to unfamiliar surroundings. The ceiling was higher than the one she was used to seeing in her Dalston bedroom, it was painted brilliant and white, and the room was large. Her bed was a large comfortable sofa, and the cushions were soft like pillows. She remembered that this was Mae Li's flat. She had been here earlier during the week, but what was she doing now? Her memory muscles flexed but were too weak to stir a response. Go back to the beginning and take it from there, she thought. Today was Saturday; therefore, yesterday was Friday. So far, so good. The day started with breakfast with her sister, as usual, then the walk to the Angeltech office for the interview and the pit of her stomach ached as she recalled the rejection, like waking to remember the love of your life had dumped you. She remembered the consolatory milky tea and chocolate in the Starbucks by Old Street and then meeting Surjit on the short walk to the pub near the Hive. Spencer insisted everybody try several beers, a roast beef sandwich with a hot horseradish sauce, and a falafel flatbread for Surjit. More drinks and then a walk to the city to a bar near Spitalfields; it had naked flames outside, a dark bar with cool and trendy people quaffing overpriced drinks. Mae Li paid for everything. They were drinking shots, tiny tumblers the size of egg cups full of toffee vodka, fruit-flavoured spirits, and some tasting medicinal.

What time was that? She remembered it was past nine o'clock because her sister messaged her to ask her where she was, and Innocence replied that she was fine, in a bar with the Unicorn Joes and not to worry. And then Surjit climbed onto the table as the rumba beat intensified, and security officers asked him to step down. Surjit slipped, and the security guys caught him and suggested he leave, and Spencer agreed to escort him off and get a coffee with some food. So they went, and it was the last they saw of them. The WhatsApp group was updated that Spencer and Surjit were getting a taxi back to Spencer's flat, having had one last drink at another pub. So that was around ten o'clock, then what? Innocence closed her eyes and thought hard, and then it came back like a jackhammer drilled to the back of her head.

"Hi, my name is Trevor. I work over at UBS; haven't we met somewhere before?" asked the tall, well-built black guy, smartly dressed in a black shirt and indigo denim jeans with brown brogues. Trevor was good-looking, with a warm, genuine smile and eyes that sparked mischief.

"I don't think so. I don't work there. In fact, as of today, I don't work anywhere," replied Innocence, her words a little slurred.

"Oh, I'm sorry, did you lose your job, or did you quit?" asked Trevor before sipping his drink.

"Neither really. I was working on a project that I hoped to receive funding for. Today it got turned down, that's all." Innocence sounded sad, she was, and she glanced down as she spoke. The brown brogues were smart.

"Can't you look elsewhere for investment? There have got to be other avenues," suggested Trevor.

"Yes, I can, but I'm running out of time, and besides, I think the reasons they turned me down are justified, meaning other investors may feel the same way," she countered. He nodded sagely,

"Tell me about it. I'm interested to know,"

"I've always played computer games, not the epic types, smaller fun pastime games, simple things please simple minds,

I guess. But, I studied this market as part of my business degree, and I had an idea to create a game that would become popular and make money. So, that's what I've been developing, a prototype, and I showed the demo and the business plans to some investors today, but they didn't like it," she smiled bravely.

"Why not? What was the objection?" he asked.

"Not different enough, market too crowded, the theme was too common, cats and dogs, candies, kittens and puppies, all things nice, sugar and spice," she laughed; Trevor laughed too,

"What's your name?"

"Innocence,"

"Innocence, you're adorable, and I like the idea of your game," he added.

"Can UBS fund me?" she asked.

"I'm afraid that's not something I can answer. I work in Foreign Exchange, I'm not sure we're the investor you'd be looking for, but I'll ask around, have you a number I can reach you on?" he closed. Innocence produced her phone, took his number, and sent her details.

"Hi, everything OK, babe?" asked Mae Li, feeling protective of her.

"Yeah, all is good, this is Trevor, Trevor, this is Mae Li," introduced Innocence.

"Clever Trevor, are you chatting up my friend?" asked Mae Li sternly,

"Er, no, we were talking about her business idea, and I have offered to ask around, that's all", stammered Trevor. Mae Li glared at him.

"Then why the fuck not? She's gorgeous, or do you prefer men, Trevor?"

"No, I don't prefer men, I prefer beautiful women like Innocence, and I have her number, so I guess the ball is in my court, so to speak," he glared back and smiled slightly.

Huh, the tennis match, we agreed to play tennis today thought Innocence back in the room; I don't feel like that at all, perhaps we should not show up.

"Morning babes, you slept, OK?" asked Mae Li, wafting into the room wearing a silk gown, it was white, see-through, and she wore no underwear. Innocence was heterosexual, but she admired female beauty, and Mae Li's figure was svelte-like and fit.

"Yes, thank you. Aren't we supposed to play tennis today?"

"No commitment made, and no, I'm not interested. How about a detox smoothie, some yoghurt, and granola?" replied Mae Li.

"I could murder a bacon sandwich, brown sauce," Innocence was reminded of the first day she met Spencer and the doorstep bacon sandwich he cradled with the sauce licked from the corners of his mouth.

"The only meat that passes my lips, babe, belongs to a big, fit fucker, and no, I don't swallow. I tell them straight, if you come in my mouth, I'll bite your cock off, tell me when you're ready to jack, and kiss your balls, but if I taste cum, then you're fucking done!"

"Who said romance was dead?" replied Innocence drily.

"Has he been in touch?" asked Mae Li.

"Who?" asked Innocence, wondering if she meant Trevor.

"Trevor," Mae Li mimicked the posh nuanced tonality of Trevor, clearly privately educated unless he was a former grammar schoolboy, no rough south London overtones on his nouns and verbs. Innocence checked her phone, an exchange between her and her sister around midnight telling her she was heading back with Mae Li. Mae Li insisted she would be safer going home with her. Nothing from Trevor, not yet. He wasn't interested in her. Finally, he politely offered to ask around for investment; that would be the last of it.

"No, he won't be in touch. However, it was kind of him to offer to ask around," replied Innocence.

"He fancied the pants off you, babe. He was eyeing you up for twenty minutes before he came over. You can tell when a man fancies you. He's got that look," advised Mae Li.

"What look, what's *that* look?" asked Innocence, sitting up on the couch and straightening the cushions.

"Like a dog eyeing a bone or a wolf prowling a flock of sheep, they may be smiling, laughing or playing it straight, but their eyes give it away, their pupils enlarge, amongst other things," Mae Li giggled, and Innocence noticed this, it was not often Mae Li did this.

"Does Spencer give you that look?" asked Innocence. Mae Li's smile dropped, and she paused.

"No, he does not, babes," and she turned away to the open plan kitchen to fetch the breakfast items, and that was what bothered her about Spencer Churchill; she wanted to shag his brains out, but the feeling was not mutual.

"Mae Li?" called out Innocence.

"Yes, babe"

"I don't suppose you have any chocolate, have you?"

"No, I don't suppose I have; now eat your fucking muesli and yoghurt, babe."

Later that evening, Mae Li clicked the red leave button from a web call with her father. He was calling her in, either representing his business interests in Europe from London or any other city in Europe that she cared to reside in or to return to China because the financial taps that untethered the cash flow to a tidy lifestyle were being turned off. She had her chance, and the outcome was not unexpected; the only sticking point now was a salary. She asked for five hundred thousand's per year, which he considered far too much without results. She reconsidered her request and then lowered her demand but conditional to an additional request which, following some debate and deliberation, her father agreed to. She decided to start working for the business on Monday morning, building the plan and company. Tomorrow was Sunday. She would go for a five-mile run-up to Regent's Park and back, listen to the strained cries of the peacocks at the zoo, and then enjoy a breakfast of bacon, eggs, and mushrooms with a cup of breakfast tea. It was an indulgence, naughty but nice, as the English said. Then she would join the call and share her news with the Unicorn Joes. She tapped out an invite to the group, pressed send, and went to her bathroom. After the bathroom visit, she was ready for bed, retrieved her toy from its drawer, lay back with her head rested on the pillow, and closed her eyes. It was time to dream.

SATURDAY

It was Saturday night. Spencer and Midnight Sun had belted out a version of "let me entertain you" by Robbie Williams at a wedding in Bushey. He was dripping in sweat as he made his way off the stage to the makeshift dressing room, usually a meeting room at the hotel where the reception was being held. Two drunken and gregarious aunties grabbed him for a clinch, and one of them squeezed his damp arse cheek before he managed to slip away to find refuge. It was like a scene from a male strip troupe. The band manager helped load some of the kits into a large van and promised to drop Spencer off at his girlfriend's house in Croxley Green on the way home. He tapped two hundred and fifty pounds into Spencer's PayPal account and wished him a good night until next week's gig, a retirement party for the local VW dealer in Uxbridge. Spencer had not heard from Chantelle today. He finally thought about her as he approached her house. She was sulking and still on the blob, so best let her mood play out. She'd be pleased to see him, at last. Spencer trotted up the path to Chantelle's parent's semi-detached home that backed onto the Metropolitan line; he had his key. The gigs paid his rent and housekeeping, with other temporary work topping up a modest monthly allowance. Still, the reality had dawned on him that his flurry in the world of hi-tech, start-up funding, and becoming a millionaire was a pipedream and that thinking of pipes, he might as well learn to be a plumber; his Uncle Gary had offered an apprenticeship. He should take up the offer while there was still time. Uncle Gary was not going to keep going forever. Still, the quarterly all-inclusive fortnights in Spain did not come that cheap, and there were other treats for which his younger second wife desired, which meant he was likely to be foraging behind u bends for some time. Spencer turned the key at the front door, but the door didn't open; something was still stuck fast. He tried again, and the same result meant he was standing waggling the key on the doorstep; he was tired and wanted to sleep after sex. Yes, she was still on her period, but she could pick up the remote; that would do. Chantelle would oblige; she always did. After another failed attempt with the key, he withdrew his phone, tapped a quick note, and then pressed to send. It was late, approaching midnight and her folks were asleep or in bed. It was rude to knock them up,

"Hun, I am at the door key won't work. Come down and let me in."

Spencer waited a few moments, then resent the message. No reply. Maybe Chantelle had nodded off waiting for him; he'd have to call. He selected the phone option and waited for almost a minute for her to answer; dozy cow, it rang out some more before, at last,

"Hi, I'm at the doorstep. The fucking key won't work. Can you come down?" Chantelle declined and informed Spencer she was tired and not letting him in; the door was latched.

"What do you mean you're not coming down? it's been a long gig, don't fuck about Chantelle; come down and let me in." Chantelle explained that she would not change her mind; he should leave and go home to his bed.

"Oh, you still sulking about Thursday night? OK, I'm sorry I didn't call or text on Friday. I went out with some business associates. I did not get my funding. I had a bad day. Spencer is a tired puppy, missing his little kitten. Can she come down and let him in, and Spencer will stroke her to sleep after kitten has stroked Spencer's lickle puppy dog tail?" Spencer morphed into a baby-toned conversation that she liked, hoping this would provide a conclusive action, which to his surprise, it did. Chantelle morphed back into her kitten-toned voice, excepting the last five words that were expressed in the most exemplary South Hertfordshire dialect,

"Kitten will not come down because Spencer is a selfish puppy, so fuck off, you cunt," and the line closed. Spencer considered his options. The tube was shut. The buses were likely finished in this neck of the woods too. A cab back to Barnet took a bullseye out of his gig money. So walk around to Mum for tonight. It was forty minutes away at a brisk pace. He skipped down the path, and his phone pinged. He knew it would. She was putty in his hands, the daft bird, and had changed her mind. It was a message on Unicorn Joe's app,

"Face call tomorrow midday. That means getting up, Spencer! Bye babes, Mae Li xxx."

Spencer found both the note and the timing of it a little odd. Maybe Mae Li had gone for the second bottle of wine. But, on the other hand, he was more preoccupied that he still had forty minutes to walk over to his parent's house. Then, at least, Daisy, the Rottweiler, would be pleased to see him. So he replaced his phone in his trousers pocket and set off at a brisk pace for the other side of Watford, signing as he went, "all by myself, don't want to be, all by myself, anymore."

Innocence sat watching T.V with Agnes, a Netflix movie about a fugitive, not The Fugitive, but a similar plot, a man on the run from the law for something he did not do. Still, her attention waned from the storyline to the more compelling matter of her future. Was she becoming a fugitive and running as an illegal immigrant in the UK? What problems could that cause her sister, who was here legally through sponsored employment at the small investment company she worked for? Could Trevor come up trumps with finding an alternative investment if Trevor ever spoke to her again? Mae Li must have scared him off, she frightened men with her aggressive and assertive attitude, but he had looked across at Innocence once more before he left the bar that evening. Should Innocence make the first move and contact him? No, that would appear too desperate, but then, that's what she was. The time inched on towards midnight, and the film ended, the man was caught, but by then, he had established his innocence, Innocence on the run, how ironic she thought. She couldn't be arsed to play casual games as she often would. She could not face gameplay for a while. Agnes had gone to bed, and it was time for Innocence to follow the same path. Her single bed was waiting in her little room with the bedside table, and lamp lit to make it cosy. She placed her phone down and muttered a small prayer; it was selfless as ever. The lamp switched off, and the room fell dark, except the light from her phone buzzing in vibration to the message received.

"Face call tomorrow midday. That means getting up, Spencer! Bye babes, Mae Li xxx"

Surjit watched his mother fall asleep on the couch. She was tired and worked long hours in the convenience store downstairs. It was not her business but a family friend, and she worked hard to maintain a rent-free allowance for her work. Food and provisions were a part of the deal, and although Surjit was never hungry, she never exceeded what might reasonably be owed. Surjit's father died from a heart attack when Surjit was much younger at school. His father smoked two packets of cigarettes a day; although teetotal, it was the fags that did for him, clogging arteries and choking his lungs that pushed a weakened heart too far one day. It was painful for his mother to serve other victims tightly cellophaned packets of the same coffin nails to other victims, nearly always too poor to consume the habit. They forewent good food and fresh items in a vicious double whammy of lousy health living, but the drug didn't care, and neither did they, existing in a mutual state of neither giving a fuck, once the habit was embedded in the nerves. He should get a job and pay down the deposit on a flat or a house, somewhere with a room for his mother. A prospective wife would have to understand that he could not let his mother work beyond her sixties and into her seventies and ultimately into her grave. He had been selfish with his dogged persistence and pursuit of Spanner, a trait any successful entrepreneur requires. But for every lucky one that boasted of tough times as their plans took shape, more maintained a meagre existence before mediocrity and normality had formed their death spiral habit. For every Del Boy that became a millionaire, a hundred Triggers were pushing so hard at their brooms that none had noticed that despite being replaced with multiple new handles and heads, new or the same old broom, they were still pushing behind a fucking broom. First thing tomorrow, CV update, Linkedin profile updated to open to offers, and search the job boards on it and Glassdoor and other tech vendors he could approach directly. His phone pinged a message which stirred his mother, who tutted, tired but sternly, but by then, Surjit had opened it to read,

"Face call tomorrow midday. That means getting up, Spencer! Bye babes, Mae Li xxx"

SUNDAY

Innocence stopped by the brick wall near Spitalfields, low enough to perch upon and check her mobile phone. She opened Strava, paused the activity, and surveyed the results. 6.5km completed in 1 hour and 5 minutes. She had 3.5km to complete, which meant over 400 calories burned for a young person of 70 kilos, or 11 stones in old money; not impressive, but well-meaning social friends would offer their kudos. Her sister followed her anyway, but another small deposit into the chocolate bank. Sadly, this bank gave no interest, as long and loyal a customer as Innocence had been. It was half-past ten, and she would comfortably manage the two miles left to return home before the midday call with Mae Li and the others; she wondered what she wanted? Perhaps to stay in touch and maybe lunch next week? It was surprising that Mae Li had sent the note. Surjit could understand doing so. After all, he had done so much to engineer the group coming and staying together, but Mae Li was the coldest fish amongst them. With a deep intake of breath, she stood erect and gathered her pace to finish the morning's exercise. There was less traffic, the air was relatively clean, and the sun peeked through the clouds, which was a consolation to her, given she was faced with finding sponsored employment or an air ticket home before the summer was out. She felt the buzz of her phone against her thigh, hidden by her tracksuit trousers, and she was too curious to let it rest, so she retrieved it from her pocket. Her heart jumped, and she stopped in her tracks as the sender's identity came into view. Trevor had sent a message.

Hi, Innocence. It is such a lovely morning, and I thought of you, so I am saying hello. I enjoyed meeting and talking to you Friday evening. Do you even remember me? You were pretty tipsy, but if you still want to meet, we could go for a walk and coffee later this afternoon, or if busy, maybe lunch this week. I'm free tomorrow. Let me know, please, or you can let me down. Just be gentle ☺ love Trevor x

She re-read the message and then again for a third and fourth time. A walk this afternoon? That would be great, more calories burned, a walk to where and from where? Would it be seriously uncool to reply yes, right now? Did she want to respond with a yes immediately? Why wait? If she lingered, he might make plans. The afternoon was only an hour and a half away. Love Trevor x. He'd sent love and a kiss; this made her feel like a schoolgirl again. She smiled and started to walk; her pace quickened. She felt emboldened. People passed her in the street; nobody knew what she knew, that somebody wanted to take her out, walk and have lunch with her. Was it too soon to call Trevor her boyfriend? That would scare him off, play it cool, treat them mean, keep them keen was the adage her mother would recount. Yeah, play it cool and don't raise your hopes too high. Look what happened this week because of that. She walked a few paces more, then stopped and tapped a reply,

Hi, Trevor, of course, I remember you, how could I not? A walk later sounds lovely, where shall we meet? Love Innocence x

She sent love and a kiss, well he had started it, and it would be rude not to, neither did it signify any expectation. Within two minutes of Trevor's invitation, he had received his reply, and the one he hoped for had boiled before his kettle that he had set after his message. He drank his green herbal tea and formed a reply, a walk around St James's Park would be perfect; meet at Green Park, walk down through it and to St James's and stop for ice cream at one of the vans adjacent to the park, the one's with the cornet base, whippy vanilla cream, and flake, called a sixty-nine, wasn't it? He'd ask her if she fancied one when they drew closer. He was sure she'd be up for it.

Surjit was stacking shelves at the store below the flat where he and his mother lived. He sat on a footstool while pushing a stack of tins on the lower shelf. Spam! Chopped pork and ham, the label read. What was the difference between pork and specifically ham? Such things could not be ignored by Surjit, and they would eat away at him unless he dealt with them there and then. He checked the internet answer from his phone to be told Ham was explicitly from the leg of a pig, whereas pork corresponded to other areas but typically the shoulder. Therefore, Spam was the front and back of a pig, or in general terms, pork. Spam was chopped pork. Not just pork but chopped pork, as if you could get pork into a small rectangular tin the size of your hand by any other means than chopping it. He examined the tin closer, and the label revealed that besides chopped pork and ham, Spam contained starch, water, salt, and ham (2%). Was this Ham inclusive or in addition to the ham detailed in the chopped pork and ham? If it was the ham inclusive to the chopped pork and ham, then it was a minuscule amount given that it was claimed that 90% of Spam was chopped pork and ham. So it was not worth mentioning unless it gave Spam an element of being a higher quality foodstuff than it was, but who would not buy Spam because it did not include ham. However, wasn't the "am" in ham that gave it the name Spam, thought Surjit?

The other ingredients were sugar, stabilizer (Triphosphates), flavourings, antioxidant (Sodium Ascorbate), and a preservative (Sodium Nitrite). Spam was a registered trademark created in 1937 by Hormel foods, which must have the most incredible advertising endorsement in the history of companies, products, and language when spam became synonymous with dodgy emails or any unsolicited digital message. He wondered how the Monty Python sketch made several decades earlier had managed to tag that specific activity with Spam. Still, however it did, spam did not go a day without being mentioned to anybody who touched a computer. Did subliminal messaging work? Indeed, if it were the case, every IT security professional bought a tin of Spam daily or at least weekly. Surjit had never tried Spam. He was not a Muslim, but neither did he eat pork or ham, not on religious grounds, but he simply did not like the taste.

Furthermore, pork was regarded as the closest flesh to humans. Hence early explorers were referred to as long pigs by cannibal tribes. Given the similarity in taste and fact, Surjit could not clear from his mind.

Surjit was about to start on a fresh box of alternate products and, no doubt, an inquisition into other useless and trivial facts aligned to whatever produce lay undiscovered in the brown container when his phone alerted him to an incoming message. Perhaps it was spam. He smiled at the irony of this thought, but he was shocked when he saw the name Linzi as the sender, and he stood up in a mix of anxiety and excitement. He drew in a deep inhalation of breath and tapped the screen to reveal the message,

"Hey Surjit, it's Linzi. We met Friday. Feel shit yesterday, did we? Remember Brighton? We could get the 13.08 from London Bridge, and we are on the beach at half-past two. Let me know. It's a nice day for networking ☺ "

Surjit was stunned and rechecked the message, sure he remembered Linzi. This morning in bed, he had reached for his sock, thinking about her. It was a ten-minute walk up to London Bridge station, he was due to finish in the shop at midday and planned to dial Mae Li's call before working through applications, but that could all wait until Monday. This was an honest date, no tattoos, lifted shoes and bullshit, just Surjit and his charm and wit. But, without the alcohol, would he revert to quiet but sanguine Surjit, pleasant, sympathy invoking, but not fanciable. He'd have to call Spencer to get some advice, which landed him with Jojo and humiliation. But think logically, she was a techie. Speeds and feeds could monitor the train speed with his GPS speedometer app, check the flight paths of overhead planes with his upgraded flight tracker, and talk about agile software development. He didn't need to look like he could play rugby to discuss being a scrum master in software engineering. Time was moving on; best to reply now and finish up the stock refresh, no diversionary anal attentive disorder like with the Spam tins; however, that was a subject he could mention later, at the right time, wait for the moment. Back to the message, he replied quickly,

"Hi Linzi, so glad you messaged me. Brighton sounds right on. See you on the platform at 13.08. 😉 Surj."

No sooner was it tapped than sent, but then he wondered if the winking emoji was a bit pervy?. Perhaps he should clarify that emoji or not; just leave it, stop being boring, Surjit, and be playful. So he opened the last cardboard box of produce with a scratch of his Stanley knife and pulled out a tin. It was custard from Ambrosia, or as it was classically known in Greek, nectar from the Gods; how apt he thought, Linzi, not the custard.

Spencer threw his arm around her, and she responded with a kiss and a gentle whimper; so beautiful, he thought. She had solid shoulders but a sweet nature, even if she was always going to be a bitch.

"I love you, darling," he whispered, and she groaned with pleasure back at him, a faint little whine as her bottom was scratched delicately by Spencer's long and elegant middle finger. He felt her tongue exploring his ear, cold, wet, a little sloppy but tickling. Spencer heard the door push open, and his mother entered the room,

"Daisy, get off the bed. But, Spencer, don't encourage her, you big soppy twat," and the big rottweiler rolled over and sprang off the bed, pushing against Spencer's abdomen as she completed the manoeuvre.

"Were you talking about the dog or me?" he grunted.

"Both of you, if you treated your girlfriend with as much love and care as you did, Daisy, you wouldn't be waking me up at half past midnight to let you in. So get up and come downstairs. There are bacon, eggs, toast and a mug of tea on the table ready for you, so get down there quick. I don't want it going cold," snapped his mum. Spencer waited for his mum to leave the room. He couldn't pull the sheets back and lay there with a hard-on. She'd done this years before, Spencer was in bed masturbating, running late for school, and his mum came in, barking orders, and snatched the duvet from the bed. She tutted loudly and walked out with nothing said as he attempted to cover his erect prick with one hand while retrieving the duvet with the other. Neither could look each other in the eye until a day later, and he thought both were reminded of the incident as he scolded Daisy, but there was no chance of her repeating the act. He yawned, stretched, and yawned again, then checked his phone; no messages. Just the one from Mae Li, it was half-past ten on Sunday morning. He'd have breakfast, take a dump and a shower, and join the call afterwards.

What could she want on a Sunday lunchtime? If it was an invite round to her gaff or even out for a Sunday lunch, she could fuck off; he wasn't in the mood. He was tired from the gig, still felt shit from the Thursday to Saturday bender, and confused about how he felt about Chantelle. Did he deserve that, to be blown out on the doorstep? Was he a selfish cunt?

As she delicately put it, she rarely swore. Must she have been angry to say this? He loved her. She knew then why he had to show it or say it? Women were strange. He loved his closest mates. They knew it, he knew it; they never had to say it or show it in displays of affection; they just knew it. He sat on the bed, his hard-on subsided, and his nuts loosened enough to scratch and pinch the scrotal skin that itched him. Fuck, please, not another dose; the scratch felt better. Daisy liked to sniff and lick his groin, which Spencer let her do. There was no sexual pleasure in it for either of them, so he did not consider it bestial or deviant, just love between them.

Daisy had thundered down the stairs with what little grace a hundred pounds rottweiler could muster, her big brown rump rocking from side to side with each descending step and her stubby tail wagging. She could smell the bacon, and Spencer always gave her the fat. Spencer selected Chantelle's name and prepared a message. With digits tapped onto a keyboard, how do people convey life, death, feelings, invitations, jokes, and everything? So many words face redundancy because they could be abbreviated or just too long to be bothered with for typing a message in text, Whatsapp or any other digital format. Spencer thought about his grandmother. They had kept their love letters in shoeboxes from years ago, sent from their fiancées, who later became their husbands. The delicate pages tied together by ribbons, written in ink on paper, faded by the years, but the words and meanings were as permanent as when they were etched on the surface and sealed in envelopes with loving kisses. The joy of receiving a love letter and treasuring the correspondence for hours, days, or weeks is now replaced by the ping from an electronic device and lost or archived minutes later. Parchment letters from pastel colours sprayed and marked with perfumes, flowers, and aftershaves, written in handwriting as personal as each fingerprint on the planet, replaced by a generic, ubiquitous, condensed font adorned with costless and efficient smiling emojis. The longing to receive words from a loved one, relieved by a postman's plod up the path after days, maybe weeks of waiting, now satisfied with a few characters tapped and sent with a love heart in a matter of seconds. Thank fuck for that, he thought as he aborted the message, replaced his phone in his pocket and skipped down the stairs to start the day with a brunch. Living in the past must have been a fucking nightmare.

"Where's Dad? Can he give me a lift to the station?" he asked his mother as she placed the sandwich in front of him on the kitchen table. Daisy edged closer to him and licked her lips.

"I don't know; ask him yourself; he's in the dining room," she replied, splashing hot water and a squeeze of fairly liquid on the frying pan that she had placed into the sink, no need to run a bowl for one pan.

"Dad, give me a lift to the station?" shouted Spencer through to the adjoining room where his Dad sat staring earnestly at his monitor in the middle of the dining room table, a cable running from it and into the boxy computer whirring underneath.

"Can't, son, I've got a job on," replied his Dad abruptly with the seriousness that made it sound like a life or death mission.

"You don't work, Dad, what job? Cash in hand?" yelled Spencer between chewing the sandwich, and he pulled the fat from the bacon, which Daisy devoured gratefully and licked his fingers. Then, Spencer applied the same hand that fed her to secure the sandwich for another bite.

"He's taken up train driving," sighed his mum, placing the pan on the drainer.

"Driving trains?" exclaimed Spencer; this didn't make sense.

"Yeah, you know, on his computer, virtual trains. So he's done the training; he sits there for hours," added his mum folding her arms like a complaining mother, pushing up her drooping chest.

"It's only a short job. It's a class 323 from Stevenage to Kings Cross, only four stops. I'll be thirty-five minutes if you can wait." countered Winston Churchill. Spencer shook his head slowly and popped the last corner of the sandwich into Daisy's drooling chops, her stubby tail wagging gratefully.

"You can pause the game Dad; it's virtual, you can fuck off around the world for 80 days, and it'll still be there waiting for you at the same point when you get back," exclaimed Spencer.

"Language, Spencer darling", chastised his mother, who added, "yeah fuck off that silly game and drive your son to the station, you silly bollocks."

"I've started, so I'll finish," Winston retorted.

"Yeah haven't I heard that before," shot back Spencer's mother. Spencer stood up and peaked into the dining room, where Winston sat studiously adorned with a headset.

"Look just a minute, good morning, ladies and gentlemen. This is your driver speaking; welcome to the 10.23 from Stevenage to Kings Cross; we're just about to get underway. We will call at Knebworth, Welwyn North, Hatfield and "Chipping Fuckbury," added Spencer.

"And Chipping, eh? Fuck off, Spence, you ruined my announcement," fumed his father. "I'm resetting the journey, that's cost you five minutes delay, and you've only yourself to blame. Good morning, ladies and gentlemen…" and Winston restarted his announcement. Spencer kissed Daisy and his mother goodbye and set out to walk the two miles to the station and left his father to concentrate on delivering his train and its virtual occupants from Stevenage to Kings Cross or somewhere on route.

"Hi guys, how are you all?" asked Mae Li, smiling, her face amplified by the face time web call.

"Brilliant, fantastic, yeah, alright", were the replies from Innocence, Surjit, and Spencer, respectively.

"Sounds great, babes, and how have your weekends been so far?" she asked.

"Brilliant, fantastic, yeah, alright", were the replies from Innocence, Surjit, and Spencer, respectively.

"Yeah, mine too, thanks for asking," she muttered drily.

"Trevor messaged me; we're meeting up later, isn't that exciting?" blurted Innocence.

"Babe, that's brilliant; oh, call me after you have to tell me everything," resounded Mae Li.

"I will. I hope there's a lot to tell," giggled Innocence. Spencer sighed audibly.

"And I'm going down to Brighton with Linzi, assuming she turns up and doesn't think I'm a perv," exclaimed Surjit.

"Er, and who is Linzi? Is this another date from the app?" asked Mae Li,

"No, I've deleted that. Spencer and I bumped into the receptionist from Angeltech on Friday after we left you guys, and she had a mate called Linzi. I asked her out. Yes, me, asking a girl out, And I thought she'd never follow up and contact me, and well, she just did, Unless you're setting me up, Spencer," squealed Surjit.

"Why would she think you are a perv, babe?" asked Mae Li.

"I replied with a winking emoji," replied Surjit.

"So long as it was winking and not wanking you're probably ok, Bro," Spencer could not help to add. The others laughed.

"So what about you, Spencer? Are you going out with Chantelle today? Such a nice day, and the sun is out?" added Mae Li.

"Nah, we split up last night," he drawled. There was a short awkward silence.

"Oh, you want to talk about it?" Mae Li asked softly.

"No, I fucked up, that's all; move on," Spencer replied. There was another short pause.

"I was talking to my father last night and informed him that my business plan still requires further funding, which is unlikely to happen in the short term. So my option is to continue with that endeavour without additional financial support from him or join his company as his international representative based in London. I agreed conditionally to do this, but there was a caveat that I insisted upon. I told him I required help from a small, talented, trusted team to work with me. First, I need a marketing and customer success manager, Innocence, who could manage the necessity for engaging digital content to reach out to new clients whilst taking care of existing contracts with respect and attainable service levels. Second, I asked for a business development executive Spencer, who could focus on growing new markets and prospects, somebody charismatic and resourceful, whilst I maintained and expanded the key relationships. We could work on your charisma! Finally, I suggested that a technical and product director Surjit must come on board to grasp the underlying new technologies embedded in his electrical products. This brainy person could embellish the added value of such emerging technology over incumbent competitors. I suggested I could work with three new hires to form a management team with three young, talented people I knew here in London. I did not mention that these are not average Joes, but Unicorn Joes like me, ambitious and who I like and could work with even if one did get on my tits a bit. Three executives could help manage this business and have the time and drive for adventurous side projects hidden from my father's view. Do you get my drift? As equal partners, formed in our own company, Unicorn Joes Incorporated, pool our talents and keep our dreams going for a billion with our ideas and new ones. I can get sponsorship for Innocence to stay in the UK. I can offer a competitive salary that will appease your mother, Surjit. And. a regular job and career will give you the start and stability you need and deserve, even if it is on your own, Spencer Churchill.

There was a combined sense of disbelief, hope and fear that this could not be true.

"Well, you're all very quiet. What do you say?"

"Brilliant" screamed Innocence.

"It'll have to be Unicorn Joes Limited unless you want to call it Unicorn Joes Inc. Ltd, to comply with U.K company naming conventions," asserted Surjit before being told abruptly to shut up by the others.

"You had better not be taking the piss, please," Spencer added.

"I don't joke about business. We'll talk details tomorrow. See you at the Hive. I've booked the acorn room from 9, don't be late, Spencer," remarked Mae Li. Innocence was overjoyed and crying. This could be the best day of her life; Surjit thanked her and swore again.

"Enjoy the rest of your days' babes. See you tomorrow," added Mae Li.

"We will, but what are you two doing? If you are alone, why don't you get together for lunch?" suggested Innocence.

"Let's not ruin this thing before it's even started," laughed Mae Li.

"Yeah, keep your mouth shut when you've got the deal. I should know this," cracked Surjit.

"What do you say, Spencer?" asked Mae Li.

"I say, tomorrow, tomorrow, bet your bottom dollar that tomorrow, there'll be sun, tomorrow, tomorrow, I love you tomorrow, you're always a day a…", but before Spencer could finish singing the verse, Mae Li closed the call.

To be continued…